A Day's Pay

A Day's Pay

STORIES ABOUT

Work

FROM THE
FLANNERY O'CONNOR AWARD
FOR SHORT FICTION

EDITED BY
ETHAN LAUGHMAN

THE UNIVERSITY OF GEORGIA PRESS
ATHENS

Most University of Georgia Press titles are
available from popular e-book vendors.

Printed digitally

Library of Congress Control Number: 2020940190
ISBN: 9780820358390 (pbk.: alk. paper)
ISBN: 9780820358406 (ebook)

CONTENTS

ACKNOWLEDGMENTS

The stories in this volume are from the following award-winning collections published by the University of Georgia Press:

Carole L. Glickfeld, *Useful Gifts* (1989)

Nancy Zafris, *The People I Know* (1990)

Robert Abel, *Ghost Traps* (1991)

Alfred DePew, *The Melancholy of Departure* (1992)

Wendy Brenner, *Large Animals in Everyday Life* (1996); "I Am the Bear" first appeared in the *Mississippi Review*

Andy Plattner, *Winter Money* (1997); "Sophia Winslow's House" first appeared as "Landlord" in the *Mississippi Review Web*

Frank Soos, *Unified Field Theory* (1998)

Gina Ochsner, *The Necessary Grace to Fall* (2002)

David Crouse, *Copy Cats* (2005); "Code" first appeared in the *Massachusetts Review*

Randy F. Nelson, *The Imaginary Lives of Mechanical Men* (2006); "In the Picking Room" first appeared in the *Portland Review*

Melinda Moustakis, *Bear Down, Bear North* (2011); "Some Other Animal" first appeared in *American Short Fiction*

Monica McFawn, *Bright Shards of Someplace Else* (2014); "The Chautauqua Sessions" first appeared in the *Missouri Review*

A thank you also goes to the University of Georgia Main Library staff for technical support in preparing the stories for publication.

INTRODUCTION

The Flannery O'Connor Award for Short Fiction was established in 1981 by Paul Zimmer, then the director of the University of Georgia Press, and press acquisitions editor Charles East. East would serve as the first series editor, judging the competition and selecting two collections to publish each year. The inaugural volumes in the series, *Evening Out* by David Walton and *From the Bottom Up* by Leigh Allison Wilson, appeared in 1983 to critical acclaim. Nancy Zafris (herself a Flannery O'Connor Award winner for the 1990 collection *The People I Know*) was the second series editor, serving in the role from 2008 to 2015. Zafris was succeeded by Lee K. Abbott in 2016, and Roxane Gay then assumed the role, choosing award winners beginning in 2019. Competition for the award has become an important proving ground for writers, and the press has published seventy-four volumes to date, helping to showcase talent and sustain interest in the short story form. These volumes together feature approximately eight hundred stories by authors who are based in all regions of the country and even internationally. It has been my pleasure to have read each and every one.

The idea of undertaking a project that could honor the diversity of the series' stories but also present them in a unified way had been hanging around the press for a few years. What occurred to us first, and what remained the most appealing approach, was to pull the hundreds of stories out of their current packages—volumes of collected stories by individual authors—and regroup them by common themes or subjects. After finishing my editorial internship at the press, I was brought on to the project and began to sort the stories into specific thematic categories. What followed was a deep dive into the award and its history and a gratifying acquaintance with the many authors whose works constitute the award's legacy.

Anthologies are not new to the series. A tenth-anniversary collection, published in 1993, showcased one story from each of the volumes published in the award's first decade. A similar collection appeared in 1998, the fifteenth year of the series. In 2013, the year of the series' thirtieth anniversary, the press published two volumes modeled after the tenth- and fifteenth-anniversary volumes. These anthologies together included one story from each of the fifty-five collections published up to that point. One of the 2013 volumes represented the series' early years, under the editorship of Charles East. The other showcased the editorship of Nancy Zafris. In a nod to the times, both thirtieth-anniversary anthologies appeared in e-book form only.

The present project is wholly different in both concept and scale. The press plans to republish more than five hundred stories in more than forty volumes, each focusing on a specific theme—from love to food to homecoming and homesickness. Each volume will aim to collect exemplary treatments of its theme, but with enough variety to give an overview of what the series is about. The stories inside paint a colorful picture that includes the varied perspectives multiple authors can have on a single theme.

Each volume, no matter its focus, includes the work of authors whose stories celebrate the variety of short fiction styles and subjects to be found across the history of the award. Just as Flannery O'Connor is more than just a southern writer, the University of Georgia Press, by any number of measures, has been more than a regional publisher for some time. As the first series editor, Charles East, happily reported in his anthology of the O'Connor Award stories, the award "managed to escape [the] pitfall" of becoming a regional stereotype. When Paul Zimmer established the award he named it after Flannery O'Connor as the writer who best embodied the possibilities of the short-story form. In addition, O'Connor, with her connections to the south and readership across the globe, spoke to the ambitions of the press at a time when it was poised to ramp up both the number and scope of its annual title output. The O'Connor name has always been a help in keeping the series a place where writers strive to be published and where readers and critics look for quality short fiction.

The award has indeed become an internationally recognized institution. The seventy-four (and counting) Flannery O'Connor Award authors come from all parts of the United States and abroad. They have lived in Arizona, Arkansas, California, Colorado, Georgia, Indiana, Maryland, Massachusetts, Texas, Utah, Washington, Canada, Iran, England, and elsewhere. Some have written novels. Most have published stories in a variety of literary quarterlies and popular magazines. They have been awarded numerous fellowships and prizes. They are world-travelers, lecturers, poets, columnists, editors, and screenwriters.

There are risks in the thematic approach we are taking with these anthologies, and we hope that readers will not take our editorial approach as an attempt to draw a circle around certain aspects of a story or in any way close off possibilities for interpretation. Great stories don't have to resolve anything, be set any particular time nor place, or be written in any one way. Great stories don't have to *be* anything. Still, when a story resonates with enough readers in a certain way, it is safe to say that it has spoken to us meaningfully about, for instance, love, death, and certain concerns, issues, pleasures, or life events.

We at the press had our own ideas about how the stories might be gathered, but we were careful to get author input on the process. The process of categorizing their work was not easy for any of them. Some truly agonized. Having their input was invaluable; having their trust was humbling. The goal of this project is to faithfully represent these stories despite the fact that they have been pulled from their original collections and are now bedmates with stories from a range of authors taken from diverse contexts. Also, just because a single story is included in a particular volume does not mean that that volume is the only place that story could have comfortably been placed. For example, "Sawtelle" from Dennis Hathaway's *The Consequences of Desire*, tells the story of a subcontractor in duress when he finds out his partner is the victim of an extramarital affair. We have included it in the volume of stories about love, but it could have been included in those on work, friends, and immigration without seeming out of place.

In *Creating Flannery O'Connor*, Daniel Moran writes that O'Connor first mentioned her infatuation with peacocks in her essay "Living with a Peacock" (later republished as "King of the Birds"). Since the essay's appearance, O'Connor has been linked with imagery derived from the bird's distinctive feathers and silhouette by a proliferation of critics and admirers, and one can now hardly find an O'Connor publication that does not depict or refer to her "favorite fowl" and its association with immortality and layers of symbolic and personal meaning. As Moran notes, "Combining elements of her life on a farm, her religious themes, personal eccentricities, and outsider status, the peacock has proved the perfect icon for O'Connor's readers, critics, and biographers, a form of reputation-shorthand that has only grown more ubiquitous over time."

We are pleased to offer these anthologies as another way of continuing Flannery O'Connor's legacy. Since its conception, thirty-seven years' worth of enthralling, imaginative, and thought-provoking fiction has been published under the name of the Flannery O'Connor Award. The award is just one way that we hope to continue the conversation about O'Connor and her legacy while also circulating and sharing recent authors' work among readers throughout the world.

It is perhaps unprecedented for such a long-standing short fiction award series to republish its works in the manner we are going about it. The idea for the project may be unconventional, but it draws on an established institution—the horn-of-plenty that constitutes the Flannery O'Connor Award series backlist—that is still going strong at the threshold of its fortieth year. I am in equal parts intimidated and honored to present you with what I consider to be these exemplars of the Flannery O'Connor Award. Each story speaks to the theme uniquely. Some of these stories were chosen for their experimental nature, others for their unique take on the theme, and still others for exhibiting matchlessness in voice, character, place, time, plot, relevance, humor, timelessness, perspective, or any of the thousand other metrics by which one may measure a piece of literature.

But enough from me. Let the stories speak for themselves.

ETHAN LAUGHMAN

A Day's Pay

I Am the Bear

WENDY BRENNER

From *Large Animals in Everyday Life* (1996)

I said: Oh, for God's sake, I'm not some pervert—you think I'm like that hockey puck in New Jersey, the mascot who got arrested for grabbing girls' breasts with his big leather mitt at home games? I'm a polar bear! I molest no one, I give out ice cream cones in the freezer aisle, I make six dollars an hour, I majored in Humanities, I'm a *girl.*

I was talking to the Winn-Dixie manager in his office. Like every grocery-store manager, he had a pudgy face, small mustache, and worried expression, and he was trying very hard, in his red vest and string tie, to appear open-minded. He had just showed me the model's letter of complaint, which sat, now, between us, on his desk. *The polar bear gave me a funny feeling,* the model had written; *I was under the mistaken impression that the bear was male, but much to my surprise it turned out that I was wrong. The bear was silent the whole time and never bothered to correct me.*

It was part of my *job* not to talk, I explained to the manager. I read to him from my Xeroxed rules sheet: *Animal representatives must not speak in a human manner but should maintain animal behavior and gestures at all times while in costume. Neither encourage nor dispel assumptions made regarding gender.*

I said, See? I was holding my heavy white head like a motorcy-
cle helmet in the folds of my lap, my own head sticking out of the
bureau-sized shoulders, my bangs stuck to my forehead, a small,
cross-shaped imprint on the tip of my nose from the painted wire
screen nostril of the bear. I can't help my large stature, I told him.
That's why they made me a bear and not one of those squirrels
who gives away cereal. I was doing exactly what I was supposed
to do. I was doing what I was designed to do.

She would like an apology, the manager said.

You say one becomes evil when one leaves the herd; I say that
depends entirely on what the herd is doing, I told him.

Look, the manager said, his eyes shifting. Would you be willing
to apologize? Yes or no. He reminded me of a guy I knew in high
school—there was one in every high school—who made his own
chain mail. They were both pale and rigidly hunch-shouldered,
even as young men, as though they had constantly to guard the
small territory they had been allotted in life.

Did you notice how in the letter she keeps referring to me as
"the bear"? I said. No wonder she didn't know I was a girl, she
doesn't even know I'm *human*! And incidentally, I added, when
the manager said nothing, you would think she'd be more understanding of the requirements of my position—we are, after all,
both performers.

The manager seemed offended that I would compare myself, a sweating, hulking bear, to a clean, famously fresh-faced
girl, our local celebrity, and I was let go. This wasn't dinner theater, he said, and at headquarters, where he sent me, I was told
I could continue to be a polar bear but not solo or in a contact
setting. This meant I could work corporate shows, which in our
area never occurred. I saw myself telling my story on "People's
Court," on "Hard Copy," but I was a big, unphotogenic girl and
I knew people would not feel sympathy for me. Plus, in the few
years since college I had been fired from every job I'd had, for actual transgressions—rifling aimlessly through a boss's desk draw-

ers when she was out of the office; sweeping piles of hair into the space behind the refrigerator in the back room of a salon; stopping in my school bus, after dropping off the last of the children, for a cold Mr. Pibb at Suwannee Swifty—and I believed absolutely in retribution, the accrual of cosmic debt, the granting and revoking of amnesty. I was, simply, no longer innocent. I was not innocent, even as I protested my innocence.

No, I hadn't molested the girl, but even as I'd sat in the manager's office I could still smell the clean spice of her perfume, feel the light weight of her hands on either side of my head, a steady, intoxicating pressure even through plaster and fake fur. I could not fully believe myself, sitting there, to be an outraged, overeducated young woman in a bear suit. Beneath the heavy costume, I was the beast the manager suspected me of being, I was the bear.

The girl had been shopping with her mother, a bell-shaped generic older woman in a long lavender raincoat. The moment they rolled their cart around the corner into my aisle, still forty feet away, the model screamed. She was only eighteen, but still I was surprised—I would have thought Florida natives would be accustomed to seeing large animals in everyday life. She screamed: Oh my god, he's so cute! She ran for me, and I made some ambiguous bear gesture of acknowledgment and surprise. Hey there, sweetie, she said, pursing her lips and talking up into my face as though I were her pet kitten. I scooped a cone of chocolate chip for her but she didn't even notice. Mom, look, she yelled.

The lavender-coated mother approached without hurry or grace. Her face, up close, was like the Buddha's, and she took the ice cream from my paw automatically, as though we had an understanding. The model was rubbing my bicep with both of her narrow tanned hands. He's so soft, she said. I faced her, making large simpering movements, and noticed the small dark shapes of her nipples, visible through her white lacy bodysuit. I blushed, then remembered I needn't blush, and that was when

3

she reached for me, pulling my hot, oversized head down to her perfect, heart-shaped face. The kiss lasted only a moment, but in that moment I could feel how much she loved me, feel it surging through my large and powerful limbs. *I am the bear*, I thought. Then it was over, and I remembered to make the silly gestures of a human in a bear suit pretending to be embarrassed. The model's mother had produced a small, expensive-looking camera from some hidden pocket of her raincoat and matter-of-factly snapped a photo of me, a bear pretending to be a friendly human, with my arm around the model's skinny shoulders, my paw entangled in her silky, stick-straight golden hair.

They left then, the mother never speaking a word, and they were all the way down the aisle, almost to the other end, when the produce manager stuck his head around the corner right in front of them and yelled my name, I had a phone call. The model looked back once before they disappeared, and though she never saw my face—I wasn't allowed to take off my head in public—it was obvious from her expression that she understood. It was an expression of disturbed concern, the way she might look if she were trying to remember someone's name or the words to a song she once knew well, but there was something else, too, a kind of abashed sadness that looked out of place on her young, milky face.

I could imagine how she must have felt, having once fallen in love with an animal myself in the same swift, irrevocable way I imagined she had. *The Good-Night Horse*, he'd been called— that heading had appeared beside his picture on the wallpaper in our cottage's bathroom at the Sleepy Hollow resort, and the words stayed in my head for years, like a prayer. The wallpaper featured reprints of antique circus posters and flyers, the same six or seven over and over, but the Good-Night Horse was the only one I paid attention to: he was a powerful black shape that seemed to move and change form like a pile of iron shavings under a magnet, quivering slightly. He was muscular, a stallion. I was six. "Katie is masturbating," my mother said, in her mockweary, matter-of-fact voice.

I would lie on the floor on my side under the toilet-paper dispenser, my face a few inches from the wall. The Good-Night Horse was shown in a series of four different postures. In the first two pictures he was wearing boots and trousers on his hind legs, but in the wild third picture, my favorite, he was tearing the trousers off dramatically. Clothes were flung on the ground all around him, his tail swished in the air, and the trousers waved wildly from his mouth. In the last picture he was, with his teeth, pulling back the covers of a single bed with a headboard, like my bed at home. "The World's Greatest Triumph of Animal Training," the poster said.

There was no problem with my masturbating, because my parents were agnostic intellectuals; they had given me a booklet called "A Doctor Talks to Five- to Eight-Year-Olds" that included, as an example of the male genitalia, a photograph of Michelangelo's statue of David. The photo was small and black-and-white, so you couldn't really get a good look at what was between his legs, but it appeared lumpy and strange, like mashed potatoes, and I found it unsettling. The book had already given me a clear picture of sexual intercourse: it was a complicated, vaguely medical procedure in which you were hooked up to an adult man and microscopic transactions then occurred. And though my parents had said, "You're probably too young to picture it, but someday you'll understand," I *could* picture it—I saw an aerial view of me, naked, and the statue of David lying side by side on a whitesheeted operating table, me in braids and of course only half his height. But this vision was the furthest thing from my mind when I looked at the Good-Night Horse.

I wasn't stupid, I knew people didn't marry horses, or any

other animal. I just wasn't convinced that the Good-Night Horse was necessarily an animal—the more I looked at his picture, the more he seemed to be a man in some important sense. It was not his clothes, or the tricks he did, but something both more mysterious and more obvious than that. He reminded me a little of Batman—and, like Batman, he might have a way of getting out of certain things, I thought. He was sensitive, certainly—his forelock hung boyishly, appealingly, over his eyes, and his ears stood up straight, pointing forward in a receptive manner (except in the trouser-flinging picture, where they lay flat back against his head)—but you could tell that he was in no way vulnerable, at least not to the schemes and assaults of ordinary men. He was actually *more* a man than ordinary men, and something began to swell in my chest unbearably after a few days, weighing me down so that I could not possibly get off the floor, and my father finally had to carry me, sobbing, from the bathroom. I was sobbing not only because the Good-Night Horse and I could never meet, but because I understood with terrible certainty, terrible finality, that I would never be happy with anything less.

And it was true that no man had yet lived up. I had been engaged once to a social theorist who was my age but refused to own a TV and said things like "perused" in regular conversation and expected what he called my "joyous nature" to liberate him, but it ended when I discovered while he was writing his thesis that he had not gotten around to treating his three cats for tapeworm and had been living with them—the cats and the worms—contentedly for weeks. And now, at twenty-eight, I only dated, each man seeming a degree more aberrant than the last. The last had been a stockbroker who was hyperactive (rare in adults, he said) and deaf in one ear—he yelled and slurred and spit when he talked and shot grackles with an AK-47 from his apartment window, but was wildly energetic even late at night, boyish and exuberant and dangerous all at once, a little like the horse. On our second and last date, however, he took me to an Irish pub to meet his old college roommate, and the roommate engaged me in an exchange of stomach-punching to show off how tightly he could clench his abs, only when it was his turn to punch mine he grabbed my breasts instead, causing the stockbroker to go crazy. He dragged the roommate out onto the sidewalk and pushed him around like a piece of furniture he could not find the right place for, and I kept yelling that it was only a joke, I didn't mind, but in the scuffle the stockbroker's visor—the kind with the flashing colored lights going across the forehead band—got torn off and flung into the gutter, its battery ripped out, and when the fight was over he sat on the curb trying in vain to get it to light up again and saying, "He broke my fucking visor, man," until I told him I was taking a cab home, at which point he spit, on purpose, in my face.

So I could understand how the model might feel. I could see how, from looking at me, the miserable, small-minded Winn-Dixie manager would believe I had no business comparing my-self to her, but, not being a bear himself, he did not understand that appearances meant nothing. I was a beast, yes, but I also had something like x-ray vision; I was able, as a bear, to see through beauty and ugliness to the true, desperate and disillusioned hearts of all men.

It was not difficult to figure out where she lived. She had been profiled earlier that month on "Entertainment Tonight" along with her sister, who at twelve was also a model, and the two girls were shown rollerblading around their cul-de-sac, and I knew all the cul-de-sacs in town from having driven the bus. So, a few days after I was fired, I drove to the house. To be a bear was to be impulsive.

It had been a record-hot, record-dry July, and the joke topic of the radio call-in show I listened to as I drove was "What have we done to antagonize God?" Callers were citing recent sad and far-cical events from around the world in excited, tentative voices, as though the jovial DJ would really give them the answer, or as though they might win something. Only a few callers took the question personally, confessing small acts of betrayal and decep-tion, but the DJ cut these people off. "Well, heh heh, we all do the best we can," he said, fading their voices out so it would not sound as though he were hanging up on them in mid-sentence. *Asshole*, I thought, and I made a mental note to stop at the radio station sometime and do something about him.

The model's house was made of a special, straw-colored kind of brick, rare in the South, or so "ET" had said. I saw the model's mother step out onto the front steps, holding a canister of Love My Carpet, but when she saw my car she stepped quickly back in-side. The model's sister answered the door. She was a double of the model, only reduced in size by a third and missing the mod-el's poignance. Her face was beautiful but entirely devoid of ex-pression or history; her small smooth features did not look ca-pable of being shaped by loss or longing, not even the honest longing of children. This would be an asset for a model, I imag-ined, and I could see where the mother's Buddha-nature had been translated, in her younger daughter, into perfection: desire had not just been eliminated, but seemed never to have existed in the first place.

"I am a fan," I said, and, perhaps because I was a girl, showered and combed and smiling, I was let in. I had also brought, as props, a couple of magazines which I held in front of me like a shield, but I was not nervous at all. I understood that I had nothing to lose, that none of us, in fact, had as much to lose as we believed. I sensed other bears out there, too—my fierce brothers, stalking through woods and villages, streams and lots, sometimes upright and sometimes on all fours, looking straight ahead and feeling the world pass beneath their heavy, sensitive paws.

The model's sister led me past ascending carpeted stairs and a wall of framed photos to the back of the house, where the model's bright bedroom overlooked a patio crowded by palmetto and bougainvillea, visible through sliding glass doors. A tiny motion sensor stuck to the wall above the glass blinked its red light as I entered. The model was bent over her single bed, taking small towels of all colors and patterns from a laundry basket, folding them, and placing them in piles. "Fan," the little sister said, and the model straightened and smiled and came forward, her perfume surrounding me and sending a surge of bear power through me, a boiling sheet of red up before my eyes. For just a moment as we shook hands I was sure she would know, she would remember the feel of my paw. But then she stepped back and my face cooled.

"I'm a huge fan," I said.

"Well thanks, that's so sweet," she said. She had taken the magazines from me automatically, just as her mother had taken the ice cream at the store, and was already scribbling across the shiny likeness of her face. "Should I make it out to anyone?" she said.

"My boyfriend," I said, and I told her the stockbroker's name.

"You're so lucky you're so tall," she said, handing the magazines back. "That's my biggest liability, I can't do runway. Well, thanks for coming by."

I looked around at the white dressers, the mirrored vanity, not ready to leave, and was shocked by a short row of stuffed bears set up on a shelf on the wall behind me. They were just regular brown teddy bears with ribbon bows at their necks, no pandas or polar bears, but they stared back at me with identical shocked expressions, another motion sensor glowing on the wall over their heads, unblinking. "Nice bears," I finally said, forcing myself to turn away.

"Oh, I've had those forever," she said. "See that one in the middle, that looks so sad? I found him in the street when I was six years old! Doesn't he look sad?"

"Yeah, he really does," I said. The bear was smaller and more lumpish than the other bears, with black felt crescents glued on for eyebrows.

"I used to make them take turns sleeping in the bed with me," the model said. "But even if it wasn't his turn I let him, just 'cause he looked so sad. Isn't that funny? I used to kiss him thirty-two times every night, right after I said my prayers."

"Thirty-two," I said.

"My lucky number," she said brightly.

"But you don't kiss him anymore," I said.

She stared at me, frowning. "No," she said. She stared at me some more and I just stood, my arms hanging, as a bear would stand, waiting. "Well, I better get back to work," she said.

"On your towels," I said.

She put her hands on her hips and gazed helplessly at the towels, as though they had betrayed her. "They're dish towels, isn't that queer?" she said. "I got them from a chain letter. My cousin started it, and I was second on the list, so I got, like, seventy-two of them sent from, like, everywhere. Isn't that pathetic—she's, like, twenty, and that's her *hobby*. You can have one, you want one?"

"Seriously?" I said.

"God, take your pick," she said. "I guess I have to remind myself sometimes that not everyone's as lucky as me, but, like, dish towels, I'm sorry."

I had to brush past her to get to the bed, the snap on the hip pocket of my jeans rubbing her arm. I took the top towel from the nearest stack, a simple white terrycloth one with an appliqué of a pair of orange and yellow squash. "Thanks, I'll think of you every time I use it," I said. I held the towel, stroking it. It was not enough, I was thinking.

"Well, thanks for coming by," she said. She had moved to the doorway and stood looking at me in the same way she had looked at the towels. The row of bears watched from over her shoulder, the slumped, sad one seeming braced by its brethren. I imagined the model and her soulless sister laughing at me after I'd gone, at my terrible size, my obvious lie about a boyfriend.

"I really have to get back to what I was doing . . ." she said.

"I'm sorry, I was just so nervous about finally meeting you," I said, and I could see her relax slightly. "I almost forgot to ask, isn't that funny? I hate to ask, but do you by any chance give out photos?"

"No, you'd have to contact the fan club for that," she said. Her face was final, and I turned, finally, to go. "But actually, wait," she said. "I do have something, if you want it."

What happened next was certainly not believable in the real world, but in the just, super-real world of the bear it only confirmed what I had known. She slid an envelope out from beneath the blotter on her white desk, picked through it with her slim graceful fingers, and pulled out a photograph which she passed to me hurriedly, as though it were contaminated. "Here, isn't that cute?" she said, laughing in a forced way, like the DJ.

There we were, her and me, her small, radiant face beside my large, furry, inscrutable one, my paw visible, squeezing her small shoulders together slightly, the flash reflected in the freezer cases behind us, making a white halo around both of our heads. Something seemed to pop then, noiselessly, as though the flash had just gone off around us again in the bedroom. Like a witch or spirit who could be destroyed by having her photo taken, I felt I was no longer the bear. "He's so cute," I murmured.

She snorted, but it had no heart to it, it sounded like she was imitating someone. Then for a moment she no longer saw me; she just stood there looking at nothing, her dark blue eyes narrowed, the faintest suggestion of creases visible around her mouth.

I had to take a step back, such was the power of her face at that moment. Then she too became herself again, and we were just two sad girls standing there, one of them beautiful and one of them something else. "Well, goodbye," I said, and she looked relieved that I was leaving—but also, I thought, that it was only me deserting her and not, as before, the heartbreaking, duplicitous bear.

On the way out I encountered her mother, who had materialized again beside the front door. It was the simple gravity, the solid, matter-of-fact weight of the woman, I decided, that made her silent appearances and disappearances so disconcerting, so breathtaking. Wasn't it more impressive to see a magician produce from the depths of his bag a large, floppy rabbit, to see the ungraceful weight of the animal dragged up into the light, than to watch him release doves or canaries, already creatures of the air, flashy but in their element? "Goodbye," I said. "Sorry."

She smiled and did not step but rather shifted several inches so that I could get past her, and then stood in the open doorway, round and lavender, smiling and watching my retreat. Only when I was halfway down the walk to my car did she say goodbye, and then her voice was so deep and strange and serene that I was not sure if I had really heard it or, if I had, if it had really come from her.

I did use the towel and sometimes thought of the model when I used it. The photo I didn't frame or hide or treat with any ceremony, but I did look at it often, trying to experience again that moment of transformation, that rush of power that had gone through me in the seconds before it was snapped.

But after a few months even the memory of it became weak. I was after all no longer the bear and could no longer remember well what it felt like to be the bear. The animal in the picture appeared only to be a big, awkwardly constructed sham, nothing you could call human. When I looked at it I felt only confusion and shame. How had I become that shaggy, oversized, hollow thing? Once I had been an honest little girl, a girl who had to be dragged away from the object of her love, but somehow, somewhere, everything had changed. How had it happened? I wondered. I studied the photo as though the bear could answer me, but it only stared back with its black fiberglass eyes, its grip on the real human beside it relentless.

The Chautauqua Sessions

MONICA MCFAWN

From *Bright Shards of Someplace Else* (2014)

My son, the drug addict, is about to tell a story. I can tell because he's closed his eyes and lifted his chin. I can tell because he's laid his hands, palms down, on the table, like a shaman feeling the energy of the tree-spirit still in the wood. I can tell because he's drawing a shuddering breath, as if what he has to say will take all he's got. He's putting on the full show because he has a new audience—he'd streamline the theatrics if it were only me. We're having dinner in Levi Lambright's recording compound, Chautauqua, in remote Appalachian Tennessee. I'm a songwriter—a lyricist—and I'm here to work on a new album with Levi, our first in fifteen years. Dee was not invited. The only other person who should be here is Lucinda, Levi's cook. But Dee just showed up, the way drug-addicted sons sometimes do.

Right as he's about to speak, I reach for the wine bottle and refill my glass, placing the bottle back down in front of me, providing a bit of a visual shield between us. He's sitting across from me, next to Levi. The kid looks good, I'll give him that. He's clean shaven, and his dun-colored hair appears professionally cut. His eyes, where the cresting chaos can most often be seen, are clear and still. They still don't track exactly right, though. Like his mother, he looks at you out of one eye at a time, like a quizzical parrot. If you look at him straight on, his thin face seems to wobble and shake like a coin on end before it flips back into profile, his mother's aquiline nose and sharp chin etched in the center of his round boy's head. On his forearm, his old self-mutilation scars have been scribbled over, I see, with a new homemade tattoo: *Trust.* I don't see myself in him at all.

"Okay? Are you sure you want to hear this? It's kind of a long story." Dee asks, though he doesn't pause before going on.

"This happened last week. I was downtown, on some crazy uppers. I think I took some MDMA that night. Maybe just amphetamines. I don't remember. All I know is I was high, really high, and I'd been dancing and couldn't find who I came with. So I decide I should go home. But when I leave the club, I can't figure out where I am. I mean, I only live a block from there. I'm walking down the street and I feel like I'm in a foreign country or something. Nothing is familiar. Somehow I ended up three miles away, in the worst part of town . . ."

I try not to listen. I've heard all this before, and I'm pretty sure it will end with him confronting the godhead. I've gotten enough midnight calls about his drug-fueled encounters with an encyclopedic list of spiritual figures: Jesus, Buddha, Allah, The Spirit in the Sky, and Mother Nature herself, who held out long arms made of saplings and drew him to her leafy bosom while nibbling a Morse code of secret truth on his earlobe. As much as I knew the source of these visions, it was hard not to be swept along by his telling. Because Dee got one thing from me: my ability to spin a story.

Sometimes Dee's language was so striking during these soliloquies that I would find myself jotting down phrases without thinking. *I can't believe you mined your drugged son for a good turn of phrase*, I'd think, looking down at the pad the next morning. Then, a preposterous jealously: *Why can't I think of phrases like that?* I'd want to use the words in my work, but that seemed somehow wrong, given what they sprang from. But to let that language, no matter how destructive its origin, simply be forgotten seemed wrong, too. So I simply recorded it on little sheets of notepaper that I stored in a shoebox under my bed. I guess I figured I'd decide what to do with it all someday. I suppose it's a bit like the newspaper clippings proud parents keep of their kids' accomplishments, for they were, in their perverse way, Dee's accomplishments.

"Man, have I been there!" Levi is staring at my son, a smile playing about his lips as though he knows he's going to hear something great. He looks at me and gestures with his fork, flinging bits of food into his drink. "Danny, remember when the tour bus got lost on the way to Santa Fe? And how we hopped out and started looking for street signs and ended up at that crazy pueblo with those cult people? The ones with all the chickens wearing stuff?"

I nod. I remember the chickens and their colorful neck warmers, scratching around in the sand while a few children sat in the sun with looms on their knees. They'd looked at the group of us—back then Levi was a bona fide rock star—with a somnolent disinterest, as if we were deeply beside the point. There's more to the story, but I don't want to tell it with Dee here. It's a funny story, and telling a funny story is an act of generosity and welcome that I certainly don't feel.

"So you were stoned and lost. And . . . ?"

Dee fixes his left eye on me and then flips his hands upward in an emphatic gesture. There's a faint purplish streak coming off his tear duct and down his cheek, like a magic marker he's tried to wash off. His inner elbow is blotchy with thick pancake makeup, but track marks peek through like the bubbles of crabs submerged in wet sand. He leans over the table, as close to me as he can get.

"I brought a man back to life. That's what happened."

———

Only one of my two sons Dale is a druggie. That's right: I have two sons by the same name—the absurd result of a tanking romance. That's why this Dale goes by Dee. He's the younger one— just twenty-four—the son of my second ex-wife, whose love for me primarily manifested itself in an intense jealously of my first wife, Gina. Vicki had the notion that she was simply a placeholder for that old passion. This was hardly the case—far from being a woman I pined for, Gina had morphed, for me, into the kind of pleasant asexuality that one associates with kin of the fun-cousin variety. I tried to make that clear, but simply hearing Gina's name on my tongue was all it took to send Vicki off the edge. "Listen to the way you make love to the very syllables!" It came to a head when she was pregnant with our son. "I want to name him Dale," she told me over dinner, a wine glass half-filled with grape juice shaking in her hand. "But Vicki, I already have a ten-year-old son by that name," I said slowly, as if to a child. "Gina's son," was all she said in reply. I gave in, figuring that naming my second son the same name as my first was such an extreme testimony to my love for her that it would cure her jealousy for good. But within a few years I had not only another Dale, but another ex-wife.

After the divorce, Vicki and Dee moved to Dearborn, where she immediately married a gruff, possessive pharmaceutical salesman who picked up the phone whenever I called her to discuss our son. So all the calls—even the later ones where we grimly discussed Dee's drug problems—were set to her husband's breathing, as if the call were coming through a conch shell. Weekend handoffs were tense, and I always felt I was smuggling the boy away as I hustled him to the car while Vicki and the husband stared through the bay window, blowing Dee kisses and making theatrical frown-faces. Once Dee and I were safely on the highway, I'd look over at him—slumped in the passenger side, his bag on his lap, his watery blue eyes turning in their sockets with a reptilian jerkiness—and feel as awkward and duty-bound as a cop entertaining a lost kid while the mother was rounded up.

I'd like to say that it was just Dee's addictions that had cooled me on him over the years, that had frayed the precious father-son thread. But there were things in Dee that had bothered me long before he started using. Even as a little boy, he was always selling himself too fervidly, selling whatever he cared about. When he was fifteen, it was Stanley Kubrick's body of work, and I spent many an afternoon watching him pause *A Clockwork Orange* frame by frame while he explained the brilliance of the shot— the shifting chiaroscuro that played against the elegant curve of a kicking foot. By the time Dee was eighteen, Kubrick was forgotten, and all Dee spoke about was music. He listened nonstop to what sounded to me like the drippings of a leaky pipe in an echoing room mixed with a duck call. Dee claimed that the absence of voices and recognizable instruments represented a higher form of music, untainted by human expression. "These sounds are incidental, you know, found sounds," he explained. "Then they're spliced and looped. That's all that's been done to them. Isn't it beautiful?"

I liked that Dee was passionate, even artistic. Unlike my other son Dale—a bakery franchiser whose imagination stretches no further than how to rebrand the cupcake—Dee seemed more like me, a thinker, someone interested in ideas and art. Yet it was hard to really engage with him. His typical response to anything I said was a wave of a hand and a wincing squint, the same gesture one would use when walking into a smoky room. Still, I loved him. I imagined that when he grew up a bit—got out of Vicki's control a bit more, saw more of the world—that he and I would have a fresh shot. The good times we had (racing down the dunes in northern Michigan and splashing into the lake, paging through catalogs of specialized recording equipment, waxing philosophical about the state of pop music) seemed to contain within them the seed of something better, something more solid. I can wait. That's what I told myself.

But Dee's habit ruined whatever fragile relationship we'd been building. He stole from me, screamed at me, punched me, came onto my then-girlfriend's mentally disabled daughter when she was staying with me (a disaster that was only averted because I walked back into the living room in time), and even accused me, during an acid fugue, of abusing him as a child. Of course that was laughably untrue—I'd hardly touched him at all, much less hit him. I'd been raised by a cold, withholding father who demanded dark and silence whenever he got home from work. When I would fix him his drink, I'd place it into his hands with the gentleness of a small spider, its legs no more than filament. I treated Dee with the same delicacy, only touching him lightly, if at all, and when I hugged him I did not even press away the air under his baggy shirt.

Vicki and I did our best for him. We sent him to the top rehab facilities in the state, even an experiential sailing adventure where the organizers likened ducking to avoid the boom to avoiding drugs, and gathering up the lines to organizing one's life and getting a job. I tried everything I could think of or read about—too much to even recall. And Dee would have good days, of course. They always do. He'd show up at my door and apologize. He'd talk in a low, exaggeratedly modulated voice, as if luxuriating in his ability to speak in something other than an accusatory shriek or a paranoid mumble. We'd go somewhere to eat and he'd stare at his plate in wonder, as if his reentry into the world had given even his limp house salad a kind of sheen. Being with him as he reentered regular life, watching him acquaint himself with all of life's serene pleasures, was bracing and thrilling. It made the world feel new to me. All he'd said and done shed off me like it was nothing. And then—relapse.

Before Tonya, my ex-girlfriend, decided she'd had enough of

me, she told me that my willingness to ride the rollercoaster of Dee's deceit, lies, and false recovery so many times was an addiction in itself. "What do you do all day? Read books about recovery. Call his phone constantly. Drive around town looking for him. All for a kid who pretends to be clean once a week, like clockwork, usually to get some money out of you. This kid will get better, or he won't. It can't be on you forever."

She was right. I'd been living off dwindling royalties from my career with Levi, refusing new songwriting work, even from artists I once desperately courted. There was no time for friends. I never bothered to see my other son, even though he lives only a few hours away. And the rooftop community garden, where I had once so enthusiastically volunteered, had taken me off its work schedule since I'd been a no-show too many times, times when I drove right by the garden to hunt down Dee, parking my car by a dark overpass or barren lot, leaping out with a flashlight and calling out his name, raking the light over the faces of those bums and strays he ran with. Each face was lit with a chemically restored naïveté, so even the roughest slow-grinned like toddlers caught in the act of scrawling on the nursery walls. I'd grabbed one I'd seen before—a man who always wore brass-buckled pilgrim shoes and drank from a horn flask—and demanded to know where Dee was. He cocked his head and called out "dee*dee*dee," a sound that rose, echoed, and converged with the faraway car alarms, bird calls, and every other ambient long *e* in the city. Dee was lost and unavoidable. I'd find him dead one day, I thought, or get killed looking for him. There's no other way it could end.

But that, thank god, is all in the past now. Five years down the rabbit hole was plenty. I no longer let myself get involved. I've let myself mourn. I've started working at the garden again, dating a woman named Natalie who knows only the basics about Dee— druggie son, liar, a sad part of my past, a toxic person, if he calls hang up. I'm even ready, now, to write again, something that was impossible when I was involved with Dee's dramas. That's why

I'm here. I want to make music again with my old partner—it's time to return to who I was before Dee. Levi has been calling me on and off over the past five years, trying to entice me to write another album. He must have been surprised when I called him and finally agreed. If Levi found out about Dee, I thought, it would be through the songs I'd write.

Dee is well into his story now. He's telling us about wandering into a neighborhood he's never been in before, still lost, still looking for his apartment. It's a bad part of town—and bad for Detroit is plenty bad—and everyone in this neighborhood is squatting in vacated homes. No one owns anything. He enters an old church. The stained glass windows are all broken. Lead solder seams that once marked out the profiles of saints now snake through open space. Someone's painted a mural of a pastoral scene on the bare lath—probably an artist trying to bring a bit of beauty, or just intention, to a place marked by ruin and randomness. Dee walks straight into the wall, thinking he's mounting a velvety hillock. He passes clusters of gang members who ignore him out of sheer surprise, the way a cat will back away from an approaching mouse, as if out of respect for the depth of its suicidal impulse. He stumbles into a huge plastic bag filled with pop cans dragged by an elderly lady riding a Hoveround stamped with the logo of a long-closed supermarket. "There was nothing keeping me going," Dee explains, "but the thought of 'getting home,' which itself, repeated in my head, was basically just a mindless chant. You know, how your name sounds if you repeat it too much? Not only does it not seem like 'you,' it doesn't seem like anything. It seems to just erase more of you the more you say it."

Lucinda makes small, sweet little coos of sympathy with regularity. Levi's two silent, sphinxlike dogs pad in and lower into the sentry position by our chairs, their legs folding under with a perfect, luxurious grace, like the smooth mechanism of a fine pocketknife. Levi's chin is cupped in his hands as he nods along to Dee's words. It's shocking how little Levi has changed over the years. His face is still handsome, just blurred at its edges, his jaw softened in flesh. This does not make him look old but rather uncontained, a face rimmed by a diffuse halo of skin. The skin under Levi's eyes, unlike mine, is pristine and glowing, bright as if someone had dropped a tea light in his empty head. And he's maintained his general expression—the familiar empathy and knowingness that used to make me feel both understood and insubstantial, as if the largesse of his person were being wasted by turning its focus on me.

"Then I walk past these screaming people. Someone grabs my shirt. I think I'm about to be mugged, but I can't get away. It's like I'm moving underwater and everyone else is on dry land . . ."

The story is reaching its climax, I can feel it. The drugs, it seems, have impaired everything in Dee but his grasp of the story arc. A bathroom break might spare me the triumphant rise of Dee's voice, the careen into lyricism. I get up without a backward glance, although I can hear Dee taking a breath, the silverware clinking again, attention turning to the dogs. The bathroom is down a hall so wide that it seems like another room. This whole place is cavernous, open-plan: cathedral ceilings, massive reclaimed wood beams hung with art prints. There are a few framed gold and platinum records on the wall and a picture of Levi and me in the early seventies, both of our feet propped up on a rock, the guitar resting between us. I had a kind of sleepy-eyed shy smile, a look that spoke of both bliss and nerves—Levi's talent intimidated me then, though I was thrilled to be part of it. Those feelings seem so long ago, and I doubt if I ever have that look on my face anymore. Maybe expressions rotate out of a person's face for good, like a song dropped from a set list.

I splash water on my face and try to clear my head. When I turn off the sink, someone's ring slides off the basin and pings around the bowl. It's a little silver seahorse, curving around to touch its snout to its swirled tail. I slip it in my pocket, since I don't want to leave it out for Dee to lift. It's late and Levi's already invited him to stay the night, but he'll be gone tomorrow morning—I'll make sure of it. No reason to worry. But why show up now? Here? I haven't seen him in a year or heard from him in weeks, and even then the calls were brief, garbled, raving pleas for money that ended when I put the phone down with a soft click, a humane death to his voice. It's like he's intuited how important this is for me, how potentially cleansing and healing, and he's made sure to inject his toxic presence. So much effort to find me, too. Vicki had mentioned where I was (why did I tell her? And she him?), and then he got online and scoured Levi's fansites and an aerial map for the compound's location. He was lost for a few hours on the twisty mountain roads but then found it—a miracle, he claims, another shimmering link on the chain of serendipity that includes the amazing story he's got to tell.

When I get back to the table, Dee is speaking in low, incantatory tones.

"The lights were flashing all around and I was so high that every one of them had tracers coming off it, as if I was walking under this glittery web. There was broken glass all around but I didn't notice it. This guy was laying there and people were screaming and running around and I guess—this is what people tell me later—that I walked up deadly calm and started performing CPR. We were so far out the cops were really slow getting there—this is Detroit, after all. I was giving compressions, like two hundred a minute, for ten minutes. This is almost humanly impossible. Some say it might be a world record. I didn't even realize what I was doing. I was so messed up I thought I was still in the club and this was some dance. I just kept going. It felt wonderful. I just remember seeing these lights going up and down and hearing this click click sound. That was the cartilage over the sternum, I'm told. The guy was certainly dead for most of that time. Then, right when help got there, he coughed, arched up under me, looked me in the eye. I just walked away and down the street . . . and all these people followed me, trying to thank me. They took me to the hospital with them and I slowly sobered up. The guy was alive. And here's the thing . . ."

Dee tries to catch my eye but I duck down and pet the dogs. "The thing is, when I felt that man—Miguel's—life return, something happened to me, too. I mean, I literally felt the force of my own life—before all the drugs and issues—leap back into me. I realized, then and there, that I would never use again. For real. And I haven't. Three weeks and going strong. It's like . . . not only did I restart Miguel's heart but my own."

Levi watches Dee with a twitching mouth that flicks into a small smile whenever Dee drives his story into a new absurdity. Of course they aren't absurdities to Levi. He's positively moved. When Dee falls silent, Levi springs forward, knocking down a salt shaker. "That is amazing, man. I have never heard anything more beautiful. You are so much like your Dad . . . you just have a way with words! God, Danny. I can't believe this kid!" He turns to me with his familiar look of awe (for what doesn't awe Levi?) and points from Dee to me and back. I shrug.

"He knows how to spin a tale," I say, echoing what the cops had said to me the first time I picked him up from an overnighter in jail.

After dinner, I head straight to my cabin, locking it in case Dee gets any ideas about dropping by for a little heart-to-heart. Then I call Natalie. She picks up right away, her voice sounding warm but a little edgy, as if whatever she's about to hear might require her to shift quickly into tough love. Natalie teaches in one of the worst schools in Detroit, where she is beloved and feared. There was a rumor going around that she reduced the superintendent to tears at a board meeting, then stopped anyone from offering him a Kleenex so he could experience the discomfort and filth his students did every day. This boldness is all the more disarming considering her face—pale, round, with an inexorable, stony quietude. Everything—from the way she kisses to the way she orders a bottle of wine—is done with a kind of resolute deliberateness, as if she'd considered the smoothest, truest way long before she had been called upon to act.

She listens for a few moments—but right when I'm getting to the nonsense about the CPR world record, she interrupts me.

"I don't think you should be putting this much energy toward him. Just don't engage. If you tell him to leave because he's on drugs, then he's got to stay to show you he's not. Attention will encourage him. Believe me, I know how this works. And it's not as if Dee has a long attention span anyway—remember what you told me about his landscaping business? He'll leave. Give it a few days."

She's probably right, but I don't like how she just rolls over the fact that I might be rattled at Dee's sudden appearance, especially when I'm just now feeling ready to song-write again. But Natalie's an emotional minimalist who doesn't need the gory details to read a situation correctly. And she's right about Dee—the landscaping idea, which occurred to him during a brief sober period, lasted less than twenty-four hours. He spent a solid twenty of those hours designing the tree logo that would go on his business cards—drawing and redrawing it in my living room, making it more and more fantastical and symbolic, using up every scrap of paper on a swirling design that incorporated the whole universe into a knothole in the tree's base. For years afterward I'd find them: a bird's nest scribbled on an old TV guide, a root system on a receipt, a bough creeping over the stamps in my passport.

The next morning, the first thing I hear upon waking is a high, squeaky warble and the sound of a lazily plucked guitar. I recognize that I'm-afraid-to-sing-for-real falsetto—Dee. And the guitar, Levi. The studio is next door to my cabin, and the unwelcome sounds come through the open window. I get up and see my computer is still open from last night, when I tried to verify Dee's story. Had he really set a world record for chest compression per minute and saved a man's life? But even if it was true, did it matter? The ridiculous turns of his life seem like just more evidence of his addiction—it's like a stoner is writing his fate. I get out my notebook and try to remember some ideas I jotted down last night. After a while, Levi knocks on the door.

"Danny-boy, get up and jam with us! We're having a blast."

I step outside to talk to him.

"Look, Levi, I'm not going to jam with him. He's a junkie. I'm sorry he showed up here. You don't want to get invested in anything he does; he's not reliable. He needs to get back into rehab."

Levi looks me in the eye for a long moment. His gray hair stands up in a fuzzed swirl atop his head, like a novelty halo. He lifts his hand briefly and makes a loose cup around his ear, as if he misheard. Then he turns both hands up and speaks.

"Are you serious, Danny? Didn't you hear him last night? It sounds like he's over all that. Why not give him a chance?"

I can't blame Levi for being charmed—I've been there enough myself—but his words make me think he's unusually gullible. Dee's story was the kind of improbable drama that users cling to. Real recovery doesn't come from the flash-pop of some crazy encounter, and Levi should at least know that.

"Levi, I'm serious. You don't know him. He's just pretending. This is some ruse, some ploy to get into my good graces or get money or I don't even want to think about what he's trying to do. You don't know the history here—"

"Danny, let him stay here for now. Come on. We'll ask him to leave if something goes wrong, but otherwise? It might be fun! We've got plenty of room here. We need a young guy around to keep us two old goats fresh . . ."

Levi glances at the main house, where Lucinda, blue scarves streaming off her neck, bobs past the window like an exotic fish. "Dang it, Lucinda's waiting for me. Totally forgot! I'm supposed to take her to the garden this morning to harvest some stuff for tonight. Did you know we have a farm share down the road? It's a great place—the old guy named Gregors owns it. When he learned I was a rock star, he said that originally Woodstock was going to be on his property but the hippies got a bad vibe from his sheep, since they all were so well-behaved and lined up for their feed. They thought he was fascist and split . . ."

"Levi, I don't want to get into too much detail but Dee—"

"Hey, Danny, I've got to run. We'll talk later. Lucinda's giving me the eye. Women! You know what's scary? Watching her weed. Ever notice how aggressive women are about stuff like that? They can be all butterflies and rainbows but let them loose on dandelions and they become these focused little wildcats all claw, claw, claw . . ." He continues talking as he backs away, his step so light on the autumn leaves that he could be mistaken for a bounding squirrel.

It's not particularly to my son's credit that he's seduced Levi with his storytelling. Levi, for all his sophistication as a performer and musician, is a strangely guileless man, the kind of person whose brilliance, you might say, comes from that ability to be seduced, to emotionally connect with anyone and anything. No matter what he sings, he finds something beautiful and authentic within the words. I've always seen him as a kind of idiot savant, a brilliant, complex performer unburdened by actually being brilliant or complex.

Levi and I had a good string of hits from about 1973 to 1980. I'd even toured with him, generating new songs on the road. But by the eighties, our music had fallen out of favor, and we both used this as an opportunity to pursue other projects. Neither of us really recreated our early successes, but Levi did as well as an out-of-vogue folk rocker can reasonably expect, landing soundtrack work ("Cloud Tears" for that cartoon, "Davy Jones' Lockdown" for that ridiculous pirate/prison film). He elevated even that schlock to the point where I had tears in my eyes when I took my kids to see them and heard Levi singing over the credits. I did okay too, for a while, and landed on the adult contemporary chart with one forgettable tune. Then my career stalled out on one particular song I'd been hired to write for an up-and-coming neo-soul songstress. Her manager was looking for a simple Motown classic that would show off the girl's voice, but I became so taken with her tone and phrasing that I wanted to do something more ambitious, a little opus, a kind of Chapin's "Taxi" with a high-flying bridge. I wrote pages and pages, fifteen minutes worth of bittersweet sentiments (nothing the girl could have sung convincingly—she was just shy of twenty), wrote long past when the manager needed the lyrics, long past when the singer put out her first and last small-label album, long past when she gave up her music career and got into real estate (last I heard). I planned on finishing it for someone else—or for its own sake—but it never got done. The longer I worked the more tight and convoluted it became, and the simple thread of loss I hoped to convey became a hopeless tangle of abstraction and symbol that I tried to unweave for years before giving up.

Soon after that, Dee became a factor, and I just never got back to writing. I don't want that failed song to be the last work I do. I want to write like I used to—for a performer who really connects with my work, who can elevate and transform it. There's truly something magical in what Levi can do—when I hear my words in his voice, it's as if I can see a pathos in myself that I otherwise can't. It used to really help me.

Soon enough Dee himself stops by. I can tell it's him by the shave-and-a-haircut knock, a knock he never fails to use even when he's a total mess and hardly knows his own name. Strange what the mind holds onto when everything else is lost. When I open the door, he begins speaking in a fast blurt, as if he's memorized what he is going to say and needs to get it all out before he forgets.

"I know you don't believe me that I'm clean. I know you think I'm using even now, and I totally get that. I understand. But I am clean. I saved a guy's life. And he saved my life. I came here because I wanted you to know."

I let him in and sit down at my computer while he sits on the edge of the bed, rubbing his hands together and clearing his voice between sentences, waiting for me to say something.

"I truly believe some higher power put that man in front of me at the exact moment we both needed each other. I remember looking in his eyes and hearing the click when I did the compressions. His eyes were just dead. He was gone. I looked into those black holes and just coaxed the universe back. I brought myself back. It happened for a reason. Everything does. I believe me coming here and you being here and working with Levi—it's all part of a healing plan . . ."

Coaxed the universe back. I find myself typing the phrase without meaning to.

"Look, Dad, I'm sorry. For everything. But you have to believe what happened that night in Detroit was real—"

"From what I gathered, the 'uppers' you were on are what gave you the strength to do those chest compressions. Seems like a great argument for doing drugs, not for quitting. And I don't get, after all the shit you've done, why some freakout with a heart attack victim in the ghetto is what turned you around. What about all you did to me? How about the time you punched me and broke my glasses? Or when you cleared out my safe deposit box? None of that triggered an epiphany? And by the way, you still owe me that money . . ."

I keep going in this vein, though the whole while I'm picturing how I would have responded just a few years ago, and it is as if that self is next to me, getting up from the chair, embracing Dee, laughing and talking to him, reliving his heroism in Detroit, sharing funny stories about ditzy old Levi and speculating on Lucinda's relationship with him. I feel sorry for that ghost self—his fragile, temporary joys and more enduring disappointments—and relieved as hell that he's not me.

Dee cuts me off in a low cajoling voice, as if negotiating with an erratic mental patient. "Okay, okay, I understand you're still mad. I understand. But I'm going to show you. Believe it." He pats my shoulder as he leaves, and the gesture is infuriatingly paternal, as if I'm the troubled son.

Levi and I are outside the main house on the back porch, sipping wine at small café table. Lucinda has supplied a bowl of fruit, placing it down between us and then turning toward me as she left with what looked to me like a gently sardonic grin, the kind of playfully doubting look I've historically found sexy. She's probably overheard her share of absurd conversations out here—moldering rock stars measuring the weathers of their inner lives with Dopplers of crystals and cleansing diets and tomes written by this or that bestselling seer. Front men gone to seed who gossip with such desperation you'd think old grudges were the sole fuel of some inner sustaining furnace. There's no doubt a parade of eccentrics traipsing through here each summer, making music or art or pretending to.

The yard is scattered with bits of refuse used as both sculptures and as seating for friends of Levi who come here to work. A metal horse trough, flipped over and bleeding rust, sits next to an old tractor seat jammed into earth. A lizard made from bicycle chains rears up next to a kinetic sculpture of a large bird, its Plexiglas and pop-can-ring feathers vibrating lightly in the wind. I've been telling Levi all about Dee—the long history of drug abuse, the uncanny way he maintains his sobriety just long enough to earn your trust before he breaks it, etc., etc. Levi nods the whole time, his brow scrunched between his dusky blue eyes. Levi looks so sympathetic, so wise, that I almost expect a profound discourse on the breakdown of familial relationships vis-à-vis art, but then he scratches his brush of gray blond hair and pops a melon ball into his mouth.

"Well, Danny, all I can tell you is what I see. He seems like a great kid. We talked last night after you went to bed and he laid a lot of that heavy stuff out for me. Seems pretty self-knowing. We got to talking about the Zen concept of letting go . . . he's real bright, you know? He gives off a nice energy . . ."

The breeze moves Levi's hair away from his forehead, exposing his oddly dewy, luminous skin. His looks have always pulled from history—he can appear as rosy and sunstruck as a cherub in the clouds or as stiff and shadowed as a daguerreotype of a nineteenth-century colonel. His speaking voice—unguarded and rich, with the slightest vulnerable tremor on long vowels—makes whatever he says sound thoughtful. With Levi, I always find myself hearing him out, even though I'd cut someone else off with a scoff if I heard such palaver. He has a way of making reason itself seem cynical, something only the spiritually bankrupt need bother with.

I take a sip of wine. The dogs have been let out, and they walk out into the yard, stopping and posing among the yard art as if engaged in a challenging modern dance. Off in the distance I can see the light in Dee's cabin. Most likely he is packing up his things now, or walking in circles holding up his phone, trying to catch a signal from Detroit. Dee's inconsequential—coming to Chautauqua is about writing again, working with Levi to make something beautiful out of the pure belief of his voice.

"And that was a pretty amazing story about him saving that guy. You gotta believe his good karma is off the charts right about now."

I've spent the rest of the afternoon trying to write, without much luck. I asked Lucinda to bring dinner to me in my cabin, thinking it would be best to focus on my work rather than let Dee's din-

31

ner theater distract me. Who knows what the next installment will be? Maybe he rescued a baby at the bottom of a lake, buoyed by a few hits of nitrous oxide. But the less I engage the better, and now the thought of returning my plates to Lucinda as the evening winds down gives me something to work toward. When she dropped off my food, she tapped my forearm with her small silver-ringed hand and told me not to work too hard. That was nice.

Nothing's come so far; the page in front of me is still empty. I think about calling Natalie, but her hyperpracticality wouldn't be useful now. She wouldn't understand what was going on here anyway—the skillful way I'm juggling Levi's sensibilities with Dee's presence wouldn't register with her. Subtleties don't interest her—the broad strokes do—will this student pass, is this student off drugs, how can I keep this one from getting pregnant. Good for her line of work, but not for art.

I write out a phrase—the stars are a scrolling readout—and I start to relax. It's a good line, good enough to perhaps build something from it. Then it hits me. This is a Dee phrase. He called a few months ago and started talking about how the stars seemed like some kind of electric readout, describing his state of mind as he wandered down the beach. I immediately scratch it out, bearing down on the paper so even the contours of the words can't be seen. I'm breathing hard and I put my hand on my heart and feel it flutter. I take a drink from the chilled white wine Lucinda so thoughtfully left, then I try again.

I watched her aurora eyes . . . Not so good, but okay, a start. I put my pen to my lips and concentrate on the line, thinking of where to take it next. Then I remember. Dee said this one when he called to describe his breakup with his waifish girlfriend, the one with the shoots-n-ladders tattoo that covered her whole left leg, winding from her ankle all the way up to the exposed white pockets of her cut-off shorts, and I presume, beyond. She was blinking out after a binge of some sort, and Dee had stayed up watching her, willing her mind to change about their future. This time I scribble the words out so roughly that the paper tears. I rip the whole sheet off and start with a fresh one.

By the flipped silhouette, I regained a planet in you, the shimmer of relief . . . It keeps happening. Everything reveals itself as Dee's. It's as if his lovely phrases have colonized my mind and pushed everything out. I don't want to use these words. I don't want any part of Dee in this work. The whole point is to move fully past all that. Back to the time before the kid was even born. But it's as if, through some sinister telepathy, Dee keeps interrupting. I try writing terrible phrases, stupid things, or just gibberish. No dice. Everything seems to pull from something Dee once slurred, mumbled, or shouted. There's not an unsullied thought in my head.

I haven't touched my food—some kind of thick pasta with flecks of fish grows cold next to me. I take another drink. Dinner is probably over by now. I could return my plates, talk with Lucinda and commiserate about the crazy talk she is forced to bear witness to around here. That look of hers—quiet, ironic, and warm—makes it clear that she has a high sense of the absurd, no doubt honed by watching Levi and the excesses that unfold around him. We could have a glass of wine and laugh at the strangeness of our companions. That will be as good for her, I'm sure, as it will be for me.

I leave the cabin and see that the studio light is on, as if Levi and Dee might be getting together for a postdinner session. Fine, fair enough. I fling the dinner off my plate into the woods. Wouldn't want to offend Lucinda with an unfinished dinner. It's dark and somewhat chilly. The crisp margins of the half-moon above look like a surgical excision in the night, a bright wedge of proud flesh. It's incredibly quiet, except for the dampened bustle of nocturnal animals waking and beginning their rounds. And a long squeak, a curse and a laugh—something being moved in the studio, someone stubbing a toe.

Lucinda joins me for a drink in the dining room. The lights are all dimmed, and a candle, still burning from dinnertime, weeps wax between us. She's lovely in this light. Her face is wide at the top, with large, heavily lidded eyes, while her mouth is small and overstuffed with a jumble of teeth, the sliver of an overbite showing even when she shuts her lips. A messy dark braid falls over her shoulder. She's the type of woman who seems ageless—there's no trace of youthful plumpness in the flat planes her face, nor is there a wrinkle. She tells me about her life in a small village in Portugal, her culinary schooling in the States, and a story about smuggling saffron in the lining of her bra on a flight after a visit home. When she laughs her rumbly low laugh, she shakes her head and winces, as if being amused is a little painful, something to shake off.

"Listen," I finally say, when we've both relaxed sufficiently. "What do you think of these two jokers? I mean, I love Levi, don't get me wrong, but we both know he's kind of a flake. And my son Dee—sorry he's here by the way—I did not invite him—I give you credit for not laughing and spitting up your wine when he was going on about restarting that bum's heart and his 'own heart as well...'"

I start to laugh myself now, wild peals. My eyes are filling with tears and a little bubble of hysteria, pleasurable and frightening, rises in my chest. I touch Lucinda's wrist to ground myself, to keep myself in the room and of this world. The warmth of her skin sobers me up, and I look at her, giving her a chance to let loose her own commentary and pained chuckle.

"I'm not sure I know what you mean. Levi is a bright man. And your son... his story was amazing. I don't know why a person would laugh at that."

Is she putting me on? Or simply making me disassemble the whole myth that Dee built around his addiction as a kind of flirtation? I laugh, to show Lucinda I'm onto her, and then comply.

I tell her his story is unbelievable, full of logical holes and crazy claims, and even if it was true, Dee's supposed epiphany and conversation struck me as cheap, sudden, and deluded. All that talk of destiny—destiny is just narcissism, a sad wish that the events of the world all ordered themselves around you. As I'm sure Lucinda knows.

"I'm not sure about all that. Some strange things are true. When I was a young girl in Barroselas, we had a saying, 'The water flows without cease.' It means your life is traveling somewhere, somewhere beyond your control. On birthdays we'd make a chain of flowers, drop it in the river, then spend the whole day following where it floated. If the chain got snagged, we would have a picnic on the bank and wait for it to either break apart or get free. It was said that the snag meant your year would be difficult and it was always right. I got the snag the year my fiancé found his Spanish girlfriend. I was so angry I cooked up everything we had in the pantry and left seven full meals on the porch. But you, maybe you don't think this way. You seem to be more of a business type person? A person who follows only facts and maybe money. That's how you talk."

So there will be no meeting of the minds. I put my head down on the table for a moment, and let the room swim. Lucinda pats my head and walks out, the dogs heaving up with a joint sigh and following her out. The sink runs and pans clang and then the kitchen light goes out. Eventually, I get up. I have the space to myself. I walk around, a little drunk, peering at all Levi's souvenirs and tchotchkes. With all the traveling he's done, you'd think he'd develop some street smarts, some healthy self-protection.

I think of what Dee would do alone in a big, opulent space like this. Steal. He would steal to feed his habit, steal out of some misguided attempt to balance out the scales of life. "You're rich," he had once said to me, after pawning off James Taylor's signed set list for something he instantly shot or inhaled into his body. "You didn't need it. It was just a fucking museum piece, morgue décor." He's stolen thousands of dollars' worth of things from me over the years, stole so much that I changed my locks every few months as a matter of course. When he'd visit I'd follow him to the bathroom. I'd make sure he was wearing short sleeves, and I'd even ask him to empty his pockets in front of me when he left, which he'd do with a baneful expression, like some pauper cartoon character.

Dee would steal. He probably already has. Levi is so innocent, so easily duped . . . There's something both inspirational and unseemly in Levi's openness, his willingness to trust all things. In a young man, it seems right and normal, but in Levi that innocence—suspended perfectly intact like some primordial bug in amber—feels spooky, unreal. How is it that he hasn't changed at all? The bubble of fame can't account for it. He was swindled out of money, swindled out of the rights to some of the best songs in his catalogue by Larry Devins, his manager in the eighties. He's been through at least two divorces, as far as I know. His father was a harsh military man who thought his son's dreams of a life in music were corrupt and delusional, and the man died right before we left on our first tour, before Levi could say "I told you so." Dee would take him for everything he had.

My eyes fall on a small jade elephant, a trinket from Levi's trip to India when he was in his full Buddhist phase. As I think of Dee and Levi—both so deluded in their own way, both so unreasonable—I pick up the figurine and switch it from hand to hand. The cool stone feels pleasant, bracing, as if it were a physical representation of the clarity that everyone in Chautauqua seems to lack. Idly, I move through the house with it, looking at old pictures of Levi and old pictures of me. Then I pocket it.

The next morning Dee and Levi are at the table, talking about something they keep referring to as "the secret weapon." I eat my oatmeal and watch the empty spot where the jade elephant had been. No one seems to notice.

"I can't wait to try out the secret weapon, man. I think you are totally right on that it'll make that track." Levi is saying to Dee.

Then he turns to me. "Danny, you've got to come to the studio. You gotta hear what Dee and I came up with. We've got an incredible track, ninety percent done, we just need lyrics. Would you give a listen? I know you've been working on the lyrics . . . maybe you can match them up with what we got so far."

I follow them into the studio, the place I've been avoiding since I arrived. Levi's walk is unchanged—eager and upright, he seems to rise up on tiptoe, as if trying to take a peek at something each stride. Dee walks with a measured, quiet step, like a contemplative monk walking the grounds, his hands clasped behind his back. Far different from the darting, manic boy who was constantly jiggling a leg or running his hands through his hair.

Levi hands me the headphones and for a moment I hear nothing. Then the music comes in. Something like a muted toy xylophone reverbing. Then, Levi's voice, strangely lilting, then falling into spoken word. Improvised placeholder lyrics and a vaguely Spanish guitar hook, and then some kind of clicking dirtied up the track. The tick becomes louder but remains muffled, like sticks snapping under a coat of leaves. Then, the guitar, this time more muscular, rising up and thinning out to a clear high sound that I feel in my teeth, like a tuning fork. And the tick, quieting. I pull the headphones off.

"What do you think?" Levi leans forward and looks me in the eye. Dee stands over his shoulder and seems to be meditating, humming to himself with his eyes closed.

"Interesting. A real departure. What's that ticking sound that starts midway? It was distracting."

Levi smiles and looks back over his shoulder at Dee, who breaks into a wide grin. Then Levi laughs and slaps my knee.

"That's the secret weapon. That sound . . . it's the click of a compressed sternum during CPR. Dee found the sample from some emergency training web video. Isn't it amazing? That sound is just so . . . I don't know . . . guttural or something. Fleshy. Bony. I love it. It's full of life, huh?"

I have quite a bounty in my pocket. The jade elephant from earlier, the sea horse ring, a brass swan incense holder, my own watch, and the ultimate prize—one of Levi's and my gold records, slipped into the lining of my coat. It all clinks and chimes in my coat like frolicsome imps playing atonal music. I'm wandering all around Chautauqua, halfway looking for Lucinda and halfway plotting how to deal with Dee. And halfway—if I can have another halfway here—just enjoying the act of roaming around with all these thoughts and desires in my head, things no one knows about. Levi thinks I'm a blocked writer at odds with my perfectly nice son. Dee thinks I'm just stewing in my cabin, on the cusp of breaking down and believing him once more, opening my heart and wallet as butterflies of acceptance and love flutter about both our faces. And Lucinda thinks I'm a cynic, a killer of mysteries, and probably a dull guy besides, compared to sweet celestial Levi. But I'm not those things. If Lucinda saw me now, she'd see that I was electric with possibility. The taken objects— and the soft clamor of their physical presence—make me feel a sudden confidence, a confidence that can come only when you hold something back from the world. Dee used to talk about the pleasures of a secret high when he was younger, that wonderful feeling of being stoned while no one knows or can tell. Extra points if you're doing something exceptionally wholesome like cooking Christmas cookies with grandma. The swirls and shifts of the room—the wild non sequitur thoughts—these are all your own to savor and conceal.

I turn off into the woods. Bars of light bend over the high branches and thin as they focus in on the forest floor. This is wild country—there are no trails, and Rosa multiflora keeps snagging me, like a clutch of fans desperate for whatever piece of me they can get. The hillside seems repetitive and smudged; nature seems to me a dull pattern, a decorative border. It's steep, and I slide on my heels a few times. An enormous rotted log, mossy and covered with the sinewy trails of some boring insect, lies across the way. It's split in the middle, right down to the ground. I pull the record out of my coat lining and take a look at it. It's the gold record for "Many a Moon." The frame includes the silver-painted record, the little certifying plaque from the RIAA and a photograph of Levi and me, riding double on a statue Civil War horse on tour long ago. I sat in front of the general, and he sat behind, hugging the stone figure with what appeared to be a rush of affection.

It was an unexpected hit for us. The song used lunar imagery to describe the way a man and a women drift apart and back together. She kept me waiting on her half-lit eyes . . . As I wrote the thing I imagined Levi and me laughing over it over a joint, wadding it up and tossing it in the busted base drum we used as a trash can. Levi had no high sense of irony, I knew, but even he would find this an occasion to roll his eyes and drop, for a moment at least, his blinding sincerity. I kept writing, pushing the lyrics into schmaltz and sugar, to baroque despair, and then, finally, an unearned and soaring end. I felt strange and elated when I handed Levi my work. He laughed just a little, said "crazy, Danny," then began to play and sing. He mugged and oversang for a few bars then let the thing fall into a kind of weird hiccupping tone, something between crying and laughing, a lovely kind of thing that kept the eye-rolling in it as well as that overarching sense that it mattered.

I pop the record out of the frame. The photo of Levi and me flutters off. I push the record into the groove in the wood. The last quarter inch or so protrudes and catches the light. I put my hands in the dirt, pull up some moss and leaves, and spread it over the edge of the record. Done and done. I break down the frame, throw the glass at a tree, kick earth on the shards.

Levi will surely notice it is gone and I already have my reaction planned. I will simply turn to Dee with a sad look, a look of deep disappointment, a look of fragile trust broken. I'll hold up my wrist and show that my watch, too, is gone. Dee will start rolling out his denials, and Levi, watching the tableaux, will see what Dee truly is—a charmer, a fraud, a spinner of tales. I want to hear his sputtering denial, see the confusion break over his face. Of course it's true that he didn't actually steal the thing, but small matter. It will give him a little taste of what it feels like to talk to him during one of his binges. The way a word in the conversation would suddenly slide off the rational, and you'd know. Every time he called and at least started the conversation with "Hello," I used to be filled with hope, since so many of his calls began midstream in what best resembled the jump cuts and shorthand of an inner monologue, as if you were simply a microphone he switched on in his brain.

I turn and run up the hill, tromping over brambles, letting others snag me and spin me around for a moment. I leap over a log into a tangle of vines and fall onto my back. The wind is knocked out of me, and I look up at the little lacework of sky through the trees, waiting on my breath. Actually, it feels like I'm waiting to breathe out, not in. It's fine I can't write anymore, I think, enjoying the breathless silence of my own body. What's the big obsession with letting things out into the world? Songs, ideas, stories . . . the real pleasure is keeping it all in. That's where the power is.

When I get up, gasping, I continue racing up the hill where Lucinda, as if fated, stands watching the dogs sniff and poop amongst the trash sculptures. Her back, draped in a golden camel cape, seems to nod and beckon as she pets one of the strange, stilted dogs. I swoop behind her and do the least expected thing: lift her up and spin her, watching her face go ashen and then, with enough revolutions, a shocking red.

"And how is the writing going? And what's happened with Dee?" Natalie asks. She sounds so aggressively no-nonsense that I half expect all of Chautauqua to crumble into the void as she talks, the house lights to flick back on, and real life to resume. Her voice in this atmosphere is completely out of place; there's nothing I could say that would make sense to her now, and nothing she could say that would be relevant here. You always get into these moments with lovers, though, and you learn to cloak experience with bland chatter rather than try to convey the impossible.

"The writing's tough. I've taken a lot of time off, as you know, but I'm slowly warming up again. Dee's still here but laying low. It's fine. I'm not letting him get to me."

I walk around the cabin as I talk and peer in the closet. A hefty pile of objects now, from both the main house and the studio. I smile when I see the bejeweled dog collar at the top of the pile. I slipped it off as one of beasts trotted by, so smoothly that it didn't even break stride.

"And you?" I ask, as I sit down at my desk. I flip my notebook open, where I've now written every interesting phrase Dee has ever said during a binge. Dozens have come to me in the last hours. I figure if I write them all down, then cross them all out, I might purge my brain of them, too. It feels good to scratch over them. As good as any writing session.

Natalie tells me all about a student of hers—a brilliant girl, gifted in math, whose boyfriend is a notorious neighborhood thug. This girl, Olivia, keeps playing hooky. The mother's doing nothing. Natalie drives into the girl's block and confronts the girl's mother in the street. Words are exchanged. It's unprofessional viewed one way, viewed another it is absolutely necessary . . . My mind drifts as she talks—words are exchanged—the cliché seems weirdly apropos, as it describes what's happened with Dee's old phrases. He's given me his words and taken all of mine.

I let Natalie talk, let her feel as if we're sharing something. Then I tell her I love her and goodbye.

When Levi, Lucinda, and Dee all appear at my cabin door, I assume they're inviting me to dinner—insisting that I come out, take a break from all the work. The second possibility is that they've confronted Dee about his stealing and are dragging him to me, like wardens, so I can pass the final judgment on him. I keep my face neutral so I can be ready for either possibility. Levi asks if they can come in, and I step aside. They all file in—Dee and Lucinda sit on the bed, Levi in the corner rocking chair and I sit at my desk.

Levi clears his throat and rearranges himself in the chair several times. Lucinda keeps her profile to me, her eyes on Levi. She's wearing what looks like one long rose-colored scarf, wrapped multiple times around her body to make a dress. I get the feeling if I grabbed one end and pulled, her whole person would unravel and I'd be standing there, holding nothing but a bolt of limp fabric. Dee's skin is sheened with sweat, and a few strands of his hair cling to his hairline in even swoops, like crown molding. He seems to be sitting in a position to best show off his "ink." His wrists are turned up so the trust tattoo shows. His right leg is crossed over his left, and his jeans ride up so the roots of the tree on his calf can be seen, reaching down into his sockless tennis shoes. The small picket fence on his collarbone pokes through a gap in his collar. A strange tattoo—is it a commentary on the emptiness of suburban striving? Does it indicate that he's within the fence—trapped—or that we, the onlookers, are the ones trapped, and he's actually on the outside, in some more authentic bohemian beyond? He swallows hard and the pickets rise up for a moment.

"Danny, we're here because . . ." Levi coughs and scratches his neck. He takes a few breaths. The yellow wood of the cabin reflects a gold light on his colorless hair; he looks like a beatific stained-glass saint, complete with the weepy eyes. He jumps up from his chair and gestures with both hands.

"I just want to say, right off, that this isn't about the stuff, you know? Material things—they've never meant shit to me, you know that, right Danny? That's not what this is about. It's about you know, just why? What's going on with you? If you want something, just ask. You're my friend. I want to give you things. You've gotta know that. So why the secretive stuff?"

I look at Dee, who is rubbing his wrists together and looking at the ceiling.

"What secretive stuff?"

"Well, gee Danny. The taking things. You've been taking things. Lucinda says you've been walking around the house late at night, just grabbing stuff, I guess . . ."

"Wait." I get up and step towards Dee, standing over him. "You're calling me a thief? When this guy's skulking around the property? Here's your problem. This kid. He's causing trouble. Stealing and pinning it on his dad. It's not the first time he's pulled this kind of shit. This is what he does."

"Goddamnit, Dad," and now Dee is up, right in my face. Lucinda is up too, her hand on him, and I can hear her begging him to be calm, murmuring some mantra about quiet waters. "I haven't done anything, Dad, and you know it. You've got the problem, you—"

And then Levi rushes over to break us apart. He's moving fast, and then he's down at our feet. We all crouch down. All six hands are on him, trying to flip him over but pulling him opposite directions. Then he's over, face up. His eyes are filmed over and his face, without the girding of his permanent smile, flattens and pools.

I used to think of emergencies as these character-galvanizing events, these moments when life does a casting call and shows a person for who they truly are. The timid and mousy become commanding heroes, barking instructions, and the brash in everyday life shrink into impotence and hysteria. So once the situation becomes plain—that Levi is in very bad shape, and that an ambulance will have a hell of time getting out here in time, meaning we have to drive—I watch as I'm moved, as if by the impatient hands of a director, into the role of the stunned, incoherent bystander, whose every move is an impediment and liability. I can't take my eyes off of Levi, who is in and out of consciousness on the floor. I feel like the whole problem is my perception, and if I could just bring Levi into better focus—make some sense of his moaning, reassemble his sliding features back into their familiar formation of gentle, pleased bemusement, all would be solved.

Lucinda and Dee are speaking in short, efficient barks to one another. Dee grabs my shoulder and pushes me back.

"Dad, Dad! Does your car have gas?"

I tell him yes, and I can hear, in my voice, a scary sluggishness as I'm now on Levi time, the slow-down of catastrophe. Dee shakes me, pulls me up, and the two of us lift and halfway drag Levi to the car. The sun is Indian-summer bright, and the slight heat brings out flavors in the woods—musky animal hair, the yeast of last year's thickening leaves, the ferment of overripe berries. The incongruent outdoors makes our carrying of Levi seem celebratory, a triumphant king paraded around by his footmen. We get to the car, and Dee morphs into an engineer, an expert in all the ways an inert body can be arranged into the tight space of a midsize sedan's back seat. He delivers rapid fire orders, tells me where to grab Levi, the pounds of pressure I should apply to each pull.

"Sit with Levi. Keep his head up so he doesn't choke. If he stops breathing, yell out. Got it?"

I climb in and prop myself against Levi's listing body. He turns his head and flutters his hands toward me. The car screeches away from Chautauqua, down the steep dirt road with all the switchbacks. Lucinda sedately narrates the route while Dee pilots the car, his eyes fixed and flat in the rear view mirror.

Levi falls onto me. Each of his breaths barely strings to the next. His head is on my lap, his eyes flutter back and forward. Expressions appear—slight smiles, squints, a pop of surprise widening his eyes and mouth—then depart, erasing more of his face as they go, like a wiping hand. I put my hands on either side of him, trying to keep him still, but his head feels like it's losing mass, emptying with each of his rough breaths, as if breathing were draining his substance rather than sustaining it. My own breath shortens and I feel the clutch of panic around my heart, something I last felt running around the city looking for Dee, sure that a pile of rags and fast food bags was his dead body. Even when it wasn't, I slid to the ground, cutting my palms on glass and junk all around me, huffing in short shallow breaths like some dog, frantically sniffing the life out of some primo scent. I focused on the creased and warped image of a cartoon dolphin on a McDonald's bag, the kind of bland commercial image that doesn't admit of life or death or anything, until I was finally able to get up.

Dee hears my breathing, and so does Lucinda. Dee catches my eyes in the mirror.

"It's okay, Dad. He'll be fine. People can look really bad and be okay. Just stay calm. That's your only job right now."

The car bounces and rolls. I put my arm over Levi and hold him. Dee turns on the radio. It's one of our songs—Levi's and mine—that I'd been listening to on the way to Chautauqua. Levi's voice fills the car. He sounds both melancholy and luxurious, like someone blinking tears back and smiling into a warm sun. The song is "When We Turn Away," a lament I wrote after my breakup with Joyce.

> *And when we turn away*
> *I see all the city lights*
> *the beach we never made it to*
> *the flowered dress I thought of buying you . . .*

Dee begins singing, in a buttery tenor, a voice I've never heard before, a voice perhaps reserved for those moments when no one

45

is listening closely. Lucinda joins in with a bright soprano with a shrill edge, a dangerous voice that soars and shears. And then I'm singing, very quietly, in a little flat drone. I'm a bad singer with terrible pitch—that's why I'm the lyricist—and I can't recall the last time I sang, even to myself. I don't ever sing my own words. But it helps me breathe. Each note is making me exhale a little longer, each pause cues me to breathe in.

The road gets rougher, and we're pitched into a series of blind turns. Dee stops singing. His forearms are so tense on the wheel that they shiver. I'm in no shape or position to offer comfort, but I want to say something.

"This is the worst part. Just this part of not knowing what's going to happen. I think hell is waiting to know if you're going to hell or not. The waiting's the hell."

"Dad, that's about the least comforting thing you could say." He catches my face in the mirror and shakes his head. Lucinda chuckles as if she's just smashed her finger.

Levi blinks up at me, recognition lapping over his face and receding. His voice, even in this ragged whisper, sounds sure.

"It's still a good line."

Let Me Tell You How I Met
My First Husband, the Clown

ALFRED DEPEW

From *The Melancholy of Departure* (1992)

No really. That's what he does for work. And you already guessed. I was in the audience. I wasn't even going to go, but my friend Sylvia said, "Come on, you study too much, we're going." In those days I was very serious. I was going to be an actress. Very serious. The only part I wanted to play was Medea. I figured there was a woman with spine. Lady Macbeth wasn't bad either, but she was too snooty. For me, nothing would do but the Greeks. Shakespeare was a little messy—all those bodies onstage at the end of *Hamlet*. Who could believe it? No. I preferred my murders offstage. That way nothing would detract from my lines. I'm telling you, those Greeks had class. Besides, what could I possibly learn from a clown?

But Sylvia said, "Come on," so I grabbed my coat, and we trudged through the Wisconsin snow to the college chapel to watch this guy. I was determined not to laugh. I was hell-bent to not even enjoy it a little. Laugh? Not on your life. And the audience! Philistines, every one. This was kid stuff, and at nineteen I was not a kid. Now, the older I get . . . well. But middle age is another story. This is how we met.

He was tall and skinny. I mean skinny. And he had this sharp nose, very Anglican-looking or Presbyterian or something.

Whatever. In the Midwest, everyone looks the same—not like anybody I knew growing up in Manhattan. They look like everybody on TV who isn't Jewish or Italian, like they've got this special farm in Iowa maybe to breed them. So he looked like that, like he sprouted up from the earth between two cornstalks in a field outside Normal, Illinois, though he was in reality from Beardsville, which, after I got to know him, I called Weirdsville. He said it was my Jewish wit. You should have seen his mother's face when she met me. But that came later.

This night, I sat in the way back because I knew he'd probably pull people out of the first rows and bring them up onstage, and I'd have died. A serious actress like myself, sharing the spotlight with a guy who did circus tricks. So I sat there, determined not to laugh, and he did his first thing, which was not so bad actually. I could see the humor in it. I could see why the audience liked him. They were not what you'd call sophisticated. What I'm saying is it was a certain *kind* of humor, the kind of thing you've seen a thousand times—Emmett Kelly stuff, the stuff Red Skelton does, good for what it is, but a little thin in intellectual content. If you don't know what I'm talking about, I can't explain it.

The thing is he was kind of beautiful, his eyes and his long, long fingers. And he was a good mime too. I had to hand him that. He made all the invisible walls and shelves and ropes seem very real. I wondered if he had studied in Paris, which would have redeemed him a little in my mind. Then he did this thing about a baseball game, he was completely different for every player, and I confess I laughed a little. Though, you live in the heartland a year or two, you begin to get some of the jokes—real cornball stuff. It catches you off guard, you have a little affection for it, but I was still determined not to give in to him. And you know? It's as if he knew that, and I swear he began playing right to me. He had these blue, blue eyes (cornflower blue, his mother called them; I always found that nauseating—I always found *her* nauseating, and believe me, the feeling was mutual, though she was too nice to admit it, but of course nice had nothing to do with it; she was a liar, a very dishonest person with her emotions).

Anyway, I noticed him looking at me straight and stern, with this big grin every time he turned towards my part of the audience. And the more I didn't laugh, the more he sort of bore down on me, grinning. I swear he could see me, even though I was so far away, and to tell you the truth, it made me very nervous because I knew he was working up to the part of his schtick when he pulls innocent people up on the stage, and I was getting self-conscious, like other people knew he was playing to me, and it occurred to me that he might be crazy enough to do something that would embarrass me in public.

He did these little magic tricks—you know, the forty-seven Ping-Pong balls that keep coming out of his mouth and his sleeves and his coat pockets? And then it happened. He pointed to someone in the first row, and a little blonde coed (I hate the term to this day, but if it fits) flounced up on the stage and started to giggle. He did everything she did, put his hand over his mouth, toed the floor, shooed her away. Then he handed her his cane and tried to teach her how to balance it on her nose, which of course got a big laugh. Then he took it back from her and made like it got very heavy all of a sudden—you know the trick—like it was a barbell, and he picked it up, raised it to just under his chin, and then sank under its weight until he fell back, hard, like it had pinned him to the floor. He stuck out his hand, and the little coed grabbed it and pulled him up.

That's when I noticed I wanted to kill her. My hands were clutching the arms of my seat, and I hoisted myself up a little. Sylvia leaned over and said, "What's the matter?" and I sat back down again. I was breathing hard. I stared straight out in front of me, and Sylvia rightly took that to mean: Don't ask any questions, I'll explain it later. Which I did. In fact, I spent years trying to explain it to Sylvia, who always listened angelically but I think never understood. How could she? I didn't understand it myself.

I wanted to pull that coed's hair out by the handful, and I remember thinking there was probably more of it all wound up in her head; her skull was full of it, like that doll, Tressy. It was a waking nightmare. As if everything surrounding that man was rigged somehow. And then the strangest thing happened; I wanted to kill him too—for making me feel like a fool, for pulling reality out from under me.

You can see why Medea held such a fascination for me in those days. We had the same problem. We tended to overreact.

By intermission I was beside myself. I ran to the ladies' room, locked myself in a stall, and wept. When I got back to my seat, I could tell Sylvia was edgy. She was dying to know. "Do you want to leave?" she said. "Not on your life," I said. And I laughed and cried all through the second half.

I didn't go up to him right after. I had my pride. I knew I had to talk to him, but I couldn't figure out a way. I asked someone, "Hey, where does he go next?" And the answer was Rockford College in Rockford, Illinois, which was not so very far away I couldn't borrow a car and drive there.

So that's what I did. I kept trying to figure out what I was going to do once I got there, because after the performance, it would be the same. People would go up to him to tell him they enjoyed it and maybe flirt with him a little, and I didn't want to be one of them. I wanted to be set apart, noticed a little apart.

Sylvia lent me her old Ford Falcon, which until the day I borrowed it had been very dependable and never any trouble to Sylvia or anybody else. And the motor was fine. It was the tire that was shot. Bam! It blew right after I got beyond the outskirts of Madison, too far to walk back, so I stood there, waving my arms at passing cars.

I'm embarrassed to admit that at nineteen I did not yet know how to change a flat tire. But then how would I learn? It's not a skill you need when you ride the subway. So I'm trying to flag down a passing motorist when this van drives by, and right off

I recognize Danny. He flashes me that big grin with an expression of sympathy on his face that could melt iron. Then he shrugs his shoulders—both hands off the steering wheel—points to his watch, and drives on. I was too stunned to even give him the finger. I stomped back to the Falcon and kicked one of the tires that still had air in it. Pretty soon, someone stopped and changed the tire. Thank God Sylvia had a spare that was okay. She was and still is I bet a very cautious and thorough person. And smart too. When she was a second-semester junior, she saw the writing on the wall. She changed her major from ethnomusicology to bookkeeping, which she could fall back on when her marriage to the dentist in Chicago didn't work out. He used to beat her up. How could she have known? He always seemed very gentle; he never raised his voice. When I knew him, he wore African shirts and sandals and clover chains around his neck. Remember the new sensitivity young men were cultivating in those days? It was a cruel joke. But what did we know? We thought we could end the war in Southeast Asia in six weeks. We thought marijuana would change the world. You have to understand: we were only kids.

About twenty miles down the road, I saw this van pulled over and a man stooped down, peering into the engine in the back. I knew right away it was him, even before I could see "Daniel Muldoon: One-Man Flying Circus" painted on the side panel. What luck! When I hopped out of the car, I shouted, "That'll teach you to drive past a woman stranded by the side of the road." And this surprised me. Believe it or not, I was a shy girl in those days. Sure, now—I see a man I like, and well, it's a different story. But then it was unusual for me to be so brash right off; I would wait until I got to know a person a little.

Danny grinned again. He looked like he was glad to see me. And not just because I stopped. He knew how to fix the van himself; it must have broken down thirty times in the seven years we were together, and he always fixed it himself. "Here," he said, "hold the flashlight."

So I held the flashlight while he banged around inside the motor with his monkey wrench. Pretty soon, he asked where I was headed.

"Rockford," I said.

"What do you know," he said. "That's where I'm going."

"No kidding," I said.

"Yeah," he said. "I've got a show at the college there tonight. You should come see it—as my guest."

"Sure," I said. "I'd like that."

"What do you do?" he asked.

"Medea," I said.

"How's that?" He pulled his head from under the hood and gave me a quizzical look.

"I'm an actress," I said. "Classical. I'm a Greek Jew, and the Greeks, I don't know, they kind of get to me. You know what I mean?"

When I saw how impressed he was, I was ashamed for having lied. My grandparents on both sides were Lithuanian. I don't know what got into me to say I was Greek. To a farm boy, what's the difference? Chicago is exotic. Why split hairs between Greece and Lithuania? But it was important right off he should know I come from people with a heritage, even though, looking back, I was taking the first step in my life that would cut me off from it.

We were married three days later in Evanston. Well, married. I should explain. It was not the sort of marriage a judge would recognize as legal, but if we hadn't moved from state to state so much, it would have been a common-law marriage. Maybe it was. I don't know if there's a federal law. I always meant to look that up. Legal or not, and I mean this, I felt more married to Danny than I did to any of the men I have subsequently married at the justice of the peace or in a Unitarian church or even in a synagogue with the in-laws there and a cantor and a bouquet.

It was the first, last, and only time we were onstage together. I sat in the front row, and when it came time for him to pull someone out of the audience, he chose me. I resisted at first, then I gave in, and once I was up there, what could I do, I was an actress; I tried not to look too stupid while he blew up balloons and twisted them into shapes. I played with him. I took the heart he made, put my arm through it, pointed to my sleeve, put it on my head, wore it like a crown. It was like nothing I'd ever done onstage. I lost all awareness of myself and the audience. I felt light as air, full of a shining beauty.

He stood erect and grim and fierce in front of me, with his hands open like he was holding a book; then he stood at my side, all bashful, shifting from one foot to the other, looking down at me and then away and then back again. Then he was the preacher again, and then the bridegroom.

Before I knew it, he slipped a balloon ring onto my wrist and played the wedding recessional on a kazoo as he marched me around the stage with everyone laughing and clapping. Then he stopped. He kissed me, and I had clown white all around my mouth. He raised his hands, came out of character and announced: "Ladies and gentlemen, I'd like you to meet Mrs. Daniel Muldoon." The audience stood up. They actually stood up and cheered, and I could see some of the women were dabbing their eyes with handkerchiefs. I remember thinking: They wish they were me; they wish they were going to have the life I'm going to have. And it was then I knew not one of them could take that away from me.

The next morning we drove back to Madison to return Sylvia's car, and that same day I packed everything I could fit in the van and told Sylvia to sell the rest. "Are you crazy?" she said, "What about exams?"

"Sylvia," I said, "exams I can take anytime. Following the man I love to the ends of the earth is a once-in-a-lifetime opportunity." Or so I thought. What did I know?

As practical as Sylvia is, I think she was a little jealous. And lonely to see me drive off with my one-man flying circus. She cried, and she kissed me. She made Danny promise to take good care of me. She stood on the curb, waving, and then made me get out of the van to hug her again. She said, "Good luck, be happy, keep in touch, be careful, and don't worry, I'll sell everything and send you the money," which she did. And then she cried again. Sweet Sylvia. My best friend in this life.

But before I left Madison, I had to call home. I couldn't just vanish. A Jewish girl disappears in the Midwest, you could find her hanging by the neck from a tree with a note from the Ku Klux Klan pinned to her lapel. So I called and said, "Hi, Ma. Guess what? I'm married. Be happy for me. I'm not pregnant. He's a great actor. We're going on the road. I'll keep in touch. Give my love to Pa. Bye." And I hung up. It was best not to get into a lengthy discussion.

We were on the road for seven years. Which is not to say we never lived in an apartment; we just never settled anywhere too long. Eighteen months in a place was about our limit. We toured big cities, small cities, all the college towns. Sometimes Danny would have to get a job waiting tables, but mostly I worked the money job to leave him free to perform and teach. I never became an actress. At this point, a number of you feminists are grinding your teeth and clenching your fists. But it wasn't like that. Danny never held me back. I lost my passion for Medea; it was no big tragedy. My interests broadened. I discovered politics. Those were the years of the revolution; there was always something you could do. I stuffed envelopes and canvassed neighborhoods and marched and got myself arrested a lot. Once or twice, Danny experimented with guerrilla theater, the stuff they were doing in the streets, but to be perfectly honest, he wasn't very good at it. He never could make himself frightening enough. He just wasn't an angry man; his heart wasn't in it.

And I knitted. I couldn't smoke during the performance, so I would knit. I knitted booties and little sweaters and blankets for the kids his sisters and our friends were having. I knitted us both sweaters and gloves and mittens and socks. Now I can't stand the thought of knitting. I must have gotten it all out of my system. It's too bad; there are times when my little boy needs something, but I figure it's simpler to buy. I don't have the time anymore.

And I watched. I must have seen Danny perform 896 times in the seven years we were together. It's not like it was the same thing all the time. He changed his act a lot, tried out new material, added, deleted, rotated his routines, and he improvised a great deal; it depended on the crowd. I can't say I ever got bored, and it's hard for me to think now what was my favorite. As much as I loved talking to him and fighting with him and watching him sleep and of course making love with him—for that alone, he should've gotten awards—I think I always loved him best when he was onstage. Not best. Maybe different. He was magic. Not altogether of this world.

Every so often, he'd pick a very timid child out of the audience and bring him up on the stage. Without a word, Danny would teach this kid how to do things, little things, something as simple as opening his arms wide and facing the audience, and everybody clapped. I swear you could see this kid changing before your eyes. He'd grin and look up at Danny, like he was beginning to know it was not such a bad thing to be a human being, no matter how little. And in a matter of minutes, Danny would have this kid sit in a chair, get him to hold on tight, and then lift the chair up over his head, hold it with one hand or balance the chair on his chin for a minute—no hands. Nobody would breathe, especially not the kid, and then he'd lower the chair, the kid would hop out all without a word, mind you—and they'd stand there together, their arms spread wide, both of them grinning, while the crowd clapped and clapped and clapped.

Children loved him. Grown men were spellbound. And women? Well. Women adored him.

I know. You're sitting there very smug, thinking that's why I left him. But you're wrong. I wasn't exactly the most faithful woman on earth either. Face it. The genitals—both male and female—have reasons that reason will never comprehend. Sigmund Freud didn't even figure it out. I left for a lot of reasons. I was getting older. I was tired of traveling. The revolution failed. And believe it or not, I wanted a child by Danny. I terminated two pregnancies—you can't mention the word *abortion* these days without some born-again Nazi trying to lob a grenade into your handbag—Danny and I both decided it wasn't time; there was no money. As I say, we were always on the road. Then when we decided it was time, I miscarried, and after that I began to get sad watching Danny perform, especially when he brought kids onstage. I grew more and more depressed. It got ugly between us. We said—I said terrible things. God, the look on his face when I told him I was leaving was enough to scorch my heart, but I had to keep saying it, "I'm leaving, no matter what you say or how you look, or how much I love you and want to stay, I'm leaving."

And to tell you the truth, I was homesick. I missed New York. I longed to live in a real neighborhood again and see people every day on the street who looked familiar to me.

So. Well. Here I am. I finished college. I'm a social worker for the city now. I have a son by the husband I married in a synagogue. This husband and I have also parted company. I'm on sabbatical. I needed a break. Marriages, like anything else, can be habit-forming. Besides, I like living alone with my son. He's six and a half. He goes to a good kindergarten run by sensible, progressive people not far from where we live.

I named him Daniel. I told his father it was for a favorite uncle, which was not entirely a lie. My father did have a business associate who was also a friend of the family, and his name was Daniel, but you and I both know who I named my son after. Maybe one day my son will. Who knows? I haven't seen or heard from Daniel Muldoon since I left, and that was thirteen years ago.

The other day I was walking my son home from school. It was my day off, and we passed a guy standing on the corner. He wore a top hat and overalls. He had clown white on his face, and he was doing tricks to make a few bucks. From a distance I saw him and my heart stopped. He was about the same height, almost the same build, but when I got closer I could see he was just a kid, maybe twenty. My son and I stopped at the same moment to watch, without saying a word to each other. Pretty soon my son let go of my hand and made his way to the front of the small group that had gathered. He wanted to get a better look. The guy wearing the top hat motioned him to come forward. He pulled a quarter from behind my son's ear. At first this took my son by surprise, but then because he is already a little skeptical and shows strong tendencies towards serious scientific inquiry, he was looking around for where the quarter *really* came from; in our household, he knows money does not appear out of thin air. The guy pulled another and then another quarter from behind Daniel's ear. My son looked up at me, as if I had the explanation.

I looked at him and shrugged.

I thought of Danny Muldoon and the first night I saw him and the look on my son's face a moment earlier. I thought of how hard I had resisted that man when I was nineteen, and how quickly I had fallen in love, of our years together and the nights I watched him perform with a timid child he had pulled from the audience, and how glad and proud that kid looked with his arms spread wide to receive the applause, his face beaming. I thought if only my father had seen that, he might have forgiven me for running off with a Gentile. He might have understood that Daniel Muldoon was not wholly of this world. He might have seen what I now saw, that Danny was a sort of Ba'al Shem Tov with laughing children on his shoulders, a man whom God had put on this earth to show us the study of Talmud was not the only path, God could be worshiped by seeming to make forty-seven Ping-Pong balls appear out of nowhere, and the purpose of living was to make life—all of it—holy.

I closed my eyes and said a little prayer for my father and a little prayer for Danny, that wherever he was he was safe and happy and still working. My son gave my pants leg a tug. "Come on, Mama," he said. "It's over." So I took his hand. It's true, you know, the momentous things in our lives almost always have small beginnings. And we headed home, my son and I, discussing the visible and the invisible, and debating the relative merits of having grilled cheese or sloppy joes for lunch.

Code

DAVID CROUSE

From *Copy Cats* (2005)

My office did not look like my office. I had asked the department secretary to redecorate it while I was on vacation, and she
had filled it with hanging plants—spidery things with long sharp
leaves. All the green made me nervous. The increased feeling of
responsibility depressed me. The plants would die and it would
be my fault. Still it was good to be back, better than being at
home where life's only choices seemed to be the noise of the television or a serene suburban quiet that made me feel like something horrible was going to happen.

When I had parked my Explorer in its familiar reserved space
that morning, I felt relief, more than anything else, to be back
where I belonged. I had even worn a new shirt—blue gray to
match my steely resolve—and polished my best shoes. The sun
was strong and high in the east as I walked to the building, and a
cluster of little birds hopped around the parking lot mechanically
pecking at the grit near the empty handicapped spaces. My travel
thermos still contained half a cup of surprisingly good coffee. If I
wasn't full of love for any particular individual, I was at least spill-
ing over with good feeling for mankind in general. Living seemed
a good idea.

"You look great," the security guard at the front desk said as I signed in. The day before, I had sprawled out on a lawn chair in the yard for a couple of hours so I'd have a healthy glow.

"Where did you go?" he asked. I wondered if I had just returned from a better vacation than I had imagined.

"Europe," I said in an attempt to be impressive and ambiguous at the same time.

"Europe," he said thoughtfully. With one word I had opened a gap between us, a distance he could be amazed by or get indignant about, depending on his mood.

"Yes," I said. "Next year I'm planning to go to Asia."

"Wow," he said, "that would be something," and he turned around the logbook and inspected my signature as if looking for a clue to my success in the fat curves of my name.

Guldeck and Cranlan met me at the elevator. "Hey," Guldeck said. "If it isn't you." He pointed at me with a thick finger, holding the elevator door for the crowd—tastefully dressed people who looked something like me. They sprayed the same juices under their arms and worried about the same things when they looked in a mirror at three in the morning. Except—and this was a crucial difference—they were not me, were they? Sometimes I didn't even feel like me.

As we jockeyed for position and I smelled their colognes and perfumes and aftershaves, it passed through my mind that maybe someone in the crowd could be better at being me than I had been. Then I thought of my empty house with its cheese-encrusted pizza boxes and half-empty photo albums and realized that someone out there right now was probably doing just that.

"I thought you weren't due back until next week," Guldeck said. He was a large, excitable man who had a way of making those around him feel rushed. Often I had heard people complain about how they couldn't think straight in proximity to him. He had the rough hands of a construction worker, someone who spent his time gripping and lifting.

"That's true," I said, "but some issues came up with a particular project. Things I had to address personally."

"No substitute for the hands-on approach," Cranlan said, and he laughed quietly as if disdaining such a simple idea. He did this often, I noticed—summarized someone else's words with a subtly sarcastic chuckle, a study in economy and control, a barely audible noise that could make you feel inadequate at a near-childish level. I would have added the technique to my repertoire if Cranlan had not mastered it so completely that it seemed inseparable from him.

The elevator reached the fourth floor, the crowd reshuffled, and the three of us pushed into the hallway. "You should know," Guldeck said. "We have a situation."

"It's another reorganization, Michael," Cranlan said. "I haven't seen it, but there's a list of names going around, circulating at the top levels."

"A list," I said.

"Exactly right," he said.

"Of the soon-to-be dead and wounded."

"We've missed your flair for the dramatic, Michael."

We entered the company's executive kitchenette, where we stood around the lunch table. I knew each of us was wondering who would be the first to reach for the tray of pastries at its center, giving up his self-control and enabling the rest to do the same. Guldeck opened the microwave and scraped at a brown splotch with his pen. "I've been dreaming about that list, you know. But I can't read the words."

I picked up a small circular roll with a swirl of gray-purple at its center and held it out to Guldeck. "Relax," I said. "Have something to eat." He eyed the pastry suspiciously.

"Damn it," he said. "Is it too much to ask to get a decent raspberry Danish? Where do they get this stuff?" He began to lift and inspect various pastries, looking them over with contempt. Cranlan was now picking apart a chocolate doughnut as a way to avoid eating it. A habit of his, I had noticed, his own nervous way to keep trim. Each day he left a pile of doughnut rubble behind for the cleaning crew to throw away.

"Whose responsibility is this?" Guldeck asked. He pointed his thumb over his shoulder at the wall behind him. "What's-her-name? I bet it's what's-her-name. She should be the first one to get the chop-chop."

"No," I said. "Not her."

Guldeck said, "I was in at seven yesterday. To get a head start on the day, you know? And I still didn't get a raspberry one. The tray was out here, but the raspberry ones were gone."

"Maybe there weren't any to begin with."

"Bullshit. I know they exist. I've seen people walking around eating them. I've seen you walking around eating them." A fleck of spittle had formed on his lip, shimmering as he talked.

Cranlan smiled. "I bet they were enjoying themselves, these hypothetical people with their hypothetical pastries."

"Considerably," Guldeck said. "Much more than I am right now eating this fossil." He set it back on the edge of the tray, two bites out of the side. Cranlan picked it up and tore it in half, scrutinized its dark and moist underside, which looked like some light-sensitive mollusk.

"Have a lemon-filled," I said. "They're okay."

"I don't want okay, Michael. I don't think I should have to settle for okay. I Stairmaster for forty-five minutes every night just so I can get away with eating this kind of stuff, and I definitely want it to be better than okay."

We stood there studying the small mound at the center of the table, amazed at its architecture. Then we pulled away one by one, and I went to my office and tried to ignore the plants. After about three minutes of staring at paperwork, I picked up the phone and punched in the extension for building supply. As the phone rang on the other end somewhere in the bowels of the building, I took a seat on the corner of my desk in the attitude of a man accomplishing things.

"Hello," I said. "Natalie?" It was Natalie. I had forgotten how good it was to hear her voice, and I forgave her instantly for not returning the calls I had made to her home phone during the last couple of weeks. "I have a question for you," I continued. "I'd like some new furniture for my office. I was thinking about an uncomfortable chair. Simple and traditional. I need to feel stoic."

"We just sent you a new chair two weeks ago," Natalie said.

I looked around my office—the bookcase littered with books abandoned by its previous occupant, the three teal-colored file cabinets along the back wall, the imported Indian carpet my wife and I had bought what seemed like years ago. I saw no such chair.

"And by the way, Michael. You said you had a question. What just came out of your mouth wasn't a question. It was a statement. People are always calling me up and telling me they have a question, but what they really should say is they'd like to make a statement."

"I'm sorry. I don't want to be part of your problems, Natalie. I want to be part of the *solution* to your problems."

"Why do you need this chair? What are you doing that's so important it demands that I drop everything and rush a chair over to you?"

"I have my fingers in a lot of different pies right now."

"Because I hate to say this, but I've heard rumors."

She was referring to the memo of course, and my subsequent absence from the office. The memo had appeared one day in my employee mailbox, folded authoritatively across the middle and signed by a vice president of something important sounding. It explained in simple, tersely affectionate language that the entire company would be more or less hibernating for most of June and this would be an ideal opportunity for me to get some much deserved downtime.

"I don't want to know," I told her, although I did. I had heard rumors too. The building throbbed with them.

"What are you working on these days?" she asked. "I mean, before your leave of absence. What were you working on?"

"Various things," I said. "Various important things. And it was a vacation. I went to Europe. But before Europe, before my vacation, I had my fingers in a lot of pies. This one project in particular keeps arriving on my desk. I add to it and then it comes back and I take stuff away."

"You're saying that its weight fluctuates."

"I'm saying that it has reached the pulsing stage. It is moving in and out. It's breathing. Like some kind of experiment from a horror movie."

"Frankenstein."

"The Blob."

"Whatever."

"Yeah. Whatever. It's around here somewhere. I expect to see it momentarily. Unless the plug has been pulled on the whole thing, which is a distinct possibility. As you know I'm a little removed from the process right now."

I lifted myself off the desk and walked to the window, where I played with my blinds, opening and closing them: small rhythms and repetitions, like an awkward attempt at semaphore. From my office I could sometimes see people in the next building. Ours was the nicer building, a full four stories taller, with a cafeteria on the ground floor.

"I'm wondering what the point of these conversations is," Natalie said. "People are beginning to talk."

"I see. A question of propriety. I have a corner office. You work in the supply room."

"That's right."

64

"The Capulets and the Montagues."

"Exactly."

"Regardless, I think you should go to lunch with me today. With a bunch of us. Safety in numbers. You can tell me what you've heard from the rumor mill. I'll buy you a drink, and I'll tell you the rumors I've heard."

"That's very nice of you," she said. I could tell she was interested in what I might know and afraid, too, should this information involve her. But she was too polite to say anything. I had noticed before that these two emotions—politeness and mild fear—seemed to charge the atmosphere in every corner of the building, like the buzz of fluorescence.

"What about my chair?" I asked her.

"That'll have to go through channels."

"Maybe I'll just buy a folding chair and bring it in."

"I wouldn't do that. You'd be stepping on some toes. Some very powerful toes. It's bad form for someone in your position."

"What is my position?"

"I'm not sure, but it's obviously essential."

"That's true," I said. "You know how when you were a kid and you asked your mom how the fridge or the car worked, and she said there were little men in there turning the gears?"

"I guess so."

"Well, I like to think of myself as one of those little men."

"I'm not sure what you mean," she said, "but I do know that a folding chair could be misconstrued."

I squeezed my lips with my left hand until they puckered. Sometimes when talking on the phone I found myself playing with my face, absorbed in the soft give of my skin.

"I have to go now," she said.

"Think about lunch," I said, and using two fingers killed the connection. I felt giddy, although I couldn't tell exactly why. I took a folder off my desk and skimmed the contents. Not much of it registered, other than the four neat columns of numbers, but it was something to keep my eyes and hands occupied as I paced the room.

I tried to get something accomplished, but I kept thinking about the blankets and pillows on my couch. I had left the lights on upstairs so that it would look like someone was home already when I drove up the street in the evening. The bed was unmade and had been for weeks, for months. Had it ever been made? This seemed to be an enormous problem, and the solution had been to sleep downstairs—on the couch, on the back porch, on the kitchen floor. I explored the house and touched my cheek to places it had never touched before. I suppose I was trying to find a way to relate. I was wondering if the house remembered me.

I had forgotten to flush the toilet. I was sure of it.

Through the closed door, I could hear the department secretary out there talking. "Yes, he's in," she was saying, "but you can't speak with him. He's brainstorming right now." I thought about playing racquetball or shooting hoops or harassing someone in the Midwest about a late package. I kicked off my shoes and flexed my toes. I loosened my tie and stretched, then did a couple of halfhearted deep knee bends.

Brainstorming. I liked the sound of that. It seemed to elevate my life to an exalted state, as if I were a quirky genius daydreaming of flow charts, brooding over a sliver-sized sixth decimal place. I took off my socks and slid my feet through the carpet. Then I balled up one sock and practiced throwing it at the wastebasket across the full width of the room, keeping count in my head.

The first shots went wide, the next three fell short, but the three after that entered the mouth of the can with a satisfying thump. I was bouncing from foot to foot but stopped to unbutton my shirt and slide my belt from around my waist and sling it over the back of my chair. I shot again, trying to release and retrieve the sock as fast as possible. My breathing grew heavy, and I bent over with my hands on my knees and inhaled through my nose in what I considered to be a virile way. I took time to snort and hawk and swallow. The back of my neck felt warm.

I took off my shirt and draped it on the chair with the belt, then retrieved the sock from the corner. It hit the wall to the right of the trash. I moved toward it on the floor but stopped halfway and went into reverse, unbuttoning my pants. I folded them on my desk. I filed my underwear in the bottom drawer where I kept empty folders and unopened office supplies.

Whenever the ball plopped into the basket, I pumped my fist and threw some left-right combinations at the air. I picked up the phone and punched the first extension that occurred to me, leaving the sock there in what had become its rightful place.

"Hello," someone said.

"Foster," I said.

"This is Schwartz."

"Exactly," I said, "just the man I want to talk to."

"Is that you, Michael?" he asked.

"It is I."

He snorted. "It's good to have you back."

"It's good to be back."

"What can I do you for?"

"Well, I was wondering if you'd heard."

"Heard what?"

"You know. The rumors."

"I have. I've heard different things from different people. Most of it seems pretty far-fetched."

"Regardless."

"You're breathing very heavily, Michael. I have a very obscene phone call kind of feeling going on here, you're breathing so hard. You wouldn't be having a heart attack?"

"Nothing like that," I said.

"Good," he said. "That's very good. I'm pleased to hear it."

"Can you reiterate what you've heard?" I asked him. "I'd like to match up my facts with your facts."

"It's a purge. Everyone knows. All departments. All levels. The company is sticking its finger down its throat. Are you having lunch out today?"

I looked at my wall clock. It was almost time to eat.

Most of the tables at the restaurant were empty. The busboys had just begun setting places for lunch, and the waitresses were talking at the bar. I immediately felt reassured by the familiar particulars—the wide wooden chairs, heavy silverware, and thick cloth napkins of a good steak place.

I noticed one of the busboys, younger than the others. He moved from table to table, wiping away the red scab from around the lip of the ketchup bottles, filling the salt and pepper shakers. "We'd like a table," I told him when he got close, and he nodded and walked away holding his stained napkin.

"We're early," Schwartz said.

"It's never too early," I said.

We were whispering as if we had just entered a church between services. We moved to the center of the room, to our usual table. A waitress met us there.

"Your collar buttons are undone," Schwartz said.

"Thanks," I said and stood there fiddling.

A small man appeared at the entrance. He held the door open with his shoulder, not in and not out, and at first I thought he was going to turn around and leave, but then he saw us and waved, and we waved back.

"Barnes," Schwartz said. "Look at how short he is. I always forget how short he is."

"The strange thing is how he can find a suit that's a size too small when he's so small himself. It seems like you'd have to expend some real effort to do that."

We took turns shaking hands, then found our places. "I'll have a rum and Coke," I told the waitress as I pulled out my chair. "As strong as legally possible. Only a splash of Coke." I made a fanning gesture. "In fact just wave the Coke bottle over the glass. That'll do."

She looked at Barnes, then Schwartz. "The same thing," Schwartz said, "except with less Coke."

Barnes opened the menu, looked it up and down. "I'll have the chicken Parmesan and a ginger ale."

Schwartz leaned forward, both arms on the table. "We're just ordering drinks, Barnes."

I nodded. "Generally we order drinks, maybe some appetizers, then unwind for fifteen or twenty minutes. Then we order the food. Then we wait for the food, which is not an inopportune time to have another drink, and then we eat the food."

"Pacing is everything," Schwartz said.

By this time Guldeck and two people I didn't know had come in and dragged the nearest table over to ours, getting a couple of nervous stares from other patrons trickling in. As he sat down Guldeck reached across me for an ashtray. "Hear the latest?"

"No," I said.

"Accounting," he said, and he tapped the ashtray against the table in a staccato rhythm, as if clicking out Morse code. One of the people I didn't know drew his finger across his throat and made a sound like an incision. Then he looked at me and smiled as if I should know him. Guldeck was ordering drinks. He was ordering lots of drinks.

"I saw it coming," Schwartz said. "They've had their head up their collective ass for some time now."

Barnes pointed at me with his fork. "Speaking of which, how's your particular project coming along? I heard a date had been set."

"They always do that," Schwartz said. "They set a date. They change the date. They change it again. Nothing is fixed. Don't worry about it." He slapped me on the shoulder.

I saw the waitress across the room, her tray loaded with glasses, moving toward us. I kept my eyes on hers as she narrowed the space. Something about the moment seemed peaceful, almost profound, and I did not want it to end. I held up my empty glass as a kind of hello. She closed the space between us with a few decisive steps and replaced it with a full one.

Guldeck was talking now. "That entire project has become our personal Viet Nam. We should just pull out and cut our losses." The waitress handed him a glass that seemed mismatched to the size of his hand. I wondered if he played football in college. He took a long sip and scowled into his lap. "You can feel good bourbon in your extremities. That's the main thing I look for."

He touched the waitress, holding her there as he emptied the glass. Then he handed it back to her. "Another round of the same. Bring everyone another of whatever they're having." Guldeck swept his hand, indicating the bunch of us.

A few more people were squeezing in around the table, and other waitresses had appeared with large plates of appetizers. Nachos and honey-glazed chicken wings. "I have an important meeting this afternoon, you know," Guldeck said to nobody in particular. "I have to balance my body chemistry."

I pulled one of the appetizer plates to me and tugged a steaming nacho loose from the coagulated cheese, taking careful bites. "You're preparing," I told him. "You're mentally girding your loins."

"That's what I'm doing. And that's what you should do too. I think Wassermann from marketing is sitting in on this thing, and you know how he can be."

That was the first I had heard of Cameron Wassermann being involved in that afternoon's meeting. And my own inclusion came as an even bigger surprise.

"Good luck," someone said, and small guttural agreements came from everyone.

When two waitresses appeared with more trays of drinks, I offered to buy the next round. It was something I figured I should do before more people arrived. The group was big enough now that the conversation had split into three or four huddles.

"Damn the youth of America to hell," someone was saying at the end of the table. Was it a joke? I wasn't sure.

Barnes was leaning over his plate, sawing his chicken into neat squares. "You know, I invested a lot of time in that project independent of anyone else," he said. No one but me seemed to hear him. By this time a dozen of us were clustered around three tables pushed end to end. Guldeck kept insisting on buying drinks for people and threatening to punch them if they refused. Someone suggested that we sing sea chanteys. It seemed in keeping with the overall mood.

Schwartz put his arm around my shoulder. "You know what I love?" he asked with real sincerity. "I love the atmosphere. There's this Last Supper kind of thing going on. That kind of feeling, you know? That kind of oh-my-God-what's-going-to-happen-next." He laughed and lifted his empty glass to his mouth.

"Please," I said. "No ironic observations."

"What's the matter?"

"Nothing. I guess I don't like your reference."

"To the Last Supper?"

"That's right. Crucifixion gives me the willies."

"The whole death thing."

"Yes. That's right. The whole death thing."

"The icy hand on your heart. The black void."

I turned to talk to the person on my left, but he was talking to the person on his left: something about how useless pennies were, like our pinkies, and we were evolving out of a need for either, and was it just a coincidence that the two words sounded so much alike?

I turned back to Schwartz. "I didn't go to Europe."

He straightened up and seemed to sober. "I know," he said, and as a smile crossed his face he suddenly looked drunk again.

71

"I hate vacations. All that being alone with yourself. All that contemplation. It's claustrophobic."

"Peeking into the coffin of yourself," he slurred softly, as if talking to himself. I noticed that he was eyeing my glass, so I slid it to him. He finished the drink for me and burped a thank you just as the next round was arriving.

"I can't stop thinking about that list," I said. Guldeck's words, sort of, but now they were mine. I looked over at him. He had an elbow on the table, open hand ready to grip and arm-wrestle the first taker. "I should go," I said. "I've been waiting for Natalie, but she's not going to show."

"Cranlan didn't make an appearance either."

"That's right. I wonder what happened to him?"

Schwartz shrugged, and we both stood. "Can you drive?" I asked him. He was listing toward one side as if he were standing on a bad leg.

"Not really," he said.

I threw some money at the center of the table. "Me neither."

"We'll flip a coin and cross our fingers," he said, and he took an awkward step toward the door. For some reason I was feeling pretty good again. Something inside me had shifted.

On the way out I collided with the busboy. Even though more than an hour had passed since I last saw him he was still hard at work cleaning ketchup bottles. One of them leapt from his hand as we crashed into each other. A streak of red splattered across my chest and I stood with my arms wide apart, looking down at my shirt. "I'm shot," I said and I staggered—although I didn't exactly mean to—and everyone laughed.

As soon as I got back to work I went by Cranlan's office and knocked on the doorframe. When nobody answered I stepped inside, moving deliberately, one hand on the wall for balance. Someone else sat behind Cranlan's desk, a small gray-haired man turning the pages of a pocket dictionary. Cranlan's bulletin board, which had previously been blank except for his business card tacked in one corner, was now covered with clippings from the comic pages: a confusion of boxes and word balloons. A squat minifridge stood in the corner in place of Cranlan's empty bookcase, a bowl of apples on top.

"Where's Cranlan?" I asked.

The man looked up, startled, watery eyed. "What?"

"Cranlan."

"Um."

"Never mind," I said, and I left.

Four or five people were gathered around the copy machine in the hall, pressing buttons, opening doors, peering inside. "Jammed," one of them said to me as if asking for help, but I kept walking. I headed to the restroom, where I bent over the sink and splashed cold water on my face. From one of the stalls I could hear the gasps and spurts of someone violently upchucking.

I tried cleaning my shirt with a wet paper towel. The ketchup spread and faded to pink. A large pale stain didn't seem to be that much of an improvement over a small dark one, so I stopped scrubbing. Instead I tightened the knot of my tie, took my pen from my shirt pocket and clicked it in and out, in and out, something to keep my hands busy while I listened. The noise from the stall gradually subsided, and Guldeck appeared at the sink next to me, looking pale except for the top of his balding head, which glowed baby red. We both stood there looking into the mirror. "Damn," he said. He took a small bottle of mouthwash from his pocket and began to gargle and spit.

I spoke to his reflection. "You've heard about Cranlan, I assume."

He swished, puffing one cheek, then the other.

"We can't afford to be sentimental, obviously," I said.

He tilted his head back, leaned forward, and dribbled green liquid into the sink. When he was finished he took hold of his lips and curled them back so he could inspect his teeth. "You know," he said, "something about the suddenness of these things seems correct. Almost Darwinian. It's like watching one of those nature documentaries."

"It's like itself," I said. I had pulled off my tie and was unraveling the knot, starting from scratch. "That's what it reminds me of. When I first came in this morning I looked around and took a deep breath and said to myself, 'This reminds me of being back at the office.'"

Guldeck was halfway to the door. He turned around, walking backward, and raised his fist in salute. "Onward and upward." The door closed behind him, and I turned back to the mirror. Guldeck would be gone by the end of the week, I realized, once some higher-up understood the incongruity of having him walking around without Cranlan, his opposite number, yin to his yang, Laurel to his Hardy. I picked up his forgotten bottle of mouthwash and put it in my pocket.

I followed him into the hall, where we moved in separate directions. I glanced repeatedly at my watch without really noticing what time it was, a reflex action that made me look determined and efficient. Or nervous and fixated, either or both, I didn't know. I was holding my tie in both hands now, stretched taut like a garrote. I had no idea what time the teleconference began. I could have been twenty minutes late or an hour early. I stopped, trying to orient myself.

Someone I didn't know pointed down the hall. "It's that way," he said, but how did he know what I was looking for? And who was he anyway? "Right," I said, although I didn't move. The floor swayed beneath me in a soft ripple like the wake from a passing boat. Then with a surge of will that seemed almost superhuman I began to walk in the direction he had pointed.

Cameron Wassermann shook my hand at the door, then stepped aside and waved his arm dramatically, motioning me to enter. He wore a loud Hawaiian-print T-shirt, untucked around his ballooning waist. His Docksiders were untied. I almost expected him to be holding a glow-in-the-dark tropical drink. There were two types of salespeople, I had decided long ago: the hungry younger ones, moving toward vague vice presidencies and company cars, and the spent older ones, moving toward retirements and multiple strokes. Cam was deep into the latter group.

"Michael," he said, "you look like absolute hell."

"Thanks."

"How was your vacation? I heard that you went to Europe."

"Yes."

"Did you like it?"

"Loved it."

"And your wife and kids?"

"I loved them too," I said, and we both laughed, although at different jokes. He was still double-gripping my fist. I wanted it back.

Still laughing, he grabbed Guldeck by the wrist and pulled him over to us. "Michael, I'd like you to meet Ken Guldeck, our director of . . ." He turned to Guldeck, voice trailing off.

"Intercorporate Situations," Guldeck said.

"Director of Intercorporate Situations," Wassermann said, and the smile returned to his wide sun-dried face. I shook Guldeck's hand vigorously.

"Pleased to meet you," I said. "You have quite the reputation." It seemed strange to be talking to someone who would likely end up as a casualty. The feeling was there as I shook his hand—the sense of being close to extinction and not wanting it to rub off on you.

"Sorry I'm late," Barnes said as he came through the door. He was wiping his forehead with his handkerchief, a gentle, cultivated gesture that made me want to grab him in a headlock. "I was moving Schwartz's computer over to my office," he said. "You should see the programs he has on that thing. Versions of software that haven't even been released yet. He must have had some contacts."

"The past tense," I said.

"That's right," Wassermann said. "You didn't hear?"

"No," I said.

"They canceled his passwords about an hour ago. He can't access a thing. If he put change in the candy machine, it would pop out the coin return."

I crossed Schwartz's name off the list that was floating somewhere in the back of my mind. We moved to sit down around the table, where blank pads of paper and pencils with new points were set at each place.

"Take a second," Wassermann said. "Get your heads in order. Visualize an optimal situation an hour from now maybe, once we've done what we have to do." He had started eating a Danish from who knows where, and he was licking sugar glaze from his fingers. I suppressed the urge to lift a pencil like a dagger and hurl myself across the table. My heart was a sieve and my negative emotions were dirty water.

I pictured a room in San Francisco with four people much like us sitting around a table much like ours, a balance that seemed important, even essential: two groups at either end of the country, arranged with the beautiful symmetry of Greek pillars or tensed football teams. That was the main satisfaction, I think, in a meeting like this. Yelling and hearing the echo of your words come back to you, the connectedness of those disembodied voices haggling and joking and coming to agreement.

Wassermann clicked the speakerphone button at the center of the table. We made the introductions, eight names and titles. At that moment it seemed that whatever happened in the next hour would resound with the clarity of something that mattered. I wanted to drop to the floor and do push-ups. I wanted to double over and be sick. That feeling always passed over me just before a meeting, only for a moment or so, before time seemed to catch and move forward again, like a skipped cog.

"Have you looked at the demo?" Wassermann asked.

"Excuse me?" asked the voices on the speakerphone.

"The demo," Barnes said. "Have you had a chance to look at it?" He raised his voice and enunciated each syllable. "You know. The demo we mailed you." As he repeated himself the word seemed to recede, becoming hazy and vague like music playing in another room.

I took a pad of paper and wrote, "It's like he's visiting his grandfather in the rest home." I slid it over so Guldeck could read it. He smiled and nodded, scratched something back.

"Axed," it said. Next to the word he drew what he probably intended to be a small axe, although it didn't look much like one. I turned the page and drew a large question mark.

"Effective Friday," he wrote in jagged letters.

"The demo," a voice said. "We have a few questions about that."

"What kind of questions?" Wassermann asked.

"Serious questions. For instance, we were wondering about this pallet shift we're getting. We called your tech support people about that. And the directory logic. Those are two of our major concerns." I noticed then that Barnes was crying, a slight wetness around the eyes that I would have passed off as a cold or allergies if not for the quiver in his lip. "We were also wondering about importing files. There seems to be a serious bug in the methodology there."

"Bug?" Barnes said. "That's a feature."

"It looks like a bug to me," one of them finally said after a long pause. The delicate balance was shuddering, threatening to break.

Barnes half stood, as if he wanted to head off somewhere but wasn't sure where, and leaned toward the speaker. "You're using the software incorrectly. We've gone over this before."

"We have talked about this. A number of times," the first voice said. "That's why it's so upsetting."

"It is upsetting," Barnes said. Agreement of a sort. Then another soft pause. Then nothing. They had hung up the phone.

Barnes was standing, staring at the wall, motionless. Wassermann had his head back and eyes closed, as if listening intently
to the single note of the dial tone. I imagined someone gently
scrolling through the network directory and noticing unfamiliar names that should have been deleted, people fired long ago.
Small markers in two columns, names and dates. Cemetery neatness. I thought of a person moving through the voice mail system, punching ones and twos, rooting deeper and deeper, from
stem to stem, and finding ghost messages from people who no
longer existed here except as dim images in the company brain.
My happy voice saying, *please leave a message and I'll get back to
you.*

"I have to be somewhere," I said.

The department secretary wasn't at her desk and neither was
her sweater, which she always kept on the back of her chair in
case the air-conditioning got too cold.

I found a Post-it note stuck to my terminal saying that the vice
president of something wanted to see me. I didn't recognize the
handwriting. A cartoon in the upper left-hand corner showed
a fat orange cat sleeping in a hammock, an image that seemed
completely incongruous. The more I looked at it the more sinister it became, and I had to force myself to put it down. I fished my
socks out of the wastebasket, put one in each pocket, and headed
toward my destiny.

I bumped into Natalie in the hall. She was holding a copy paper box packed with odds and ends: papers and folders, a framed
photograph of her cocker spaniel, a baseball she would toss from
hand to hand when having a bad day. "Walk with me," I said without stopping, and she moved up alongside.

"Did you hear?" she asked.

"I heard," I said.

"Where are you going?"

"This way," I said. "I'm going this way."

"What?" she said. "Where?"

"Outside. Then to my car. After that I'm not sure. Maybe far away. Far away would be good." I had reached the elevator. A young boy held the door for me, a bike messenger dressed in ripped jeans and retro-chic wraparound sunglasses. "Come with me," I said to her. She looked at her box of things. I thought of the empty closets in my house, the unread newspapers, the bed that seemed to grow wider the more I looked at it, the vast spaces to fill.

"You know I can't," she said.

The kid smirked and sniffed and looked as bored as a person could look. "Fine," I said and stepped into the elevator. The kid had already punched up the ground floor, and the doors closed behind me. I turned to him, pointed at his sunglasses. "I'll give you fifty dollars for those."

When I got outside I broke into a run across the parking lot toward my Explorer, clicking off the alarm as I went. I slid the air-conditioning to full, gunned the engine for effect, and moved past the guard post, going twice the speed limit as soon as I passed the yellow-painted speed bump. I glanced to my left when I reached the stop sign at the exit of the industrial park, accelerating into the turn with the kind of relaxed intuition that comes from doing something again and again. As soon as I rounded the corner I slipped the car into fourth, then fifth, letting my hand linger on the stick shift, feeling the vibration of the engine that seemed to be focused there. I sped up more, just to experience the change of sensation against my palm.

In five minutes I had reached the main road, which was clogged with four o'clock commuters getting a head start for home. A few cars were turning around on the highway on-ramp, driving up over the curb and across the neat grass strip that separated the two roads. I tapped the dash with both hands, keeping awkward time to the song on the radio as we lurched forward, merging with the main flow. There was something almost biological in the way the cars clung together, bumpers almost touching bumpers, like blood cells pumping through an artery. The radio played a dance song, slinky sweet, turned so low I could hear only muffled drums and some semblance of a voice.

The traffic picked up speed past a truck with emergency flashers on. I imagined the insides of each vehicle, thousands of synchronized parts sparking and clicking: a seemingly simple thing turned frighteningly complex. I cranked the radio louder, punched up an all-news station. I reclined my seat, leaning my head back so that I felt as if I were sitting dreamily in a dentist's chair, letting some drug work itself through me. There was a busy, antlike desperation in the way the cars tried to narrow the space in front of them. People leaned on their horns if someone else grew lax and let the car in front gain too much distance. We all have to work together here, seemed to be the consensus, like it or not.

"It's a real battle out there this afternoon," the traffic reporter was saying. "It's congested. It's constipated. It's complete entropy." I looked to my left out the window, and I could see a helicopter circling in the distance. I wondered if the man on the radio and the man in the helicopter were the same. My foot moved to the brake, and I heard a sharp honk from behind me, then a second, longer this time. I slapped my horn twice in reply and then held it down until the car to my right leaned on his. Two more horns behind bleated out together, then another one ahead—sporadic bovine noise, instinctive call and response. When I closed my eyes I pictured the line of cars as a procession of clumsy animals, starved and lost, migrating blind to an unknown destination. "Bumper to bumper," the reporter was saying.

I dropped my car into park and set the brake, then opened my door and stepped out into the breakdown lane, into the shiny bits of glass, as fine and delicate as broken shells on the beach, and the sand and litter and shredded tire rubber. The person in the car in front of mine turned her head and stared. I didn't stare back. I was taking off my jacket. I was taking off my tie. I was straddling the guardrail, and then I was scrambling down the embankment. In passing I remembered that my car engine was running, that the door was wide open like a crippled bird with only one wing. More horns were beginning to sound from further away, until we were all joined by that beautiful, aching music.

The stones chaffed my feet as I walked, and I wondered if the woods were surrounded by highway like a small island. The trees were getting thicker and I had to duck under branches. A wet leaf the shape of an arrowhead was stuck to my bare chest. I was cold and warm at the same time. Except for my boxers, I was now as naked as an elk. Then they were off too. I clutched them in my hand and then dropped them to the ground, leaving a trail behind me for other lost souls to follow when they went over the edge.

Meeting in Tokyo

NANCY ZAFRIS

From *The People I Know* (1990)

During a business trip to Tokyo I engaged one of the secretaries in a conversation about curry. I was up from my home in Kyushu, but I let it be known I knew my way around this overwhelming city. "Let's take the subway to Akasaka and have curry at that Indian restaurant," I suggested. I had to cough before mentioning its name. But she knew what I meant. She accepted and that was that.

From the Indian restaurant we slipped by taxi to Shinjuku, where the lights and noise were even more excessive. We wove through the crowds until I found a coffee shop I liked. It bordered the blue cinema district, and during our conversation the distant catcalls from porno revues scratched at the edge of our voices.

It was through this seedy district that we strolled on the way to her train station. Giant billboards rose above the theaters and illustrated pivotal scenes from this movie and that. Beyond them, lights of hotels blinked purple and red and I made a move to hold her hand.

At the Seibu Shinjuku station I bought a ticket in order to escort her up the stairs, and possibly farther. We barely made it. The warning whistle suddenly blew, the doors swished open, and she stepped inside the train without me. As the second whistle sounded, I reached in and pulled her out just as the doors were sealing shut. I guided her down the stairs and back out into the theater district. My hand at the small of her back met pressure but no resistance as I guided her up the hill toward the colorful hotels. From the Pachinko parlors came the metal waterfalls of victory. Afterwards I made sure she boarded the final train at 12:08. I attempted a brisk businesslike wave, then returned to the coffee shop we had sat in earlier and thought about what I'd done.

I had to confess some forethought in selecting a coffee shop where the clangor of flesh-peddling and Pachinko games could brush against our privacy with disconcerting sensations. But the rest was accidental. That she caught her train at Seibu Shinjuku in the middle of the cinema district, thereby requiring a visual romp through scenes of torture and sodomy, was simply a stroke of good fortune. And although the audacious timing of pulling her through the doors between the two whistle blasts had secured the seduction, this flamboyance was no more than my sudden desire not to make the long commute to her apartment.

During our brief passionate struggle, she called out my name. "Mister Naoka!" she cried. I admired her skillful secretarial juggling between abandon and deference, but when another wanton outburst came addressed in the honorific, I couldn't hold back at the comedy. I burst into a laugh, although I managed quickly to disguise it as my orgasm. Wouldn't my old friend Ashida like to see the honorable Mister Naoka now? I chuckled to myself, but my amusement flickered to sadness at the thought of my lost companion. This secretary I was with, attempting to bluff me with outlandish gyrations, never realized that she herself had been faked out.

As I sat alone in the coffee shop, the same waiter who had served us earlier took my order. He arranged a clean ashtray on the otherwise empty table, and in front of that placed a hot towel. I ordered Coffee Kilimanjaro. From behind the bar the steward took the order and commenced his operations with the affected strokes of a bartender. A line of coffee beakers was displayed before him like glass barbells. He undid one of the barbells and poured boiling water into the lower bulb. The flow of water grew long and dramatic as he lifted the kettle higher. At the instant he cocked the kettle to stop the flow he looked up at me with the hint of a smile. As if to flaunt the perfect precision of his movements, he wore white gloves.

The pleasure with which I viewed his refined movements recalled my own theatrical precision in hauling the secretary through the closing doors of her train. Were I to repeat the action, it would be all the more pleasurable for its added calculation. A military step properly performed is, after all, the most pleasurable to watch, despite its endless repetition.

I settled into my seat. Although the coffee shop was fairly large, each setting was cramped. The low easy chair forced me into an unnatural delicacy by springing my knees against the underside of the table. If I leaned back comfortably, which the cushions encouraged me to do, my legs jacked the table in the air. It recalled a memory. One evening early in my career I was called upon to dine with some American businessmen. When we sat down on the floor to eat, my crossed legs sprang up like crowbars and dug into the Americans sitting next to me. My Japanese companions swelled with pride at my uncontained lankiness. I stood a head taller than these Americans who, like me, must also have been chosen partly because of their (obversely) accommodating sizes: they were all short. During the meal their fingers kept searching out the handles of their emptied coffee cups. Ah, I surmised. "Refills!" I called over in Japanese. Then I switched to English. "Let's have more coffee," I said in a friendly way.

I sipped on my Kilimanjaro and remembered the episode. It was ten years ago, at the beginning of my career. I was living in Tokyo and felt Armageddon all around me and fancied myself suicidally carefree. In my mind I was constantly describing how I must appear to others: So tall . . . So confident . . . There's nothing he won't do . . . I wish I were like him . . . During these early business dinners with Americans, such descriptions of myself swam through my head. As I plowed right into Western-style meals with my fork, I almost had to keep myself from laughing out loud.

The Americans and I finished our food in sync while across from us my Japanese co-workers and superiors were hardly halfway through the torturous process of eating European-style, tidbits of rice nudged precariously onto the backs of forks and doomed to slip off before reaching any mouths. When they noticed they were lagging far behind the Americans, they simply ended their meals and went hungry rather than risk possible impoliteness. But when we all ate Japanese-style, the tables were turned. My co-workers practically swallowed their bowl of rice in a single gulp while the Americans became the dainty ones who clenched lower and lower on their chopsticks until they were clamping onto their food with a pincer movement of fingers rather than sticks. Again I somehow managed to time my eating to suit these Americans twiddling over their food like crabs.

My co-workers asked me why the Americans seemed to like me. I said it was because when I saw food before me I ate it. I forgot where I was or how I should behave. I just grabbed the fork and got up the rice the best way I could. "You should do the same," I suggested, but I knew they wouldn't. They had to follow the lead of our superiors who sat across the table trying to coax loose vegetables onto an upside-down fork. Sometimes their efforts were so futile it was nerve-wracking to the extreme. Across the table their shaking hands were all that I could see. My focus grew so intent that when I looked up from their trembling fingers I expected to find my friend Ashida, my lost friend Ashida, his nervous shaking hands, the cigarette bobbing up and down. The things I would then think about my superiors . . . I had a lack of respect for them for which I alternately praised and berated

85

myself. Though I still obeyed the multiple conventions of work hierarchy and social etiquette, I liked to think that a sheen of slick weariness separated my own conformity from the others' and proved attractive to the American customers simply through its unexpectedness.

Around this time, when I was still living in Tokyo, an American began working in our office and I observed him. His name was Sandy. As he was taken around and introduced to everyone, he showed us each his styrofoam cup with a 7-Eleven logo on it. He seemed extremely amused at having found a 7-Eleven store nearby, and everyone bowed happily, pleased to have pleased him. By the second day he was practicing behind-the-back bank shots into the wastebasket. He was still civil enough to return our greetings. "Good morning," I said to him in English as I passed. "How's it going?" he answered with a casual nod and flipped a wad of paper.

Later, when I asked him a question about English, he looked up slowly. "Say what, guy?"

I went no further. After carrying the sound of his utterance back to my desk, I repeated it over and over until it clicked into three words. I wrote them down. I didn't know what they meant.

By the end of the week this new American employee began avoiding us. He retreated to his desk and sat behind it whenever he saw any office workers approaching him with an inquiry. As they spoke to him, he lowered his head and went through a disconcerting little ritual. He turned his wrist inward and fiddled elaborately with his watchband until he finally unhooked it. Then he spread the watch before him on the desktop, the bands splayed flat like tortured arms, and leaned heavily over the watch to check the time. Only then did he look up to listen.

His questioners immediately bowed, thanked him for his time, and left before asking him their question.

Throughout the day the quiet of our office was interrupted by his jarring spells of laughter. When we looked over he would be alone, reading our advertising copy. He had fashioned his laughter into a falsetto wheeze, which was very disturbing.

Although he didn't know any Japanese except isolated words that he sprang on us like karate chops while we stood by with compliments (*Him*: Idiot! Boring! Nice! Idiot! Double idiot! Thanks! Ah so! Well! Uh, like uh! Idiot! *Us*: How superbly you speak!), he made no such concessions when he spoke to us in English.

> *Him*: I wannahaisdahbaahhortheresaprahifyoudahhhtohan bats dayorelse.
> *Us*: Yes, I see.

Then the follow-up later that day.

> *Him*: So whassatory?
> *Us*: Yes, I see.
> *Him*: Kaaa . . . RYSSS! What is wrong with you people?

This last sentence he always spoke slowly and clearly, and each day it would be the only sentence we understood. What is wrong with you people? We slunk away.

One morning I gave him the ad copy I had written: *If you always use it, it will refresh your skin and make smooth. And then unconsciously you will take back healthy and clear skin.* For the rest of the day he whinnied deliriously whenever he looked at it. I couldn't stop hearing his laughter. Even in the rest room, where I entombed myself in a stall, his sour revelry slid under the door and found me. Beneath me the toilet began to shake. Oh. An earthquake. I would go gladly to my death.

No. Just a tremor. I was still alive.

Late in the afternoon Sandy handed my ad copy back to me and said in a colorless voice, "Yeah, it's perfect." Then he said in Japanese, "Splendid, right!"

By now my embarrassment was so profound that I left work not thinking of his silly attempts at Japanese and how I could ridicule them, but of my own horrible English and the howling of his American friends when he repeated my advertising slogan. The friends would reach into their breast pockets and take out their notebooks to write down another funny example of Japanese English. They would be gathered in a restaurant and their happy derision would be loud and public and fueled by beer.

My face burned and perspired. I tapped a folded handkerchief to my upper lip while the other commuters regarded my condition without turning their heads. In the succeeding days I struggled visibly to do better in my job—for some reason I struggled still harder to please this American—and soon thereafter I was transferred to the island of Kyushu where missionaries and potentates had once made their stand but where nothing much happened anymore.

I grappled with the reasons for my transfer to this southern island. I reviewed the advertising campaigns to which I had contributed my efforts. I had done nothing on my own; how could I be at fault? Had I unknowingly perpetrated something like *Snatch*, a new candy bar marketed throughout Hokkaido and readied for Honshu, before someone came forward and explained that the English we were so proud of meant a woman's crotch? I repeated the English phrases I had used, hoping to find in a foreign grammatical structure the personal accountability that didn't exist in my own world. If I was personally at fault, I wanted to know. If I wasn't, I wanted to go somewhere else.

I didn't want to go to Kyushu. For one, it carried the small stain of an unpleasant memory. For another, I had dared to hope for a transfer to the United States. In the U.S. I planned to call on two American girls Ashida and I had met during college. I imagined capturing the casual tone of their life-style and moving easily among several American friends. But the picture was now marred by the loss of Ashida and the introduction of a wife who spoke no English and was country-shy.

After a time, the picture of my sitting at an American bar

and talking sports faded. After several years, the snapshot went blank. I was now settled into my job in Kyushu, and a few times each year I traveled to Tokyo. At home I never spoke to my wife. I kept my head down at the dinner table. Sometimes I watched myself with horror as I handed her an empty rice bowl in a peremptory, silent command for her to refill it. What had happened to me? When I came home and she served me tea like an obsequious office girl, I didn't know what to think. She retreated to whatever personal memories her teacup held, and I retreated to mine. It was impossible to sip tea without feeling akin to the myriad other moments in your life when you were doing exactly that: nothing but sipping tea, the insignificant moment held like the eye of a hurricane while life swirled around you. Sometimes the aroma of musk in calligraphy ink affected me in the same way, but the memories it provoked were more exotic and gravid. A teacup rolled about in your hands like a common egg, inert, mundane, the gift of everyday life. Memories inspired by tea were just the things that had happened.

What had happened was that I grew up in a small town near Kanazawa where I attended a public high school and was thus for all practical purposes fated to a college on the second or third tier. Knowing this, my friend Ashida and I worked hard but we didn't kill ourselves. Why stay up half the night, week after week, and nearly ruin our health when the result was as good as foregone? But our teachers didn't see it that way. Each week I heard the squeak of a bicycle and the metal scrape of the kickstand, and in would walk my teacher for his weekly visit. I stood rolling my eyes until my mother pushed me and I shuffled in and bowed. This time it was the new English teacher, Ikeda-sensei.

We took our places on the tatami floor and my mother served tea and bean pastries. Ikeda-sensei introduced himself to my mother and offered his brief autobiography, the schools he had attended including a seminar at the University of Hawaii, as well as his trip to the U.S. and the states he had visited. My mother and I nodded in unison as he listed each state. When he mentioned one we couldn't place, I went in search of a map which we then spread over the table after my mother moved the teapot and cups of tea to the floor beside her. We hunched over the map. Ikeda-sensei's finger landed with a thud. "Idaho!" he pronounced triumphantly. "Hmm!" we exclaimed. "So big!" The states of the U.S. were generously splashed on the map. Our own country was a delicate sliver choked by water, nervously scratched on the atlas by a rapidograph.

We folded the map and my mother brought the tea and pastries back up to the table. She emptied our lukewarm cups and refilled the teapot with hot water from the thermos. She poured the tea almost immediately. Then my teacher began. "Your son is a good boy. Everyone admires his size and strength." My mother smiled. Ikeda-sensei cuffed my shoulder and laughed. "Yes, it's true," he said. "Look at him."

Both my mother and he looked at me and smiled approvingly.

"But he is not working as hard as he possibly can. Each morning he comes to school fresh-faced and apple-cheeked while the other students are pale and wan."

My mother, in her kind voice which rose higher and sweeter as the words grew more polite, explained that she had accepted the fact that I no longer had the credentials which would lead me to a top school. So now the kind of effort which required sleeplessness was for those private high school students who realistically had a shot at a major university.

"Yes," Ikeda-sensei explained, "that is generally true. But only last year we had a student who got into Tokyo University."

"Ohhh!" my mother exclaimed. She nodded appreciatively. Then we all fell silent and looked down. My mother picked up the teapot to refresh Ikeda-sensei's tea, but he declined and pushed his fists against the tatami to hoist himself up.

"Well then," he said, "it's agreed that we'll try harder." He turned to me and bowed. With a catch in his voice he addressed me directly. "I will try harder as your teacher not to let you down." He bowed deeply and sincerely.

I felt very moved by my teacher's declaration, and indeed I felt my mother beside me draw in her breath and hold her mouth tight. I followed Mr. Ikeda outside and stood by his bicycle. He patted my shoulder. "I don't want you to ruin your health. You're growing big and strong, and you need your sleep. But your class-mates are working so hard. Can't you work just a little bit harder to show them you appreciate their efforts?" I felt tears come to my eyes. He patted me again. "There, there," he said. Then he pushed off on his bike. Despite a dangerous unsteadiness in his balance, he turned his head and lifted a hand. Even today I see him clearly, waving to me from his wobbling bicycle.

Two years later I was an improved student, and what's more, I was over six feet tall. The now monthly visits from my teacher changed in tone. Most of the conversations revolved around my height. Due to my build I was treated like a star, and I developed an easy confidence with my teachers, who complimented me on my physique. During conferences they treated my height as though it were an obscure area of scholarship. They asked my parents detailed questions:

Was anyone else tall in my family? No one?

What kind of tall behaviorisms did I have as a child?

When did my parents first have an inkling that I would be tall?

What did this inkling feel like?

I hated it when my father had come home early enough from work to be present at these conversations. He embellished insig-nificant details until they became full-fledged anecdotes. A fond-ness for round things to stick in my mouth became the mad de-sire for an American basketball which, being only a year old, I was unable to communicate verbally to my parents. But my fa-ther, who had this inkling that I would be tall, figured it out. "I knew it for a certainty," he explained, "when my son desired steak for breakfast." Seated cross-legged on the tatami, he posed his arms atop each knee before delivering the punch line. "That's what American athletes eat," he said.

My teachers appeared just as limber in jumping over the gaps in logic and voicing their approval. "An amazing thing, to want steak for breakfast. He actually said this?" My mother nodded. Gradually, when called upon, she had learned to invent these small details as well as the surge of parental pride she felt upon first noticing them. After one of these conferences she was so embarrassed she said nothing over dinner, and turned on the TV to cover the silence. On the nightly singing show the introduction of Hideki, who was the raging adolescent heartthrob, was preceded by a near-hysterical recitation of his vital statistics, climaxing with his height—183 centimeters. My height exactly.

Oh well, I thought, if all else fails at least I have one thing going for me. Meanwhile, my friend Ashida stayed short. Nobody asked his parents when they first had an inkling that puberty wouldn't affect him. He remained nervous and small, a timorous, innocent hoodlum punished with several weeks of extra mopping duty after the teachers caught him with a cigarette.

I always wondered what the teacher said to Ashida and his parents during his home conferences. One day I asked him. "Ikeda-sensei says I need to be a better student," Ashida said. "Toguchi-sensei says I need to avoid delinquent behavior." He held up his cigarette. "Aso-sensei says I need to be more outgoing. Ito-sensei says I need to maintain my friendship with you through loyalty, more outgoingness, better scholarship, and less delinquent behavior."

"Ito-sensei said that?"

Ashida snickered jumpily and inhaled on the cigarette. He was the nobody I almost was, and after high school we spent two years at a *ronin* preparatory school trying to get into a college. We tried to pretend we were really the masterless samurai the term *ronin* originally meant; after all, the masterless samurais were the ones on TV who got to grow out all their hair, and that's the first thing we started to do after getting out of high school. Ashida grew his hair long and unkempt and refused to have it trimmed at all. Split ends eventually layered it until it swung in the air like a grass skirt. My own hair was bushy and grew over me like a black rain cloud. Seen together, we were an ugly sight. We were warriors in search of a master.

We comforted ourselves by listening to the albums of Inoue Yosui, our favorite singer. On the inside jacket of one of his albums Yosui had charted his personal history on a graph. Small photographs punctuated significant events, and there he was in high school, short-haired and severe in his black military uniform. At one-year intervals after the high school photograph, intersection after intersection on the graph recorded this notation:

Took entrance exam.

Failed.

But Yosui learned integrity from failure and became a famous musician who refused to appear on TV. Likewise, we planned to learn integrity from our failure and thereby avoid becoming company men (although we planned to accept any TV offers that came our way). Like us, Yosui came from a small village and often wrote nostalgically of his hometown. There is a famous saying: The farther you are from your hometown the more nostalgic you become about it. We projected a nostalgia for our hometown through our desire to escape from it.

After two years of *ronin* we were both accepted at a mediocre college near Tokyo. Our life burst with freedom and leisure. For the first three years, armed with Yosui albums, we watched with equanimity the nearly insane April rush of new graduates swarming Tokyo for jobs. During the summers, coddled by parents who had already divined our busy future as company men, we were free to do as we wished.

One of these summers, during a trip to Kyushu, we actually passed through the town where I now live. We met a woman on the train and innocently fell into conversation with her. She appeared to be quite sane until well into her chatter. Suddenly all that changed. She began to tell us something, but her own spurt of laughter cut her off. When she recovered, she started again. During the war, she said, her brother died in the A-bomb explosion while she was riding her bicycle beyond the epicenter. I nodded, more out of wariness than sympathy. To this day, she continued, she wondered whether he exploded or disintegrated. Upon saying this, she dissolved into a crazy cackling, and to my shock, Ashida joined her. Together they laughed like hyenas, a maniacal lethal siren, while I sat soberly and stared at them.

Finally she stopped long enough to tell us that she was going to set herself on fire to find out the real story. "Then I'll know!" Her mouth blew open to release more dammed-up snorting. Beside me, through the spasms of his laughter, I could see Ashida trembling. Since I was hardly amused at any of this, the woman turned on me and began to taunt my seriousness. She invited Ashida to join in. Ashida indicated approval with fluttering nods and groped for a cigarette that immediately flew out of his nervous hands like a comedic prop. Then the woman dismissed us both with loud insults and stood up to move to another seat. No one on the rest of the train acknowledged that any of this was happening, so as the woman searched for another seat she hurled personalized commands to each of the other passengers who were ignoring her.

"Take off your hat!" she barked to this one.

"Take out your teeth and look at them!" to another one.

"Take off your hair and use it as a wallet!" she commanded a poor elderly man with a black toupee.

With each insult she stood by their side and waited for a reaction. There was none. The woman cackled louder and louder at their neutral masks and feigned deafness. This isn't laughter, I remember thinking, it's something else but I don't know what.

A few years later I heard it again. The same kind of malicious stage laughter emanated from Sandy, the new American employee, as he sat at his desk while each morning our female office workers ceremoniously served him tea and he ignored them, preferring to bring in coffee from the 7-Eleven store. Each morning he drank the coffee in great fits of hilarity while a confusing cloud of nostalgia engulfed me. His laughter billowed throughout the office in high-pitched convulsions; it continued daily and people were afraid to ask the joke. When he was on the phone engaged in loud and shameless personal conversation, our heads were turned and studious. He erupted in a braying that dared us to eavesdrop and mocked us for the attempt to understand his English. Indeed, it seemed to me, this laughter sloshing about his upper registers was an excess of spit. Soon he would scuttle away like a cockroach, emerging later from other Far Eastern cracks when he sniffed gullibility nearby.

And yet I had redoubled my efforts to please this person. I knew things were going downhill when I found myself reddening uncontrollably at the thought of him mocking the advertising copy I had submitted. *If you always use it, it will refresh your skin and make smooth. And then unconsciously you will take back healthy and clear skin.* What was so bad about it? I was determined to ask.

I waited until he was away from his desk so he couldn't perform his ritual with the wristwatch. Then I went up to him with the ad copy he had snorted at but not corrected. As I began my carefully rehearsed first sentence, the American removed his thick college ring and began polishing it against his shirt as though it were an apple. He polished and polished, studied it, and then polished it some more. Then he took out his shirttail and screwed it back and forth through the ring. He blew on it and slipped it back on his finger.

Finally he looked at me. "*Omai!*" he exclaimed with exasperation, addressing me with the crudest form of "you." Instinctively I jumped back at the language he had used, just as he must have known I would, and instantly I knew I had lost.

"Thank you very much," I slurred quickly in English. To my disgust I found myself bowing and scurrying away. I sat at my desk, heaving. Unaccountably, the image of my teacher atop his bicycle swelled before me. I felt the beginning of tears. What had happened to me? How had I come to this? Perhaps I had only climbed a single step each week, but each week I had climbed imperceptibly higher. Suddenly I had accepted the stakes; when I looked down, the stakes were too high.

I waved my arm at the waiter and he hurried to my table with the check. I was the only one left in the coffee shop. I could sense that the waiter and steward wanted to shut down and go home. "Another cup of coffee," I said.

A flicker of perturbation crossed the waiter's face as he readied himself to protest. After a second's pause, he bowed. "Coffee Kilimanjaro correct, sir?"

"Yes," I said.

The steward, beginning to slump on his stool, jerked to alertness and began to prepare the coffee. Again I found myself oddly thrilled by the formalized precision of his technique. I remembered the thrill of sweeping the secretary from her train without a second to spare. Again I loved the exact timing of the train attendant's two whistles. Those hurrying up the stairway, upon hearing the first whistle, could decide in an instinctive assessment of distance and footspeed whether or not to make a run for it. They knew the timing of the whistle blasts. They knew the speed of the closing doors. They knew how to hurtle themselves in sideways as the pneumatic jaws were sealing—and hurtle they did, just as I was reaching in and pulling the secretary out. Whatever our varying intentions, wherever our destinations, we had this in common. The beat of time was engraved in everyone's bones. All of us, scurrying strangers, were united by this. I wanted to turn on the stairway and greet the rush as the first whistle sounded. "My friends!" I wanted to shout. "Run!"

And should the attendant ever vary the beat between the two whistle blasts? Should a minute ever decide to be 61 seconds, even for a second? I would have remained faithful to my wife, but mathematics would be lost. Departed friends would return. The world would make no sense.

Wasn't mathematics simply an attempt to explain everything in relation to the perfect circle, which itself needs no explanation? Wasn't there a reason why the Yamanote Line remained the connecting link to all the other trains, going around in one huge circle, the trains never more than a few seconds off? Wasn't there a reason that the bums chose this train for their naps, their dreams hurling round and round, the invisible numbers of their lives swirling into the brief visible circle of perfection, and, thus refreshed and newly imbued, could get off where they started?

And wasn't this why Ashida and I had spent an April day riding and riding the Yamanote Line while our appointments for job interviews were left behind like straggling passengers on the platform, a blur in our lives that we chose to ignore? Ashida claimed it was impossible to commit suicide on this line: all the pedestrian walkways were guarded by high fences that curled inward like fingers to prevent them from being scaled. Neither failure nor suicide were tolerated—putting us, we joked, in a no-win situation.

But our brief bluster of rebellion ended, and on our last day in Tokyo Ashida and I went to all our job interviews. That evening we celebrated with sushi and beer at a cramped, homey restaurant. From there we walked to Olympic Park and Ashida, in a burst of euphoria, began to run around the track. I climbed the pedestrian walkway to watch. How ironic, I thought, the overpass was unbarricaded, nothing to prevent me from throwing myself under the churning legs of a passing runner.

I leaned over the edge to yell at Ashida. I could hear him coming but could see nothing. Then his figure broke through the darkness, a visual Doppler effect to his sound. Before I could focus running sounds to running forms, he passed under me in a swish, furthering the sensory illusions. I knew he couldn't be going that fast, but by the time I completed this thought he was gone. He disappeared for a long while. The track was huge; a stadium sat in the middle of it and even in the daytime one couldn't see across it.

In a few minutes Ashida appeared again. He went around and around, and in the long gaps of his absence I stood in the stillness and waited for my body to sense when he would approach again. Beyond my sight and hearing, a breeze was building. I was filled with a sudden pleasure at the exact way his dark form moved with the dark that itself seemed to be moving, chasing its sliding monolith until he caught up with it and then surpassed it and only then became visible to the inferior human eye. He ran on and on and my pleasure increased, not because of his competitive pace or the quantity of kilometers he was accumulating, but because of the circle he was completing again and again. In a secret way I longed for a similar motion that would take me from job to home and back again.

When the wave of stillness felt timed to end, I waited for the sound of gravel to kick up. I waited longer. Thinking Ashida might have exhausted himself and was walking back, I extended the rhythm of his absence to its breaking point, but still he didn't come. Finally I climbed down and walked the track myself. I mounted the steps to the stadium's bolted doors and looked around. Then I checked the walkway again, and then called his name. It was hard to say it. The human voice, the voice of reason, was not contained within this circle.

Ray's Boat

FRANK SOOS

From *Unified Field Theory* (1998)

Ray looked down the dinner table at his assembled friends. Sitting with their chairs pushed back, a coffee cup resting here and there on a knee, they looked the very picture of satisfaction, maybe even bliss. On the table, the casserole dish was almost empty of its bricks of lasagna; the sticks of bread smeared with butter were all gone. So was the salad, so was the wine from the big two-liter bottles. There was still some cheesecake left. Somebody might still want another piece of that.

Ray looked on the flushed faces, the distended bellies of his guests, and thought everybody should eat like this. The world's leaders ought to be brought together and made to eat Sherri's wonderful lasagna. With so much blood tied up in the digestive track, the world could be made a safer place. He called for a toast. Nobody had any wine, but they had their water glasses and their coffee mugs, and with some effort they pulled themselves toward the center of the long table. Ray smiled. This disparate bunch overcame their drowsy inertia for him because they were his dear friends. "To this green world," he told them.

Nobody asked what his toast was all about. On this summer's evening when the trees, the grass, the lettuce and spinach in Sherri's garden threatened to push through the newly installed bay window right on into the dining room, people might have thought they understood him well enough. Besides, Ray was known by his toasts.

At one memorable dinner he had toasted, "To socks with no holes." They ate that one on a partially refinished door straddled across a couple of sawhorses. They ate surrounded by buckets of paint and ladders and Ray's saws and hammers and drills. Then, only Ray had a sense of how his old house was going to come together or had the confidence that he and Sherri would reach a point when they could stop camping out in their underheated bedroom, could stop buying black beans and lentils in fifty-pound sacks at the feed store.

Ray's sock toast had marked the day when he would stop augmenting his wardrobe from stray articles of clothing picked up off the roadway. Back then when he rode his bicycle to work, he told people, he saw a wealth of things left to rot on the shoulder. T-shirts, knit hats, socks, gloves. Sometimes even pants and underwear. Once he found two brassieres left on a picnic table in a park, but Sherri wouldn't wear them. Surely, she said, there were limits.

But if there were such limits, Ray could never comprehend them. Now, with his house wrapped around him, newly plumbed, painted, and furnished, proof that he really had peeked into a brighter future, who could deny that he wasn't some kind of visionary?

Eight-thirty—people would have to start packing it in soon. Ray was thirty-one, most of his friends were about that. Their kids were somewhere along the route from diapers to preschool. Little ones were going to start falling apart in the next half hour. No more of that 2 a.m. shit, no more sitting around listening to Ray's tapes and talking. No more getting a little high.

"Wait," Ray said, "I got to show you what I found today."

Today, as he went to his job as foreman of a small crew of carpenters and painters who specialized in repairs to two-hundred-year-old houses, repairs for people who wanted only the best and could afford it; today, in his good-as-new pickup that he'd fixed up himself; today, Ray saw this guy dragging a big canvas bag out to the curb for the trash men to pick up. He wheeled over and asked what, exactly, that sack was all about.

"Junk," the guy said, "crap. You don't even want to hear about it."

"Well," Ray said, "I could take it if all you're going to do is send it to the dump." And the guy was more than happy to give him the bag and oddly shaped boards and bent steel rods, all the paraphernalia that went with it. All of it was piled in a heap in Ray's garage right now.

The men excused themselves from the table and poured the rest of the coffee into their mugs on the way out. After promising they wouldn't be long, they headed downstairs to the garage. But kids had already broken out of the bedroom with weary tears and recriminations. Ray's party was coming to a close and people would have to hurry to maintain this happy sense of equilibrium long enough to bathe their babies, put them to bed, and finally climb into bed themselves, where they would be free at last to share their built-up sense of well-being and love and of the rightness of their lives.

"Look at this," Ray said. The canvas fabric of the boat itself was already spread on the floor, looking like the flayed hide of a strange animal. He picked up two pieces of wood and slid them into a metal sleeve, twisted, and—ta da!—instant oar. "If the rest was this simple," he said in a make-believe mournful voice.

But by then men were taking up the various wooden shapes and turning them over in their hands, saying to each other: "This must be the transom, and that thing maybe will unfold and make the keel." "These steel hickeys must be the ribbing." Ray had, of course, already seen that much of the design, but it pleased him to watch his friends make it take shape.

By placing the steel rods through a double thick length of canvas webbing, the men began to assemble a ribbed backbone for some prehistoric lizard. The side door to the garage cracked open and a child's face looked in, not Ray's kid but another. "Mommy says," the girl started, but it was at that moment that Ray held up the skeleton and hollered out, "Looks like a whale! How'd you like to wind up in the belly of this thing?" The child scampered back up the stairs to the dining room.

With some pushing, the men were able to get the transom to pop into the stern of the boat skin. But that's when they lost Chuck, which was too bad since Chuck was a sculptor who was selling pretty well these days now that he'd gotten into a gallery in Richmond and one in D.C. too. Once he and Ray had put up flimsy apartment buildings together. "How are we going to finish this thing without him?" Ray said. "I mean, we need somebody whose brain works in 3-D."

But Chuck left anyway with his wife the printmaker and their bawling kid who'd overshot her bedtime and gone hyperactive on them. "I hate it when that happens," Ray told Len and Terry who were left, who had figured out the steel ribs weren't in the right order to fit into the slots along the canvas gunwales of the boat. "Great, terrific," Ray yelled at them, only now he saw that the canvas strip that held the ribs maybe should have gone in before the transom if the keel was to help stretch it the length of the boat.

His own child appeared at the door. "What is it, princess?" he asked her. With her long blonde hair and her ballerina tights, Bonnie really did look like a princess from one of her own storybooks. She whispered in his ear, "Mommy says it's past our bedtimes."

"Uh-oh, it's past our bedtimes," Ray told his pals.

"Oh man, you aren't kidding," said Len, who went to high school with Ray but got a law degree and turned into a Republican. Which goes to show, Ray thought, that life's a pretty crooked road. Take Terry, who sold a little dope, played drums in a country band. Who knows what all he did to pay the bills? But here he was in Ray's garage with Len.

Not for long. Len and Terry left. Ray heard the good-byes and the front door shut, maybe he could even hear Sherri throw the dead bolt. Alone, then, he sat on the floor and considered how the slim metal battens must fan out in some sort of umbrella fashion to make the bow.

Nobody had time for fun anymore. Now it was day-care, now it was deals. Real life, Ray's pals were fond of saying, had snuck up on them. Caught in house payments and car repairs, the shit they pledged themselves against not so long ago, not one of them would say it was a mistake. Like insects, they'd simply gone through a fast and unimagined alteration from larva to adult. Nobody even had a chance to say, "Now what?"

Ray and Sherri had two kids. Anybody could see Bonnie was daddy's girl. Ted was still a tiny baby in diapers so it was hard to say for sure, but Ray and Sherri worried about him. Ray's mom, if she was still alive, would say Ted wasn't right.

Ray sat on the floor, slapping a metal stay against his shin. Not right in what way? So far nobody could say. Sherri seemed to worry more about it than the doctor did. Ray listened for the noises his house ought to make. The ventilation fan in the attic ought to be shutting down about now if the thermostat he put in was working. Bonnie had been so quick to learn everything. Maybe Ted was just slow. Hell, Einstein was slow; there was nothing wrong with being slow.

They'd figure it out; put enough heads together and you can solve just about any problem. That's what Ray thought. Ted would turn out okay, just like the boat. Ray considered his boat a marvel. Sure, he still needed to do some fiddling with the ribs and patch a couple of holes that had been poked in the canvas hull. Above him, he could hear the drumming of Bonnie's feet as she ran from the tub to her bedroom and Sherri's heavier step following.

Ray's house didn't grow quiet. Directly above him in the kitchen, Ray could hear Sherri banging pots, running water and abruptly shutting it off. The rhythm of her movements alarmed him. Whenever something pissed her off, it always caught him by surprise.

Ted had been slow sitting up. They'd sit him on his rear and he'd just topple over like those sock-em toys Ray had as a boy. Only Ted didn't roll right back up. He was slow crawling, and now he was only walking clumsily, hanging on his mom's leg, not talking at all. Bonnie, though. Bonnie was a lucky girl. She was just like Ray. When he was a kid with a big dopey grin, strangers at the grocery store would fish in their pockets for pennies so he could work the gum machine. He knew doors would spring open for Bonnie the rest of her life; all she had to do was smile.

Ray made a list of stuff he needed to pick up from the shop or buy at the hardware to fix his new boat and went back up to the kitchen. He was surprised at the carnage left there. Red sauce ran down the cabinet fronts, a cone of coffee grounds spilled over the counter. Plates were piled in high crooked stacks. When Sherri turned around from the sink she was crying.

"Hey, hey," Ray told her. "That's what we got a dishwasher for, right?" Except Ray hadn't allowed for enough of a slope in the drain pipe, and it tended to get stopped up. It just had in the middle of running a load of pots and pans, and had disgorged itself all over the floor.

"You're no help," she told him. But he was. He was like the goddamned Cat in the Hat, charging into her kitchen, more a force like weather than any kind of human being. Whenever he pitched in, things ran wildly out of control. Dishes slid out of the over-filled drying rack, silverware went crashing, water sprayed across the room and hit the new wallpaper in the breakfast nook.

Now he was on his knees feeding a plumber's snake into the dishwasher. Sherri said, "You know how Ted is if you don't get him settled down." She said, "You know what it's like to get Bonnie her bath and get him put down at the same time." He knew, he knew. Maybe she was losing her delight in his disorder. Before the kids, her placid days at the county library could use an infusion of Ray's wacky attacks.

Ted started hollering from his bedroom. Poor little guy would be waking up this way throughout the night now, sweating, rolling his big blue eyes around. Nightmares might be what it was, and him not even able to tell them about it.

When, exactly, was it that Sherri saw she was getting tired of Ray? When was it that she began to realize that one of the reasons she could stay on at the library year after year when nothing ever changed, when it was the same work of being quietly pleasant every day, was Ray? He was like a radio turned up way too loud, but locked a room away and out of reach.

When he got her on the phone, the sound of a power tool whirring in the background, he never apologized for not being where he said he would be. "Ray, we're supposed to be taking the kids to the pool," she said.

"No problem. I'll meet you there in the truck. Pack me a couple of sandwiches—ham, mustard and mayonnaise."

"Ray," Sherri could say, but the phone would already be dead so there was no chance to explain that the kids were already in their swimsuits, Ted was in his car seat bellowing, and she would have to stop for gas too since he left her with an empty tank.

Whenever Sherri thought of Dr. Roger Armstead, she thought of a big brown dress shoe, worn over in the heel, a hole in the sole, scuffed, with a broken and knotted shoelace. He was a big man, six-three or -four with long brown hair shot with gray and a thick gray beard. Every day he wore wrinkled and stained khaki pants, a light blue dress shirt, also wrinkled even if he put it on fresh in the morning, and a blue and orange striped tie. The man was her boss at the library and from the beginning she found him mildly repulsive. How was it she agreed to have lunch with Dr. Roger Armstead?

Dr. Roger was what he liked to be called, and everybody at the library knew a version of his story. Once he was a history professor at UVA, but they let him go. Maybe it was for drinking, maybe it was for not doing his work or hitting on coeds. Whatever, they let him go. His family, though, was rich; his family went way back in Virginia history. Probably they lent Thomas Jefferson money once. So Dr. Roger came to be director of this small branch of the Albermarle County Library, which was okay since it wasn't a real library and since there were enough people who knew what was what to take up the slack. Meanwhile, Dr. Roger spent his days arguing about history and politics with some of the old men patrons who didn't seem to mind his lax personal hygiene.

Knowing what she knew, Sherri went to lunch with Dr. Roger Armstead at the all-you-can-eat Chinese buffet place. "How is Raymond?" he asked her, and "How is pretty little Bonnie?" and "How is Ted coming along? Are you still worried about him?" Sherri answered these questions while she felt like she was having a lucid dream. One part of her mind was sour and alert and told her this man probably had to sneak around that very morning and ask the other librarians the names of her husband and kids, that his was a clever act, assembling his next thoughtful question out of the clues from Sherri's previous answer. An ex-bullshitting professor. But another part said, that's okay, relax, you need this. You need to sit down and talk to somebody about yourself. And it felt good that somebody was a man.

She agreed it would be fine to swing by his house and drop off some papers on the way back to work, telling herself she was curious to see if it was as messy and nasty as his office and the Oldsmobile they rode in. When they pulled into the drive of Dr. Roger's tall brick house, he rooted around in the rubble in the back seat until he found some yellowed papers in no way distinguishable from those he left behind. "Won't you come in?" There was another little voice in her head, the voice that was around from her excitable girlhood readings of Edgar Allan Poe and H.P. Lovecraft, saying, *Don't open that door, don't go down that hallway.* Her more adult voice, the voice of a librarian and mother of two, said, *Don't be so silly.*

The house was, in fact, messier and smelled like a dirty man, a little like sweat, a little like pee. Stacks of old newspapers and magazines slid from every flat surface down into the middle of the floor. "My research," said Dr. Roger. Sherri wondered what sort of research he did, then she wondered how much of this material had been carried off from their very library without authorization. Underneath the papers and the dust was fine old cherry furniture and oriental rugs too. These had been worth something before the moths got after them. Maybe the furniture still was. Back in the kitchen, Dr. Roger could be heard making them drinks.

"How about a gin and tonic?" he hollered. Sherri walked in the direction of his voice. "Oh, oh you shouldn't have come in here." Dr. Roger's kitchen had been white once, but now it was yellow with a fine patina of fuzzy dust hanging to the greasy walls. The enamel around the eyes on his stove had grown tentacles of grimy rust and his sink was brown. "My mother was a saintly woman," Dr. Roger told her. "I keep this house out of respect for her memory."

In this way he mocked his sloth and made Sherri feel sorry for him while at the same time she knew he was trying in his clumsy way to seduce her. She found herself oddly grateful for the effort and accepted his offer of the drink, though she rarely drank liquor at all.

Loving Ray would be enough to wear anybody out. He turned each day into an obstacle course, not so much to be got over and around, but to be knocked down. Even Sunday began with the whine of a power tool. Maybe he was putting in a new window sash, or a new radiator in his truck, or building a jungle gym for the kids. Whatever, he ran from job to job, and none of them ever quite got done. The radiator might wind up fully installed but lacking a thermostat, so for a week he would have to take the station wagon to work until he found the time to stop at the car parts place. The window sash never got painted, and the jungle gym remained an odd assortment of four-by-four posts standing in the backyard.

"Think of it as a temple," he told Sherri, "like Stonehenge. On the first day of summer the sun is going to come up and sit right on top of that post." He ran over to the post and rested his chin on top.

"Don't be silly, Ray," she told him, and from behind her Bonnie on her powder blue tricycle said, "Don't be silly, Daddy."

It would be wrong to think these projects had been forgotten. In Ray's mind, his work was always in evolution. Part of his brain scanned his basement and garage inventory for the bolts he bought for the jungle gym and the weights for the window sash he'd salvaged from a fire damaged house. In the middle of the night Sherri would wake up to the light in her eyes while he wrote notes to himself, sketched ideas on the pad he kept beside their bed.

"There's a million ways to get things done, a million ways to make things work out," Ray sang to himself while he carefully, carefully worked his pry bar under a dry rotted floor joist. The trick was to take out the joists one at a time and replace them without damaging the floor above. Ray liked his work and didn't especially mind being chief since everybody on his crew was a pretty good worker. Except the new guy. All day Ray had been thinking about the new guy. For one thing, nobody was sure what the new guy did. He wasn't a carpenter; he wasn't really a painter, though he claimed to be.

Ray would come up from under the house and find this guy, Dave, sitting on the ground smoking, gazing at the windowsill he was supposed to be scraping, sanding and caulking like it was one of life's bigger mysteries. "Hey," he'd say, "just taking a little break. What's up?" It occurred to Ray that since it looked like he himself was taking a break maybe Dave thought taking breaks was okay. And it was, everybody took a five-minute break in the morning and in the afternoon. But somehow Ray knew this guy's breaks ran longer.

"Maybe I could see if anybody wants a Coke or something," Dave said thoughtfully.

Ray found some money in his pocket for a soda and told Dave to go around and see if anybody else wanted something from the store before he went. Shortly he heard Dave gunning the engine in the company van and remembered Dave wasn't supposed to be driving. His license had been revoked.

One of the painters came around the house. "We got to talk about that guy," he told Ray.

"I know, I know. What do you want me to do?"

"Tell the bosses. Tell the bosses to fire him."

The bosses. Ray tried to stay away from the bosses as much as he could. They bid the jobs, got the contracts. As long as Ray's crew brought the jobs in on estimate, they stayed away. Everybody on all the crews was happier that way.

Occasionally a boss came by driving one of the green Chevy station wagons that matched the green Ford vans the crews used. All of them had the company name printed discreetly on the side. On a good day, Ray liked to imagine Charlottesville being crisscrossed all day long by the station wagons and vans— stitching it back together through careful, crafty workmanship. Two-hundred-year-old houses don't stand up all by themselves. On a bad day, Ray thought of the green vehicles as locusts or alien invaders, taking over the world silently, sneakily unless somebody woke up and noticed.

He got that feeling sitting in the air-conditioned seat, a gallon of newly tinted paint between his feet, listening to a boss bitch him out about a guy on his crew who wasn't shaving every day, or about eating their lunch under the big oaks in a client's front yard. All the time, the radio softly bleated, "Jesus, Jesus, Jesus," since the bosses always tuned to the religious station. Taking over the world through niceness and neatness, Ray thought.

Dave was tight with the bosses. They hired him through the pastor at their church who found him while sharing a moment of prayer at a minimum security prison. When he came to work, he had no brushes of his own and wore a black T-shirt featuring the name of a rock band and a large cannabis leaf. His clothes, the bosses said, were leftovers from his former life and, just now, were the only ones he had. Praise Jesus for the gift of Dave's repentance.

God's world is full of such miracles, the bosses would tell you if they thought you were worthy of sharing their insiders' knowledge. One by one they had been converted from Sunday golfers to acolytes of a true faith, though they were still a little cagey about revealing their clean new souls to prospective clients. This they professed to believe: The world as we know it is coming to an end right around the corner, and in its place a new heaven on earth will be established for a chosen few. Wondrously, that new heaven would resemble the rolling Virginia piedmont with each hilltop crowned by a red brick mansion, the countryside scourged of strip malls, condo developments, trailer homes, and plywood minibarns. It would look rather like the Old Virginia of Mr. Jefferson's time had he only been their kind of God-fearing man.

On her way home Sherri stopped at a convenience store and bought some breath mints. She really had nothing to hide; she just didn't want to have to explain to Ray all the things she had seen and heard. Dr. Roger's cannonball, for example, a real Civil War cannonball he had dug out of a pasture in Manassas. There's probably a law against that now, she thought. There was probably a law against it then. But since Dr. Roger's family had entertained Major Mosby right in the room where she was sitting, Dr. Roger felt that gave him the right.

It seems he came from a long line of people who felt they had certain special rights. His father had been a judge, and his grandfather before that, and to hear Dr. Roger tell it, they had devoted their legal lives to pushing the unwashed back from the breastworks. He winked so Sherri, up from Nelson County with two years at the community college, understood she was one who slipped through. "It's nothing to be ashamed of," Dr. Roger told her.

Until she and Ray moved into town, she had never imagined it was. She told Dr. Roger her own family had fought in the War Between the States.

"On which side?"

"The Rebel side, of course," she said, suddenly feeling proud over something that hadn't meant that much to her before.

"They were fools, then, weren't they?" Dr. Roger said. He said Johnny Reb died defending an institution that held nothing for him. He had been tricked because he loved the land too much. You shouldn't love anything that much, Dr. Roger told her.

He had made his own life a monument to indifference. He had shambled through the same University of Virginia where his family had previously distinguished itself and then been drummed out of the law school after representing the work of another Virginia gentleman as his own. His old man pulled some strings to get Dr. Roger instated in the graduate school of a neighboring state university so he might come home to teach in a position created just for him. In the same manner he spilled his corn flakes onto the kitchen floor, clipped his nails over the fine carpets in the sitting room, he had pissed his sinecure away.

"Your poor momma and daddy," Sherri said. She wasn't sure if it was the right thing to say or not. It just came out.

Dr. Roger just smiled, "Oh hell, he didn't care about me."

"Your mother, then." Sherri had the notion women could be counted on to love people more than ideas or things.

"Yes, Mother." Dr. Roger cocked his head and looked into her face, blinking his big old eyes.

Sherri thought it was time to be getting back to the library.

Nothing had happened, had it? Except Sherri knew even as she walked back into the warm sunshine from Dr. Roger's musty house she would mention none of it to Ray. The way he was, and he really couldn't help it, you couldn't keep anything to yourself. He had to be poking into everything.

When Sherri drove up from picking up Bonnie at her dance class and Ted from day care, Ray was sitting in the open door of his truck reading. "Who can find a virtuous woman? For her price is above rubies," he told her.

Sherri blushed, but Ray had his nose in the book and didn't notice. "Ray, what are you talking about?" She could hear her voice bouncing around inside her head like she was listening to herself on a tape recorder.

He held up a green pocket Bible about the size of a deck of cards. Dave had given it to him; Dave had given one to everybody on the crew that morning while they were riding the van out to Farmington. Guys who were used to purposefully taking up all manner of tools held the pocket testaments nervously, tenderly, then put them away in their shirt pockets or dinner buckets. Nobody said anything.

Just as they pulled into the driveway of a pre–Civil War manor house in need of minor sprucing up, Dave spoke. "I'm wondering if anybody might want to join me in a moment of prayer?" Everybody sat real still, but they were all looking at Ray. Another carpenter, the guy riding shotgun, said, "No," and got out and slammed the door.

Ray said, "Well, Dave, I guess we all have our own ways of getting ready for work."

"Huh." And all day Dave sulked around, doing even less than he usually did. At lunch he went to the back of the large yard and ate by himself.

What could you do with a guy like that? Ray had nothing against Jesus, but work was work. Still, the little green Bible was a kick. He took it out at lunchtime and started at the beginning with old God himself rolling his voice out on the waters. He started reading slowly in a deep, serious voice, "In the beginning," but everybody told him to put a sock in it. "No kidding," Ray said, "we could start reading to each other at lunchtime. Not just this," though he thought to himself he liked the sound of the Bible, its rhythms reached back to his kid days and put him at ease, "but Louis L'Amour books and detective stories, you know?"

They didn't know. And neither did Ray. Not really. Now that his house was pretty much finished, now that his imagination had some time to run loose, he was wondering, what else was there?

"You know what I mean?" he said to Len. They met for breakfast once a week before they went off to their different jobs, and they were both pleased about the impression they made: Ray in his carpenter's jeans and dirty ball cap, Len in his slick suit. They must be special people to be such friends.

But Len didn't know. The law, he thought, was a wonder in itself. Every time you thought you got to the end of some problem, it seemed like you went down a trap door into a whole new way of thinking. It was all words, all the way you put together words, all different every day.

"Well, sure," said Ray, "that's just like a house. You're never really done, there's always something else. But I mean something different. Something that isn't a house or the law. Something else."

Len said maybe there wasn't anything else.

"Even in the woods?"

"Even in the woods."

"Even in the woods with your hands in your pockets and you not thinking about cutting down a tree you're not supposed to or catching a fish out of season or pissing and having somebody accidentally see you?"

Len said no.

Ray said, "Maybe there's a way of thinking that just doesn't have anything to do with the law."

Len said, "That would be chaos." He said our social fabric was thin as ten-cent toilet paper, and without the law there we would fall right through it. And he picked up his greasy napkin and poked a hole in it so Ray would see.

"No kidding?" Ray said. "You believe that?" Then he said they should go fishing for smallmouth bass in his new boat, and Len agreed they should do just that. The question was when. Len was busy all the time these days, even on weekends. Still, it had been a long time since they went fishing together, since either of them had gone fishing at all. As soon as Ray finished the boat, maybe they really would.

Sherri said she'd hate to be married to that guy. Which surprised her. She used to think Len was cute, sly and sexy. Back then he put words together in ways that made you laugh. Now he sat at the table with his hands made into a church steeple and lined his nose up at you like he was taking a bead: one false move and blam-o. Len's life seemed like it had turned into a big argument, and he had to win it.

"I'm glad you're not like that," she told Ray and meant it. She was still feeling bad about eating Chinese food with Dr. Roger. Besides, it gave her gas. Maybe they would have steaks for dinner. They weren't good for you, even Ray agreed with that, but he still liked them, and eating a steak made him feel like he had amounted to something.

"I bet Len has steaks all the time," Ray told her.

No, Sherri said, they took casseroles and stuff out of the freezer and nuked them. Len's wife was a lawyer too. They had one kid, a prissy little boy with a real big head. He was already reading on the fifth-grade level, and he was just in preschool.

"Well, Bonnie's prettier, aren't you honey?" Ray said.

"He's dweeby," Bonnie said.

"Ted now." Ray took Ted out of the car seat and swung him up over his head, down between his legs, threw him a couple of feet in the air, and caught him.

"Ray!"

"It's okay. I'm getting him ready for a future in outer space." He pulled Ted's face up to his own. "Right, buddy? You thinking your deep thoughts in there? You happy?"

Ted giggled and snorted.

"See? He's all right. He just doesn't have any complaints."

Nonetheless, Sherri insisted they make an appointment for Ted at University Hospital. In Nelson County when they were kids, you went to the doc when you were sick, and that was that. People grew up the way they grew up, and that was that. You loved them anyway. Maybe, Ray thought, some old ways were better.

Ray's crew knocked off, gathered up their tools, and headed for the van. The smell of marijuana rolled out its doors. Everybody looked at Dave; Dave sniggered. Work was getting to be this way, a series of little trials for Ray.

On the way back to the shop, nobody said anything. Then one of the guys said, "I don't know about you, but I need this job."

"I kind of like a job," somebody else said. They were all looking at Ray now except for Dave, who was slid over by the cracked open window letting the wind blow over him, looking like he was all blissed out.

"Okay, okay," Ray said, "everybody who needs a job hold up your hand." They all did, even Dave.

"Good. That's settled." And he drove on.

Terry knew Dave. Only he called him Crazy Dave. Crazy Dave used to hang out with the garage bands that played for frat parties over at the u, a kind of roadie for bands that never got to go on the road. Shit-faced every time you saw him.

"Was he any good at it?" Ray wondered. He was still hoping Dave might turn out to be good at something.

"What's to be good at? You run around with a roll of duct tape and make sure all the equipment is plugged in. Somebody who knows a little bit runs the sound board." But Terry didn't know Dave had been in jail or found Jesus in there. It figured, though, Jesus or Buddha or somebody like that. He would be the type.

Ray showed Terry the little Bible Dave gave him. "I've been reading in it a little."

"You can pick those things up all over the place—the jails, the detox places, soup kitchens. They're always trying to get you when you're down."

"I kind of like the Old Testament part."

"You better get rid of that guy," Terry told him.

"You think so?"

"Fire him, Ray. Christ, you've fired people before, right?"

But Ray never had. He always just let things in the crew roll along until they sorted themselves out somehow. "Listen, I nearly got my boat finished. Let's you and me and Len go fishing."

"Ray."

"I'll talk to him."

But he kept putting it off. There was Dave, still eating lunch by himself, out under a huge old oak tree, studying his own scuffed up little Bible. What if—and this was what was really bugging

Ray—what if this guy was really onto something? Here were these Children of Israel always getting it wrong, following false prophets, worshipping golden calves; you could bet they'd miss the genuine article when it came along. Across the yard, Dave chewed a big hunk off his sandwich, grinned, and wagged his head just like he knew what Ray was thinking.

After dinner Ray told Sherri he wanted to work on his boat, but really all he wanted to do was go sit in the garage and look at it. Ray thought his boat a wonder. A hybrid of umbrella and bicycle, it only looked complicated until you got used to it. Now all its ribs were ordered in their webbed canvas spine, and he had solved the problem of the folding wooden keel. Driving home from work one day, Ray saw how it would work. It was just a matter of opening the keel on its hinges over the top of the canvas spine and locking it against the transom and the point of the bow where the metal battens fanned out. All put together, Ray's boat had an optimistic sense of motion. He saw it was a miracle of design. Steel, canvas and wood, the reliable old materials of the mechanical age. You look at them every day, and one day you see how they could be made into a collapsible boat. Some clever guy, somebody a lot like Ray, had thought of this boat. All it needed now was painting.

Upstairs he could hear Sherri doing the dishes, his job. Tonight she was cutting him some slack, probably because she had been on his case so much about Ted. He thought he wanted to explain to her about Ted, about just giving him some time. But really what he wanted to do was explain to her about himself. Inside him, strangely shaped notions were growing. He could quit work and ride a bicycle across the country, for example, or build a small airplane in the backyard, then circle the globe in it. A little voice kept telling him to go do it and find out.

The door bumped open and Bonnie came in carrying Ted.

"Honey, you aren't supposed to be carrying him around like that; you'll hurt yourself. Him too. Put him down so he'll walk."

"It's okay, I do it all the time. You just never see me." She leaned against him and looked at the boat. "That's a silly boat. I wouldn't ride in a boat like that."

"What are you talking about?" Ray said. "This is a great boat. This is a magic boat, a boat that goes in a bag."

"Mommy says it's rotten junk, and you're stupid if you think you can make something out of it."

He was going to tell her how little Mommy knew about it when Ted, who was pulling himself around the room by holding to the walls and shelves, grabbed hold of the stubby cord to Ray's Skilsaw. Ray hollered, "Ted!" and in two big steps grabbed the saw just as it slid from its shelf. Ted looked at him, but it was a blank look, a look that registered neither panic nor fear.

"Take him out of here," Ray told Bonnie. "This isn't a place for little guys. This isn't a place for fooling around."

In a house full of the sounds of hammers and saws and drills, couldn't the sound of Ray's voice be one more noisy thing? He and Sherri never hollered at each other, even when they argued. Still, when was a voice a voice and not just another noise?

Ray decided right then he would paint his boat green. He took down a can of green enamel porch paint, opened it, and carefully stirred. He saw that he had been saving this quart of paint for a job just like this. Ordinarily he didn't like to paint; that's what God made painters for. But sliding the fresh bright paint over the canvas hull, pulling a river of green with his brush, and covering up the dirty brown, Ray was seeing the boat make itself new. Maybe everything was still possible, he couldn't be wrong about something big like that. Ray's boat was ready for some river or lake, some new place he had never explored. Ray was ready too. He and Len and Terry were going to fish in this boat; they had all promised.

There was something needful about Dr. Roger that people never saw around the library, where he could be high-handed and mean to the patrons. Away from the building, he could sometimes be courtly and shy. He was a fat middle-aged man. Maybe nobody had ever loved him. Not his daddy. Not his mother either, no matter what Dr. Roger thought. How could she have stood by and let him ruin himself like that if she did?

Dr. Roger started asking Sherri to go to the Chinese place every week. Sometimes she tried to get out of it; sometimes she tried to suggest some place different, but he wouldn't hear it. "All you can eat. Isn't that the American way, all you can eat?" Real Chinese places didn't serve Jell-O, she told him, and the next time they went he made a point of eating a bowl of red Jell-O. "Here, taste that and tell me whether it's strawberry or cherry. I can never tell the difference," Dr. Roger said, poking a wobbling cube on a spoon in her direction.

Was he making fun of her when he did this, or not? Sherri couldn't tell, but she knew she didn't like it, and she didn't like it when he called their lunches out of the library "dates." "I've got a date with Miz Sherri for lunch today," he told the other librarians in the morning, "so don't go getting your hopes up. My social calendar is filled."

Often he protracted their absence by making up specious errands. One day as they drove all the way downtown to pick up some special kind of pipe tobacco he said he could get only at this one little shop, they passed a young woman wearing white shorts and a sports bra riding a bicycle. Sherri watched Dr. Roger's eyes roll to the rearview mirror as they passed. "Look out," she told him when the car started to drift to the left. "Oh, oh," he told her. "There ought to be a law. They do that to indulge themselves, you know. To make fools out of old men like me."

"Who? Who's they?" She was only teasing, but Dr. Roger didn't say anything.

When he parked the car, he caught her looking at him in the mirror. "Sometimes you think you can trust somebody. You take them into your confidence, and they let you down." His voice got heavy and slow. "They betray you." He sighed a purposeful sigh. "Stay in the car; I'll only be a minute."

The trouble with Ray was that he could make everything he needed in his workshop. Hadn't he remanufactured his house right up around him? Where did Sherri come in? "You're a good cook; you're a good lay" was what he told her. He meant he loved her. And he would do anything for the kids. But what did he need from her? She thought he might disappear down into that workshop one day and get ahold of a project so big and complicated he might stay there forever.

When Dr. Roger came back, he made his voice sound cheerful and offered to buy her a drink.

Those stories she'd heard at the library about Dr. Roger and college girls must have been true. Like those girls who wore tight shorts on bicycles, Sherri was thinking, they knew what they were up to as much as he did. He hurt them; he took advantage. But he got hurt too.

"Don't you have any hobbies?" Sherri asked him.

When Ray cracked open the inner office door, he saw the bosses kneeling on the gray industrial carpeting, down on one knee like high school ballplayers in their pregame locker room. The secretary, who was like all the other secretaries he had known in construction outfits, a pretty young woman in a short skirt, tiptoed around them with the coffee makings. When she looked up and saw Ray, she made a violent chopping gesture. When he made to shut the door, she slipped out beside him.

She grabbed the tail of his T-shirt and twisted it into a knot. "Are you crazy?"

"What's going on in there?"

"What's it look like? Ray, you better get out of here; you're in trouble with them already."

But before he could pull out of the parking lot, one of the bosses hollered to him and came jogging toward the van. "Ray, what's your question?"

"Nothing. It was something, but I think I can get it worked out."

"Do you?" The boss's face was heavy and lined, the face of a guy who drank too much, who had a closet full of secret debts and family troubles. "We're praying for you, Ray."

It was good to work with a bunch of wise-asses, good to take the edge off. "Woo woo," they hollered as soon as the van rocked out of the parking lot, "We're praying for you too, Ray," and "Praise Jesus, He wants you for a sunbeam." Dave sat in the very back seat grinning. Seven thirty in the morning, and was he out of his gourd already?

It was good, because Ray was feeling scared. Not of the bosses. They were assholes, as lost as he was; anybody could see that. Ray was scared of the wide world opening out on him in a way he had been too busy to notice before. Hadn't he always said there wasn't a problem anywhere the right combination of time and money couldn't fix? Ray knew he had been blessed with more time than money, but that was okay. He had just revised his estimation: Time and the right tools.

Now he considered that he just might be mistaken. People, for example. People could get in such a way they couldn't be fixed. He wasn't thinking about Ted or even Crazy Dave. He was thinking about Sherri, how she got to be the way she was. She had been at the library so long she was starting to see their whole life as a matter of neatness and keeping your voice down. A book on the wrong shelf was as good as a book lost, she told him. Which was maybe a good way to think of books, but he wanted to leave room for possibilities, to allow room for whatever he hadn't thought of yet. He was thinking that when he needed to talk to somebody he went to Len or Terry and not to her. But Len had his laws and was so balled up in them he couldn't see anything else. And Terry had his drums. When things got too bad for him, he just went out in the shed behind his house and wailed. An hour or so of that would mellow anybody out. A good example of time and the right tools, Ray thought.

He never stopped to consider what would happen when time and possibility worked against him. He could not picture the day when Sherri went back to Dr. Roger's house, this time going in with a bellyache and resignation to see his rare and famous Civil War sword. Dr. Roger kept it in his bottom dresser drawer under piles of black socks. "You can't go wrong with black socks," he told her, "just get up in the morning and grab a couple."

Sherri looked into the open door of Dr. Roger's closet full of rows of blue shirts on hangers and more thrown up on the shelves still in their shrink-wrap packaging. Beside them were four or five pairs of wrinkled pants. His bathrobe hung on the door with his slippers, those leather slip-ons she always associated with corny old cartoon variations on dogs, newspapers, and fetching, kicked off on the floor below.

This is how it was, then, with the bedclothes thrown back to show an elongated yellow stain the approximate shape of Dr. Roger running down the middle of the sheet; Dr. Roger's mother, a horsy intelligent woman, staring critically out of a tarnished silver frame from the dresser top; and Dr. Roger himself grunting to his feet with the long sword and scabbard in his hands. Sherri looked at the sword with tassels hanging from its basket. Once they had been golden, but now they were faded to a pale pea green. Dr. Roger offered the sword to her, and in reaching for it she saw in his face a look of greedy anticipation bordering on joy. Sherri burst into tears. Dr. Roger wrapped her in his damp, hairy arms and pulled her to him, the cold sword pushing against her bottom. They stood this way in the middle of his bedroom for some time while she cried and cried like Bonnie when she dumped over on her tricycle.

By high summer, stands of cumulus clouds twenty stories tall come rolling up from the tidewater and across the piedmont until they stack up against the Blue Ridge. By lunchtime it would already be humid enough to make Ray want to step out of his clothes and wring them out. By three o'clock the clouds would have packed and darkened, and Ray's crew would start to climb off their ladders and unplug their power tools and make ready to hop in the van and run back to the shop with the slapping wipers on high speed and still not able to keep up with the rain water rolling down the windshield. They passed people standing soaking at the bus stops, cars stalled out in intersections. All around them, water ran down the parking lots and roadways, into gutters and storm drains, down, down the shingles of the world, cleansing away the carbon monoxide and sulfur dioxide in the air, the spilled antifreeze and motor oil on the highway, the bird shit and corrosion from the statue of Lewis and Clark and their doughty men, carrying it all to the James, the Rapidan, the Rappahannock, those beautiful green rivers of Virginia where in their time Captains Meriwether and William were known to wet a line in the springtime.

How could they have guessed? How could Mr. Jefferson himself, sitting up in his big old cluttered house always in need of some work, the French doors thrown open to get a little air moving, sitting there puzzling over a mammoth tusk, how could he have known? Sending those two redoubtable country boys over hills and valleys to the westward would wind up making life hell for little fishes.

All of which set Ray to thinking about what you aim for and what you get. Right here at the stoplight where water ran off the bronze hats of Lewis and Clark and made them look like they had just walked up from the bottom of the ocean into this unexpected world. Take a right and you're at University Hospital, where doctors with wires, electrodes, and a ray gun were all set to tell him and Sherri what was going on inside Ted's little head.

"Not so smart," Ray said. He meant getting off the bypass and driving through town, but he might have meant something he just now only felt and could not say. He moved as a wheel inside a wheel, inside lots of bigger wheels. The kids, Sherri, the house— these were things he thought he had planned for and wanted, but maybe they were all part of a bigger kind of movement he couldn't see or understand, that he had no more planned for than he had budgeted time for day and night or space for land and water.

In the parking lot outside the shop, the guys on his crew threw open the van doors and ran like hell indoors or off to their cars. Crazy Dave crawled out like he had been napping back in his seat, stood in the rain stretching, pulled his T-shirt off, and turned his face up to the sky. After a while the rain slacked off and more light came back into the day. Dave started off slow and easy to his car, and Ray went after him.

Ray had been meaning to talk to Dave for some time, hadn't he? He had been planning to tell him to get off his ass and make an honest effort, to stay straight on the job and not bullshit him because there was a difference between how you handled yourself around the guys and how you handled yourself around the bosses. He needed to tell him to take some of his payday and buy his own brushes. Instead he said, "Thanks for the Bible."

"No problem," Dave told him as he started to climb in his sky-blue Pinto. Somebody from the bosses' church had given it to him; all he'd added was the stereo tape deck and the two carton-sized speakers leaning against the back seat.

"Hey," Ray said, "I've got this new boat. I've been thinking about taking it out and doing a little fishing."

"The old back-to-nature thing," Dave said, like he already knew all about it.

"Something like that." Ray felt like Dave was looking him over from his orange ball cap advertising his favorite brand of chain saws to his work boots spattered with wood glue and paint as if he'd seen him for the very first time. "What I mean is you might like to go."

Dave took out his cigarettes and shook the pack around, peeked into the hole torn in the corner, then reached in with one skinny finger and pulled out a one-guy joint hardly fatter than a pencil lead. Before he lit up, he took a little look around him. He pulled on the joint, then offered it to Ray. "Maybe," he said through the smoke leaking out of his mouth, "maybe I could." If Ray took a hit, it would hardly leave any for Dave, but taking it seemed like the right thing to do now. Dave grinned, "Jesus got into fishing too."

When Ray got to his truck, he felt a little like puking. A hit on an empty stomach will do that to you sometimes. But it was something else. For one thing, he'd promised Sherri he'd give up marijuana now that Bonnie was getting big enough to know. He rolled down both windows and turned the vent window in so it would blow straight at him. The streets were already steaming anyway, and the humidity was even higher than before the storm. No, Ray decided, it was that Dave guy. He wasn't sure he wanted him in his fishing boat, hadn't meant to ask him. But when the time came, nobody else could go fishing. Len, well Ray could have guessed how it would be with Len, the family thing, the billable hours at his practice. He said he had to protect his time. Terry's band had a gig at a club in Bethesda; this could be a big break for them. Ray thought he'd heard that one before, but never mind. He even called Chuck, who he hadn't seen since the night of his big dinner. Ray was embarrassed by that, but Chuck was busy anyway. His wife was having an opening at a new gallery in Baltimore. If it went well, they would drive over and dance to Terry's band afterwards.

By now, it was moving into fall, a drizzly day and a little cooler. There was an honest chance of getting some fish if you knew where to go. Ray thought he did if he could find the place, up in the mountains, a little green lake he had fished once as a boy, somewhere off the Blue Ridge Parkway. He put his collapsed boat in the back of his truck, put in his rods and reels, the same old stuff he and his daddy had used, cleaned and oiled up with new six-pound test line. He put Ted in his baby seat and Bonnie next to him.

Sherri had already made it clear she didn't want the kids to go. Even Bonnie was too little, she said. She said her say the night before, when Ray sprung the trip on her at the last minute the way he always did. Bonnie would do all right, Ray said; she'd do fine if he baited her hook and took her fish off for her.

A picture of Ray's fishing expedition formed in Sherri's head as an illustration from a children's book, the half-rotten skin of the boat wobbling like Jell-O under a little girl wearing a bright yellow slicker and a perplexed expression. A child who knew better, but didn't know how to say so. Like Jell-O, she thought, forgetting that once Ray's immunity to all things ridiculous had been a reason she loved him. In another picture, she saw the child in the swamped and sinking boat reaching out of the page, crying out. That child was Bonnie. "Why don't you take Ted too?" she told him.

"Okay," he said. And she saw herself trapped by her own contrary impulse. Isn't that the way it always is? A fairy queen left waiting for all the ugly consequences she brought on herself?

So she stayed back in the bedroom, fretting and listening to Ray in the kitchen pouring Bonnie her Coco Puffs, feeding Ted his cream of wheat, crooning, "Would you like to swing on a star? Carry moonbeams home in a jar?" in that bouncy Ray voice designed both to put them at ease and excite them.

"It's raining, Daddy," Bonnie told him.

"That's all right. That's good. Fish like it when it rains; they don't mind getting caught so much."

"Oh," she said. Sherri could hear the doubt seeping out of her daughter's voice. And why not? Ray had been doing the same thing to her for years. With Ray, there was always a hitch, always something more than he let on. Just like that conniving Cat in the Hat, he came around talking about fun, but only made trouble.

He hadn't mentioned Crazy Dave. He hadn't mentioned that all four of them would ride in the cab, where there were only two retrofitted seat belts and a piece of nylon rope strung between to hold down the baby seat, or that Dave would smoke his Marlboros all the way up the mountain.

Sherri watched out the window as Ray got the kids and his gear loaded. Maybe he would take a step back and look at the truck and the boat and the weather, take a look at himself and what he was getting into, and just give it up, quit. But Ray had never done that; what made her think he'd do it now?

She made herself a pot of tea and put it in a quilted cozy shaped like a laying hen. Ray was right; this was what she always said she wanted to do. She went into the living room and looked at her little shelf of books. They didn't keep many books that weren't shop manuals. Why keep books when you work in a library full of them? was what Ray told her.

She took down *Wuthering Heights*, the kind of book she thought she ought to read on a dreary day, wrapped up with a quilt and a cup of tea. But did she really want Heathcliff coming into her house, in his muddy boots, dripping with rain and smelling of sex? She walked around all the rooms and looked out the windows, hoping to be surprised by a different view. Then she put on her raincoat and got in her station wagon; maybe she would go shopping or just go for a drive.

There were parts of Charlottesville Ray didn't know about.

Crazy Dave lived in one, toward downtown and off to the east, in a little house needing paint set down in a cinder yard. Ray saw it was the kind of neighborhood where folks pooled up who worked at all-night gas stations and convenience stores when they had jobs at all. Folks who left school at sixteen, walked off jobs, walked out on marriages, and nobody—teachers or kids, bosses or spouses—was sorry to see them go.

Dave sat on the fender of his car, picking the sleep out of the corners of his eyes. He had no fishing gear, only himself in a windbreaker advertising an out-of-business nightspot. It looked to Ray like he was shivering a little. When he made to climb in, Bonnie scooted forward to the edge of the seat. "This looks like a place where trolls live," she told him. Dave smiled a little smile. "The gal my roommate's dating, she looks kind of like a troll. Maybe it is."

"Then we better get out of here." Bonnie cut her eyes at Ray.

All the way out the valley and on up Afton's Mountain, Bonnie held herself balanced with one hand against the dashboard, not wanting to touch any part of Dave and risk catching his cooties. Sherri could be that way too, blaming Ray when there was nothing to be blamed for, blaming him for what anybody could see were facts of the human condition. Dave was another person, different, but worth some consideration and respect. He woke up and lit up a smoke. "Shitty weather," he said.

"You shouldn't say that, it's cussing," Bonnie told him.

"What'd I say? 'Shit'? Shit's not cussing. Cussing's taking the Lord's name in vain. Shit. Shit's something you do, something everybody does."

"It's not nice." She looked at Ray and said, "Is it, Daddy?"

"Nice? What's not nice?" Dave was looking at Ray too.

"In our family, we don't say nasty words or swear words, honey."

Dave rolled his eyes up to the roof of the truck and blew out a plume of smoke. Then he said in a tired voice, "I know about you, man. I know about your kind of people. Nice people. Jesus don't know from nice."

"Jesus was nice," Bonnie said.

"You don't know what you're talking about, kid." And Dave rolled into a Technicolor movie of a Jesus seven stories high, trampling out the grapes of wrath like Godzilla in a bathrobe. Tall buildings would topple over; cars scatter off the highways like dried-up leaves. Every corner of the ocean would be swept clean of ships; whole pieces of the planet—football stadiums, parking lots, missile silos—would just be vaporized and replaced by big trees and little bushes full of berries. All the earth put back the way it was. "I bet you never thought of that, huh," Dave said, still talking in his soft, weary voice. "Heaven on earth, sure, but where would all this crap go?" He punched his cigarette at the windshield, but meant the highway they rode on, four-lane from sea to shining sea.

"Daddy," Bonnie said, and Ray could hear a panicked urgency in her voice.

"What do you expect me to do about it?" he asked Dave.

"Do about it? Why, you can take your foot off that accelerator and pull over and get out beside this truck and pray. Pray to Jesus. Down on your knees. She's big enough," Dave said, flipping his cigarette at Bonnie, "she's big enough too."

"Daddy," Bonnie said again, but Ray didn't answer. Instead he announced into the cab as if he'd just discovered it himself, "We used to come up here when I was a kid."

"That's nice," Dave said and took a drag on his cigarette, looked out the window, and fidgeted. Everybody was red in the face, maybe from the overheated cab.

"Daddy," Bonnie said again.

Ray had to pull off on top of Afton's Mountain just as they turned south on the Parkway so Bonnie could be sick. "Sorry," Dave said. He leaned against the bed of the truck while Ray sat on the grassy roadside holding Bonnie crying on his lap. It wasn't raining much at all now, but the fog had rolled over the road. Ray always marveled at how easily a child threw up, the vomit just seemed to slide right out her mouth and onto the grass. All her breakfast, the brown wads of cereal, the tiny bites of toast, the juice, was right there. He offered to take her into the little nearby restaurant and buy her another, but she shook her head no.

Down below them, under the fog and clouds, on the slick and rainy streets of Charlottesville, Sherri drove herself in the approximate direction of Dr. Roger's house. The dark heavy sky brought up the color, the yellow in the traffic lights and fireplugs, the greens and blues in the college students' slickers. Flashing between the beating wipers, color threatened to overwhelm her. Did she let herself know where she was headed when she put the key in the ignition? Sherri felt the presence of another car looming up behind her, urging her into a slower lane. She held her ground. He was an awful, awful man, yet he could serve some purpose in her life. She felt she was in danger, and she decided she wanted to be.

Nobody prayed on the Parkway roadside. Instead they climbed back in the truck where Ted lay sleeping in his baby seat. Ray thought about turning around. If Sherri hadn't been so pissy when they left, maybe he could have. They drove on. Crazy Dave had his vent window pushed all the way open so Bonnie wouldn't get sick anymore, while Ray ran the heater full blast to try to clear the window glass. All he could do was run the truck along the white line marking the shoulder and look for the turn to his lake. Ted was waking up and starting to squirm around in his car seat. Pretty soon he'd start hollering.

"We should go home, Daddy," Bonnie said severely.

"In a little while," Ray told her.

When Ray caught a glimpse from the road above, he wasn't sure it was a lake or a gouge in the green mountainside, a deep dark hole seen through the fog. "That's it." He could have heard it in his own voice; he didn't really want to go down there.

Ray's boat, which had looked sturdy and competent in his garage, was a puny thing threatened by every sharp stick and rough-edged rock down on the windy lakeshore. The hull wobbled with the small waves running under it. Maybe it would be more stable with four people, the cooler of sandwiches and pop, the rods and the can of worms holding it down. Dave said, "Hey, man, maybe I could take one of those rods and try fishing off the bank."

Standing on the side of this small lake, Bonnie was thinking even if her daddy was a smart man, he couldn't know everything. What did her daddy think a little boat could do? She was afraid for him; she saw him as somebody who needed taking care of. What could a princess do with a daddy like that? Bonnie started to cry.

"Okay," Ray told her, "you can stay and fish with Dave or you can come in the boat with Ted and me." She looked over at Dave, who shrugged and smiled, then climbed into the boat. Ted hollered and flailed his arms around. "Look at that, Ted's ready to fish."

"Oh Daddy," Bonnie said.

Ray pulled the oars, and the boat moved out into the lake. Really, he thought, it rowed much better than you would think. The wind began to fall off, and as it did, the fog settled down on them. While Ray rowed, Crazy Dave, the pickup, the shoreline, and the mountain behind it all disappeared. All around them was whiteness and the sound of lapping water. Ted heard it and was soothed; he left off crying. Bonnie heard it and thought maybe this time her daddy would be all right. His funny boat would take them wherever he wanted to go.

And so Ray took up one of the old casting rods with a push-button reel and broke a fat worm in half and put it on the hook, cast it out for Bonnie and told her to watch her bobber. He did the same for himself. They sat in the foggy lake and waited.

No fish came for their worms.

Ray thought, how about it, fish? How about it, world? But the world had balled him into a big wad of cotton and gone off and left him. Where were his friends? Now was when he needed them, not to give him off-the-meter legal tips, or to put him onto some hot new bands. He needed them to sit in his boat with him in the fog and not get any bites either, to stick around until it was nearing nightfall, when they could all go home, take a hot shower, and eat dinner. Where were they now?

He looked at Ted and saw how his eyes took in the foggy color of the sky and returned it. "Having fun, buddy?" he asked him, but Ted didn't say anything. What if he never said anything? What if he turned out to be one of those big old guys you saw going around the shopping malls with a broom and a dustpan? A shaggy forty-year-old man trained up to the level of a good bird dog? Roll the window down and let him stick his head out on the way home and that would make him happy.

Fish had yet to come for their worms.

How long had it been? With his paint-speckled watch hanging on the gearshift in his truck, Ray had no choice but to sit in his boat in the fog, his boy asleep in his baby seat, his daughter gazing out at her bobber. Nothing but his bobber off to his left and Bonnie's off to his right, both of them still. Ray waited. He listened, and every now and then he thought he heard a plunk that could have been Dave casting from the bank. Ray wanted to call out, but he didn't.

Ray had been claustrophobic as a kid. Once his brothers and sisters had locked him in the coat closet under the stairs, and after a short while the pressing smells of mothballs and wool, the wooden limits he felt in all directions, caused him to holler out and go at the door so he had kicked out the bottom panel by the time his mother got there to let him out. There he had stood in the middle of the living room, his eyes still getting used to the light, still feeling the presence of a nearby power.

Now it was different. There weren't any walls holding him in, only fog. But the fog seemed like it might go on forever, the lake below them might be the kind he heard stories about when he was a kid, the kind where divers went down and down until they ran out of their air supply and came up without ever finding the bottom. How could he row his boat when one direction seemed as good as another?

Ray got scared. He got scared of everything. It wasn't just the things he wanted to happen, the things he always thought he could make happen, but everything that might and could happen whether he wished for it or not. It was as if the shores of this small lake were getting farther and farther away from him. Once again, he wanted to call out, but didn't. There was no point.

Then, as it often does in the mountains, the wind came up lightly and started rolling the fog away up the mountain. If Ray could have seen it from up above, it would have looked like a kid tearing the paper away from a present. Across the lake, the head of an old man in a roll-top hat popped out of the fog, then the rest of his body appeared in a cloudy mist shot through with golden sunlight. It looked as if he rode on a throne on top of the water. He turned his head toward Ray and his children and hollered out, "Howdy there. I thought I had this place all to myself."

When Ray and Bonnie hailed him back, he heard in their voices the forlorn cries of sailors set adrift. "What's the matter, not catching anything?" And he rowed toward them, working his oars one after the other like a bicyclist. He lifted out his stringer and showed them many shining fish, crappie, ring perch. "You got to fish down deep to get these," he told them as he took Ray's stringer and gave them half his catch.

"We were scared," Bonnie told him, "we were lonely."

"I expect so," the old man said. "Hardly a fit day. Now, you all go home and eat those fish." And he brought his boat about and rowed off into the lake.

Crazy Dave lay curled up asleep on the seat of the pickup, his rod thrown in the bed. When Ray opened the door, Bonnie said, "What's that funny smell?"

"Nothing to worry about," Ray told her. As they climbed in the truck, the mountain came out into the sunlight and stood there as it always had, stoop-shouldered and worn.

What, exactly, had happened after Sherri pulled into Dr. Roger's arcing driveway hidden by hedges? When Dr. Roger met her at the door, he had tried to act surprised. But beyond the marvels of cannonballs and tarnished swords, what else could such a guy have for Sherri? She wondered this herself, sitting alone with a drink in a grimy bar for college students. Her clothes, made foul and unfamiliar, did not seem to fit her right. She needed a bath, but that would mean going home and she wasn't ready for that. She wanted to give the rescue squad a chance to find the bodies, the police a chance to come to the house, for them to find nobody home so the guilt would fall fully on her shoulders.

When she was good and drunk, when the bar was full of college boys who grinned at her like they knew all about it, she made her way back to her car through the fresh, damp evening air. She drove home without seeing a sign of a policeman, and found her house pouring light from every window onto the rich green lawn.

Clean and bathed, Ted sat in his high chair, Bonnie at the table in her PJs. Ray was flipping a fish over in the skillet. Her family beamed at her. She saw Ted, she saw Bonnie. She saw that Ray remained the very Ray who had pulled out of the driveway that morning, and she thought she loved him still. And yet she felt the events of her own day hovering between them. Like a ghostly presence, what happened between her and Dr. Roger would hang around in the air of the house until she had the nerve to tell Ray what had happened. She wondered if she ever would.

"Somebody else caught those fish, Mom," Bonnie told her.

But Sherri already knew that, didn't she?

Some Other Animal

MELINDA MOUSTAKIS

From *Bear Down, Bear North* (2011)

Ruby opens the pen and Sitka stands up on his hind legs, puts his paws on her shoulders as if to say listen, listen closely and she, not expecting this greeting, falls on her back. He hovers over her, licking her face, the warmth of his breathing a comfort, but anyone watching from a distance would think she was being mauled. She doesn't fight or flinch or shield herself with her gloved hands—she doesn't move. Sitka nudges her with his nose. Ruby stays still, the snow sinking beneath her. He growls and tugs on her blue scarf with his teeth until she chokes and hears the yarn tearing and she sits up. Then he releases her.

Mrs. Stern had stopped by to check on Ruby and said, "I got a job for you and you can't say no." For the next two weeks, Ruby would learn how to properly care for the dogs.

"I'll be right there," Mrs. Stern said, on the first day, when she answered Ruby's knock. "Let me get my boots." Ruby's mother, Kitty, had met Mrs. Stern at a poker game, a new night out after Ruby left for school. She said Mrs. Stern could drink all of them under the table, schnapps and more schnapps. "I liked her immediately," said Kitty. "She didn't act like a goddamn bridge player."

Mrs. Stern walked down the steps in a black down-filled coat that went to her knees. Her hair, curly and brown with streaks of silver, frizzed underneath a wool hat with earflaps.

"I know," she said. "I look like a bag lady."

"Mrs. Stern," said Ruby. "Thank you for—"

"For the garage," said Mrs. Stern. She handed Ruby a key.

"Thanks," said Ruby.

"Please, call me Marsha," she said. "And thank *you*—we get to leave all this for a month." She waved her hand at the firs burdened by snow, the flakes falling to the ground. She jiggled the door to the garage. "Damn thing," she said. "Sometimes I give it a little kick."

Mrs. Stern headed toward the bags and cans of dog food, but Ruby was distracted. There were shelves and stacks everywhere—boxes of rice, macaroni, cereal, cookies; cans of peaches, corn, fruit cocktail, olives, soup; jars of pickles, mayonnaise; one tier dedicated to peanut butter. Four refrigerators hummed along one wall next to a free-standing freezer the size of a couch.

"I don't notice," said Mrs. Stern. "I forget. Ira. I call it his bunker. Something with the war. 'What?' I used to ask him. 'Where is this army we have to feed?' But I gave up. There are worse things he could do."

The malamutes eat twice a day, at ten in the morning, when the sun rises, and again at five in the evening—the sky settled in darkness. Ruby measures out the dog food in the garage. She's down to three cans of tomato soup, crackers, and a can of kidney beans at home, and she used the first check from Mrs. Stern to pay her utilities. She won't be paid again until the Sterns come back from their trip. The Sterns' garage is warmer than her mother's house—she has the thermostat set at fifty to save money. And her peanut butter has run out. She's eaten a spoonful at a time and she eyes Mr. Stern's jars. She could take one home, rearrange the rows, but she knows he'd notice. Every box and package and can is in meticulous order, rows and columns uniform, at attention.

Kitty died in June, right before solstice, during the night that wasn't night, the sun never going down. "I'm living two days for every one," she said. Kitty used the extra light as an excuse to tie more flies and paint beads, keep her focus from being sick. When she couldn't tie them herself, she gave Ruby instructions from her bed. Chuck, Ruby's father, had started the business under his last name, Silashouse. What the fishermen didn't know was that Kitty made half of them, and when Chuck left, she made all of them. Silashouse flesh flies were known for hooking rainbows in the murkiest rivers, the zonkers were known to get bites when most fishermen were skunked, and the beads—coral and swirled with glimmering ivory paint—were said to look exactly like salmon eggs. The Silashouse specialties, though, were voles and mice. Fashioned from deer hair and wire, their beady eyes glinted with startling conviction, and Kitty heard from Mr. Forne, the storeowner, that many were staged in pranks and practical jokes.

Kitty had made enough to live on, to be buried, and to let Ruby pay the bills for the past six months. Last week Mr. Forne called Ruby, said he'd sold everything and had one last check. "Why don't you take over Silashouse?" he said. "I'd help you." But she couldn't. All the supplies were shut away in Kitty's room.

Ruby framed her life: Twenty-two years old. Dead mother. No money. No other family in Anchorage—they all live in the lower forty-eight in places like Nashville and Omaha and she doesn't know them. And by the sound of those places, she doesn't want to know them. Nashville—gnashing of teeth. Omaha—oh my god. And she's in Anchorage—an old boat surrounded by ice.

———

Ruby braces for Sitka's weight, one hundred and fifty pounds of exuberant dog, and wraps her arms around him as much as she can. They sway for a few steps and when Ruby feels she might fall, she says, "Sitka. Down." She imagines him, in another life, as a music-footed dancer in a tuxedo.

Ruby has a routine: water, feed, sled, shovel, lock the gate. Some of the malamutes are show dogs, others were weight-pulling sled champions. They have sly, grinning expressions and plumed tails and thick, padded coats—white with charcoal coloring on their hoods and backs. Sitka, Mrs. Stern told her, turned out too large to be a show dog, but he is a natural at weight-pulling. She pointed at Orca, named for the black mask of fur on her face. "And this girl was too pretty to show. They can't have blue eyes. What a stupid rule."

"Mush," says Ruby. The four dogs—Sitka, Orca, Gersh, and Cosmo—lurch, and the sled moves forward. The Sterns have ten acres of woods and the dogs crisscross a path through them at the slow, steady pace of stocky wrestlers, thick-boned and muscular. After about a mile, Ruby yells "gee" to turn right and head back. But the sled halts. The malamutes stand still with their ears perked up in black-tipped triangles.

She hears a rustling and turns. The man is wearing snowshoes and aims, eye on the scope of a rifle. He lowers the gun and puts a finger to his lip. "Shhh," he gestures. A stranger in the woods with a gun, a broad brown jacket and a rabbit fur hat. The man takes a few more steps, passes in front of Ruby and the dogs and kneels. He takes a shot and Ruby follows his line of sight to a moose, and from the size she guesses it's a bull that has already shed his antlers. The dogs start howling in long-winded coyote calls, Sitka an octave above the others.

The bull strides a short distance through the trees and collapses on its front legs, buckles to the ground face first, snow flying around him. He raises his head, struggles for footing, and falls again. Ruby holds onto the sled, ready if the barking dogs lunge and try to go after the wounded animal. Confident in his one shot, the man stands up. He approaches the sled with the rifle pointed at the snow, pats Orca on the head. The dogs, all at once, stop howling.

"Hey there, girl," he says to Orca. He looks up at Ruby, crinkles his eyes. "Well, you're not Mrs. Stern," he says. "She's an old battle-ax. I'd say you're more of a pocketknife." He smiles at Ruby through his dark, reddish beard. She doesn't smile back. The bull, a dark form through the trees, struggles halfway up and groans.

"So, pocketknife, do you have a name?"

"Fred," says Ruby. She puts her hand inside her jacket where she keeps a pistol.

"I doubt that," he says. "But what do I know? What do you do, Fred, when you're not sledding with dogs?"

There's a succession of grunts and huffs from the bull and the smell, not of blood, but the threat of blood.

"Aren't you going to take another shot?" says Ruby.

The bull falls again—felled branches snap.

"Don't need to."

"It's not moose hunting season," she says. But she would take a shot and end the bull's struggle if she had a bigger gun.

His name is Josef, he's a taxidermist, and he lives on property west of the Sterns'. He made a deal with them: any moose he tracks and shoots on their land, he gives them a fourth for the winter. Ruby thinks of the big freezer in the Sterns' garage, how it must be filled with years and years of moose meat. He has to walk back and drive his snowmachine and haul the bull home, gut him.

"After that, I'll bring some over for you," he says over the moans of the bull's slow death. "Then you'll be less likely to report me as a poacher."

"No," says Ruby.

"Don't tell me you don't eat moose."

"I do," says Ruby. And she wishes she hadn't said so.

Josef pats the dogs goodbye. "Couple of days," he says. "I'll stop by."

On the trail back, Ruby follows the plot: Woman meets stranger in the woods. Stranger kills woman. Or woman kills stranger. Or start again: woman meets stranger in the woods. Stranger lures woman with moose meat. Woman becomes strange. It never ends well.

The cupboards and pantry and fridge at her mother's house are almost empty. Ruby finds a can of tuna and eats from the tin with a fork and stamps her feet to keep warm. She quit school in Eugene, Oregon, to come help her mother—she chose the school because Eugene sounded like the name of a man who listened to jazz, wore cabbie hats, and kept butterscotch in his pockets—the opposite of Chuck, who she knew in pieces, shards her mother told her and the postcard he sent once. Ruby was seven and her mother went out to check the mail and, after flipping through the stack, handed her a glossy square of blue water, Niagara Falls. He'd written, "Kitty and Ruby, I got married. I thought you should know."

Kitty went back to the vise where she was tying flies. "That's that." She wound the whipping finisher around the hook. And then she stopped for a second and looked at Ruby. "Don't ever fall for a man who eats steak for breakfast." She turned and let out a nervous laugh and then she said, "That's fucking ridiculous," and buried her face in her hands.

All the fly-tying supplies, the hooks and fur, are shut away in her mother's bedroom. They came and took her mother's body and Ruby closed the bedroom door and hasn't opened it since.

Ruby locks the gate to the kennel with the padlock. She should get in the truck, her mother's green '79 Ford, and head home, but she unlocks the gate, steps inside the fencing and walks to Sitka's pen. He cocks his head to the side, questioning.

Sitka has to lie down to fit in the cab of the truck. Outside, the snow falls in lazy swirls, powder blunting the edges of everything, smoothing over the points of trees. For so long, Ruby has waited for a sharp stick, a sudden jab that will make her stop wearing her mother's slippers, their tattered flaps like slack mouths, and sitting on the bathroom counter, her feet in the sink, staring and looking for a trace of her mother in the mirror's reflection. Kitty had olive skin, hazel eyes, a smile wide and thin, and freckles dotting her high cheekbones. And Ruby, fair and blank, had checked her toes, her back, her legs for one marking, one freckle, and found nothing.

Sitka fills up the house. His presence and size overwhelm the spaces and rooms that Ruby alone has been occupying. He takes up most of her bed, his brow to her back, as if praying. Ruby listens to his breathing, a habit, waits for his light snore and the airy rhythms of sleep and when she's sure there isn't a hitch between breaths, she uncurls her fists from the pillow's corner and closes her eyes.

In the morning, she stands in front of Kitty's bedroom door, her hand on the cold metal knob. Maybe, with Sitka there, she will open it. "On five," she says to him. But her hand trembles and she stops counting at four. If she could open the door, she would gather up her mother's fly-tying wire and thread and feathers of blue, yellow and red, and dyed rabbit fur, and elk hair and deer hair and all the beads and tinsel and hooks, and she'd weave a shawl, bright and fringed, and go to the cemetery and dig up the coffin, wrap her mother's body and carry her into the woods where she should have been buried.

Ruby steps on the brake and the dogs slow down. Tracks and then a wide depression in the snow. Dark spots where blood must have been. The bull was shot here. The bull died here and was dragged off, butchered. The doctor. The butcher.

"I'm glad they're getting chopped off," Kitty had said, holding open her shirt and looking down at her chest. "Cross-eyed pieces of shit. I mean, look at them, Ruby."

"That's not funny, Mom."

"It is."

"No," Ruby said.

"If I say it's funny, then it is. Goddamnit, if we can't laugh I might as well croak." Kitty took her shirt off, stood in the living room topless.

"Mom."

Kitty shimmied. "Tell me they don't look cross-eyed."

Ruby bit her lip. "You're having surgery—"

"Fuck you," Kitty said. She reached for her shirt.

"Fuck you," said Ruby—quiet.

Kitty stopped buttoning and looked up. "Say it again. Like you mean it."

Ruby said it.

"Thank god." Kitty said. "We've got a little bit of normal back."

Every night Ruby says it will be the last, but she brings Sitka home with her. She and Sitka sleep face to face. "If you were a man," she tells him, "you'd smoke a pipe. You'd have a voice like gravel and honey and I'd make you read to me." She cups his jaw. "And you'd never wear flannel." Sometimes she wakes up in the middle of the night, panicked, because she doesn't know where she is, the darkness in the room spinning into phantoms of other places, convincing her she's back in Oregon, or that she heard her mother calling. Once, she wakes and pats the bed and when she feels fur she screams and jumps up—she forgot she'd been sleeping next to a dog. Sitka jumps up too, stands on the bed, and from across the room, he is a monster, a wolf creature. She flicks on the light. "We're sleeping with this on tonight," she says. But Sitka fidgets and tosses his head from side to side until she turns the light off.

———————

Sitka stands in front of the open truck door, refusing to obey. "Come on, boy," she says. "Get in."

Sitka runs around the truck, and then bounds toward the kennel gate and stops in front of the lock. The other malamutes leap against the chain fence and yelp.

"Sitka, come here."

He ignores her and nuzzles the gate. Ruby walks toward him and he dodges and backs toward the woods.

"You're not funny," she says.

He pounces toward her and skids in the powder, and before she can reach, he leaps away.

She stands near the truck and points. "Let's go home."

He flings his head and throws off the wet snow and jaunts to the kennel gate.

Ruby drops to her knees. She pretends to stab herself in the chest. "Sitka, help, help. Oh my god, I'm dying." She falls as she had practiced for a theater class the last term at school before the phone call, her mother's voice unraveling, pleading.

Ruby waits and waits. He's testing her. She clenches her teeth against the cold and thinks of heavy things. A boulder. A mountain. A body filled with cement.

Sitka barks and the other malamutes join in, echoing his get-up, get-up yap. He runs at her and Ruby tenses as he jumps over her back, but she is stone.

He creeps up to investigate and sniffs her ear.

She snatches his collar. "Got you."

He's dragging her, snarling, and she's holding on and yelling, "Stop. Stop," and he does. A growl in his throat. Teeth bared.

"It's me," she says, not looking into his eyes. "Sitka, it's me."

His mouth softens.

Ruby takes Sitka to the house, and this night, shuts him out of her bedroom. He presses against the door and whimpers. She knows he won't sleep in the living room with the lamp turned on, but she won't sleep without the light cutting the darkness and slipping through the doorframe. And she knows she won't sleep with him so close. Fangs and teeth and wildness. His long-legged shadow stretches toward her, walks miles across her floor.

Orca and Sitka are pawing at the front of their pens so Ruby lets them out into the main run while she exercises the first sled. When she returns, the gate to the kennel is wide open—she forgot to lock it. Sitka and Orca are gone. "Whoa," says Ruby. The sled stops and she dismounts. Orca appears out of the trees and pads toward her, tail wagging.

"Sitka," she yells. "Sitka."

Ruby closes the gate and paces in front of the kennel. The snow is heavy, a blizzard is in the forecast that night and there are dog tracks all around from the sled. What she needs is a snow-machine and the Sterns don't have one. The nearest one would be at Josef's—hunter, poacher, neighbor. She unharnesses Candy-rock, then Iditarod, Mitzy, and Chance. She locks the gate, pulls on the lock to make sure, and then drives down the long, winding driveway. Most malamutes, Mrs. Stern had said, given a chance to escape, will run and keep going and never turn back. "They'd make it to the Arctic if a bear or some other animal didn't get them first." Ruby turns right, west, and stops at three mailboxes, jumping out of the truck and brushing off the snow to read the names. The third mailbox reads Josef Emmit and then she notices the sign—J. Taxidermy. There are two buildings when she comes to the clearing, a small pine cabin with a porch and then a shop, open for business. The lights are on and she stomps the snow off her boots before going in.

The door jingles as it closes behind her. There are raccoons and bear heads, king salmon on the wall, the living dead in every corner. One moose stands, peering out the window, his magnificent rack sprouting like open palms from his head.

"Fred," says Josef. Ruby turns to face him and his gap-toothed smile melds into concern. "Everything all right?"

Ruby rides with Josef, her arms around his waist, trying not to hold too tight or be so close, but the frozen air stings her eyes. "These are my babies," Mrs. Stern had said. She ruffled Mitzy's ears. "Ira said no children, not in this crazy world. So I have my pups."

The snow hails down in a fury and they ride up the ridge, make a wide circle from the edge of his property into the Sterns'. They don't have much time before the sun sets, before the blizzard arrives, full force, a white-out. Ruby searches through the binoculars for a clump of black, a dog of a spot.

After an hour, Josef slows the snowmachine and points back to the direction of his place. He shouts over the engine. "We won't find him today." He reaches into his coat pocket and holds out a silver flask. Ruby declines and Josef takes a swig. The snow is thickening in the air.

The Sterns will be back in ten days. Ruby sees Mrs. Stern's eyes widen, taking in the news—as if Ruby had aimed a gun and shot her in the gut.

Josef parks the snowmachine. "You want a hot cup of coffee?"

Ruby has to get home. Her feet are numb, her hands, her face.

"Wait here," he says. He returns and hands her four packages of moose steak wrapped in white butcher paper. She isn't hungry, doesn't think she'll ever eat again, but takes them.

"I'll do a run everyday," says Josef. "I'll tell the neighbors to keep an eye out."

Ruby puts the white packages of meat in the freezer at her mother's house. She opens up every cupboard and scans the empty shelves for a hidden can or package of noodles. Then she moves a chair in, stands on it for a closer look at the bareness, the stray macaroni, the cracker crumbs, the dust of flour and spices. She should have borrowed the peanut butter. She paces the four corners of the kitchen, trying to ignore the animal noises coming from her gut, worry wrestling with hunger. "Stop it," she says to her stomach.

She sits on the couch, in front of the television, flipping through channels, hitting commercial after commercial of hamburgers and pies and dancing french fries and food, food, food. "You," she says to the television, "are a torture device," and clicks the off button. "You," she says to herself, "need to stop talking to appliances." At least when she brought Sitka home with her, she thought he understood what she was saying, at least she was talking to something that was alive.

She goes to bed, but after two hours, is still too hungry to sleep. She faces the freezer, grasps the handle. Sitka hit by a truck. "Mrs. Stern, I'm so sorry. I thought I locked the gate." Ruby drinks a glass of water instead. The nurse who had come into her mother's hospital room after the doctor gave his dooming verdict, a year at the most, had said the same thing, "I'm so sorry," and touched her hand. But it wasn't the nurse's fault. That Ruby felt obligated to respond to her and didn't know what to say made the sentiment cruel. There was another nurse, one with a ponytail of brown hair, who sat down next to Ruby in the hallway, and said nothing, and held her hand, traced a circle on her back. She stayed with Ruby until someone called her away. This one, her mother and Ruby called Nurse Nurse because "She's got that knowing way," her mother had said. "She's magic."

When Ruby approaches the kennel, the malamutes push their eager noses through the wire mesh. They know Sitka has escaped. They all stand on three feet of snow from the blizzard. She opens Timber's pen after shoveling the main run, and he rushes out and leaps at the caged dogs who start barking and rattling the fencing. She releases and harnesses the dogs to the sled one by one, first Timber and Cosmo as pair leads, Cosmo as a substitute for Sitka. Then she harnesses Chance, who snarls at both of them.

"Hey," says Ruby, and she chokes up on his tug line. She switches Chance with Cosmo. Timber and Chance in the front. Orca and Cosmo are paired behind them. The four dogs charge the packed snow. Ruby scans the woods for movement, for tracks, for a sign. She leaves out three bowls of food along the sled route to entice Sitka back. She calls his name and her voice echoes, small and insignificant. At the top of a hill, the dogs start barking and running faster. Chance is leaning to the left to move closer to Timber. "Whoa," says Ruby. They don't listen. She hits the brake and the sled stops and she plants the snow hook. Timber springs onto his hind legs and Chance rises up to fight him. They twist their tug lines over the main line, which pulls at Cosmo and Orca, who start barking. "Stop it," says Ruby. She stands at Chance's back and reaches for his tug line to pull him away—she knows not to get between two fighting dogs. But then Chance falls backward and the force of one hundred and thirty pounds knocks her down and she lands on Cosmo. Cosmo, in self-defense, attacks and catches her arm, his sharp teeth ripping into her jacket. She tries to pull her arm away, but he clamps down. She buckles with the pain. She's shouting and flailing—she shields her face with her free hand and then he yelps and lets go. Orca has him by the back leg, and she's pulling him away from Ruby. He throws his head back, snapping the air in Orca's direction. Ruby scrambles to a safe distance. Four big, fighting, snarling, tangled dogs. Wolves in parkas, that's what they are. She checks her arm and there's a little bit of blood. The barking pitches into a frenzy. Ruby takes out the pistol and aims for the sky. She fires. The malamutes cower and look at her. Orca lets go of Cosmo's leg. Then Cosmo tenses up with a growl and Timber lunges in his harness toward Chance. Ruby shoots again. They settle, but now, in the distance, the dogs at the kennel are barking because of the gunshots.

A spot of Cosmo's fur on his hind leg is matted with blood. She approaches, kneeling. "There, boy," she says to Cosmo. "I'm just trying to help you." He's keeping his weight off his injured leg. She needs him to lie down in the basket in the front of the sled and have the other three dogs pull them back to the Sterns'.

Ruby sits near Cosmo and waits a moment. "I'm going to un-clip your harness," she tells him. She holds out both hands in front of his eyes. "Please don't bite me again." He bares his teeth. She pulls her hands in. Woman shoots self and four dogs in the woods. Stupid dogs. Stupid life. "Let's try this again," she says. She moves slowly, presents her hands to him, and inches closer. "We're all going to keep calm. Orca is calm. Timber is calm. There, Cosmo," she says. She pets his ear. Her other hand smoothes over his head and shoulder to the harness. "Almost there." She holds the har-ness lead and coaches him to the basket. He whimpers as he limps. "We'll call the vet and get you fixed up," she says. Her arm starts to pulse and ache.

She leaves Cosmo on the sled and the other dogs in their har-nesses and calls the vet. The assistant tells her to wash the bite on her arm with soap and hot water and bring the dog in. "No, you have to send someone here," Ruby says. She loses it on the phone, dissolves. "You don't understand," says Ruby. "I have no one." They make an exception.

The assistant, a short, thin woman named Sam, has known Mrs. Stern for ten years. Sam muzzles and then bandages Cosmo, says he won't need stitches. She inspects the punctures on Ruby's arm and then disinfects the bite and wraps it in gauze. "You're going to be fine," she says.

Ruby finds a crumpled box of saltines in the Sterns' garage and takes it home, her compromise for not stealing a jar of peanut butter, her consolation for being bitten by a dog. She devours one entire sleeve on the drive. In her mother's kitchen, she heats up water with a chicken bouillon cube found in a dark corner of a cabinet, and then fills a bowl with the broth and more saltines, smashing them as they soak. She takes a bite. "This is disgust-ing," she says, her upside-down reflection in the spoon mouthing the same words. She unwraps a package of moose steaks, runs water in the sink to defrost them apart, and cooks them on the stove. She sprinkles dried garlic and oregano. Sitka dead or cold or starving. "I know," she says. She takes a bite, burns her tongue. Sitka crumpled and broken, bleeding. "I know," she says again, chewing. The more she eats, the more she's crying. "What the hell is wrong with you?" her mother would say, is saying. And Ruby's mouth is hot, her throat, her hands. "Nothing's wrong with me," says Ruby. "What did you expect?"

"What did *you* expect," says the voice. And Ruby follows it to the door of her mother's bedroom.

"Tell me," says her mother.

Ruby throws opens the door and flicks the light. She attacks the table, empties a bin of elk hair and rabbit fur on the bed. Feathers and beads fly. She throws yarn and string and rips open pouches and unspools tinsel. She burrows in the nest she's made, covers her head with a pillow.

Her knee finds the first one. She didn't notice them before, but there are three small bumps underneath the sheet—two mice and a vole her mother made—she would have delighted at Ruby finally discovering them, her loud choke of a laugh shaking the mattress. Kitty gave a stash to Nurse Nurse who in the last months called with their adventures. "This one new hire was being a real bitch so I glued a mouse to a bedpan and you can guess what happened next. . . . I put one in the cotton ball canister and oh my Lord. . . ."

Ruby holds the vole in her hand and cries.

Ruby doesn't take out the sled for two days. She's allowing her arm to recover is what she tells herself. When she's not with the dogs, she drives around, searching for Sitka. She doesn't sleep— her thoughts telling hunters to stop shooting, wolves to leave him alone, the woods to point him back to the kennel. Then, for the first time, Ruby decides not to feed them—one day won't matter. But then she thinks of Mrs. Stern. Ruby puts on her coat and snow pants over her flannel pajamas and trudges out to the green '79 Ford.

There's another truck already parked in the Sterns' driveway and Josef is propped against the kennel gate.

Before Ruby asks, he says, "No sign of him."

She wishes she could harness all the malamutes to the sled and have them pull her and the house and the kennel off the edge of a snowy cliff.

"Thought I'd check on the rest of the dogs," says Josef. He realizes what he's said. "Not that I thought—"

"I know," says Ruby.

He points at Cosmo's bandaged leg. "What happened there?"

She tells him the story as she opens the pens and collects the empty food bowls. Josef helps her carry them into the garage. He marvels at Mr. Stern's collection, the bunker of food. And she's embarrassed, as if she's showing him a part of herself, the stored up things collecting dust and waiting to be opened, slashed, consumed.

"I wonder," he says. He moves toward one of the four refrigerators.

"Don't," says Ruby.

Josef opens the freezer door—a stock of ice cream. He chooses a carton, chocolate, lifts the lid. There isn't a spoon so he pats his pant leg and retrieves a pocketknife, scooping some into his mouth with the blade. Ruby leans her back against the counter, arms crossed, and he stands next to her, his shoulder almost touching hers. "You want some?" he asks. "It helps with dog bites."

"How about that flask?" says Ruby. He sticks the blade into the ice cream and hands her the whiskey. She takes a sip, concentrates on his face, the white scar that slashes his left eyebrow in half. "How old are you?"

"Old enough to be divorced and have a son." Because his voice cracks, because she's tired of winter and worrying and mala-mutes—she surprises herself and stretches up on her toes and kisses him. He backs away, startled. "Fred," he says. "You sure?"

She could say it was a mistake, she didn't know what she was thinking. Stranger gives woman moose meat. Woman kisses stranger. Or undresses him. "But not here," she says, as if the food-filled garage were a church, a sanctuary, hallowed ground. Woman and stranger naked in dog kennel. Dogs watch.

"Wait," he says. "You're just a kid." He sets down the carton and walks past her to the door. As he's closing it, he turns and says, "But you need anything—you let me know."

"Kid?" says Ruby to the jars and shelves around her. She carries the food bowls out to the kennel. The malamutes eat as if what is placed in front of them will be stolen, snatched away.

The next day, Ruby resumes the sledding schedule. She's lock-ing the kennel gate and pauses. A muffled bark. Sitka? There it is again. Ruby races into the garage for Mrs. Stern's snowshoes. She walks out and the dogs rail against their pens, the metal ringing shrill and constant. "Sitka," she yells. She follows a track she plowed earlier on a sled run. In the half light, the branches darken against the backdrop of powder white. Above the tree-tops, the stars appear—iced winks clustering over the ridgeline. Another bark. "Sitka," she yells again. The kennel answers with a chorus of barking. Sitka is out there, miles ahead of her. Maybe she could drive to Josef's for the snowmachine. But that might scare him away. Maybe she could reach him, call him home. But the glittering snow and her throbbing hands tell her the tem-perature is dropping. Woman freezes to death in the woods. Bears eat frozen woman. Or wolves. The malamutes are howl-ing now and she hears Sitka, his sharp cry rising above their long, lonesome bay, and she knows that this is as far as she can go—and she waits, before turning around, for all of them to stop wail-ing at the moon that isn't there.

A Good Investment

ROBERT ABEL

From *Ghost Traps* (1991)

"What is it, darling?" Victor spoke mildly, even though he had asked his wife not to disturb him when he was in his study, and had sometimes responded to her intrusions with impatience and sarcasm. But tonight he was not really working very hard. He closed the portfolio with an air of bored satisfaction.

Janice had an abstracted look on her face, as if she had just forgotten the reason for this violation of Victor's Law. She did not speak for so long that Victor felt it necessary to prod her along. "Is it something important?"

"I'm sorry," she said. "I thought it was. I suppose I'm being silly. I was sitting there, and I was suddenly afraid."

"Afraid?" Victor said, a little disapprovingly, for he detected a slight slur in her speech that suggested she had been drinking again. She was growing entirely too lazy and in consequence was losing both mental sharpness, which had always been consider-able—one of the reasons he married her—and her formerly fine figure. In her Victor thought he was seeing in the flesh an example of what was meant by "going soft," and he didn't like it at all.

"I thought I saw a face," Janice said, and then laughed un-pleasantly. "Outside, at the window."

Victor grew serious, capped his pen and stood up. "I'll have a look," he said.

"I'm not sure," Janice said, folding her hands on her stomach.

"Well, we'll make sure."

"What should I do?"

"Do?" Victor squeezed her shoulder as he passed by. "Stay by the telephone. If I shout, call the police."

He stopped at the hall closet, rummaged for a flashlight, and found the one he carried with him on the boat, one that would float if you dropped it overboard. He wished now he had one of those which were long and silver, for that kind could also be used in a pinch as a club. His son Robert was always hounding him to buy a pistol, but Victor had avoided doing that, he said, because he did not believe in guns and the country was too violent a place anyway. But the real reason was that he did not trust himself enough to own a gun, and there were plenty of people he had fantasied using one on, including his own wife. But as he went through the front door now, he thought, yes, a pistol would be a comfort.

He flicked on the light, looked quickly behind the shrubs along the front of the house, then moved to the left side, flashed along the walls and into the shrubbery, then doubled back across the front in case a prowler had been there and was trying to elude his search by circling the house. Victor didn't really want an encounter with any prowler, but could not stop himself from making this artful little move, for more than he feared running into a thug he feared being thought stupid by one. Most likely, though, the prowler was all in Janice's mind. She had been damned moody lately, scared silly of every little thing.

Victor moved quickly up the driveway past the garage and sprayed the light back and forth over the rear of the house and the back lawn. The swimming pool glimmered blue and green as he spanned it with the light. He checked the side door to the garage—it was locked—and flashed the light through the window. Nothing was awry, and in fact the interior of his car seemed inviting and peaceful, doubly insulated from the world. The night itself was calm, a bit humid, but very pleasant. Of course, that wouldn't matter to murderers. A nice night for a murder, that's all they would think, Victor surmised.

Light fanned across the lawn now as Janice opened the back door and peered into the darkness.

"Victor?"

"I'm right here."

"I called the police. They said others had complained, too. A car's been sent. Maybe you should come in."

"I didn't find anything . . ."

"Victor!" Janice shouted, pointing up, and Victor turned and aimed the light where she had indicated, absurdly high. The beam swept to the gable over the garage doors, over a pair of black shoes, then two bare, dangling legs, settled on a little, fat man, squinting, chewing, dressed only in cotton briefs. The man's flesh seemed too pale, garishly white in the flashlight beam. He chewed slowly, as if only mildly perturbed at being discovered, or like some animal just prodded from hibernation.

"Victor! Get in here!"

"Yeah, yeah," Victor said. "Call the police. Tell 'em what we've got." In Victor's eyes, the man had no intention of moving. In fact, he seemed in a little bit of a predicament, a cat up a tree, and in any case was too far away to be immediately dangerous. He clearly wasn't armed.

"*In* here!" Janice's voice cracked.

Victor backed to the rear stoop, keeping the man fixed in the beam of light. Janice snapped on the spotlights over the garage and the whole yard was illuminated, the flashlight superfluous. Victor kept the beam on the man's face, however, sure that it kept him disoriented and unable to see well. Victor had been on the other side of flashlights himself, blinded by that insistent, irritating brilliance. The house was only a few feet behind now and he felt safe enough, if just a little uneasy. He could hear Janice reporting to the police, and the words seemed almost comic: " . . . on the roof of our garage, and he's naked."

Victor snapped off the flashlight and the pale white figure dissolved suddenly into a dark, pathetic lump. Victor continued to observe the man, wondering how such a creature, so doughy and flaccid, could have grappled his way to such a height.

"Hey, fella," he called out. "What are you doing up there anyway?"

"Just leave him alone and get in here," Janice, behind him again, insisted. "*Please*, Victor."

"Hey, fella," Victor pressed on. "You want something? Water?"

"Don't you go near him!" Janice said.

Before she had even finished her plea, Victor was aware of the beginning of something, like the *meow* of a cat, a high-pitched, grating sound that, in the wake of Janice's voice, emerged suddenly and clearly as a wail of grief. The man on the roof was attempting a song of sorts, and he leaned back with his hands in his lap and raised his voice in a cry of such sirenlike sadness that Victor trembled, as if chilled.

"Oh!" Janice whispered. "Oh God, Victor."

"Are you hurt?" Victor called. "Do you need medicine or something like that?"

The man's only reply was to wail all the more loudly and more plaintively still.

Victor was about to call out another question when car lights splashed the front of the garage and a powerful beam fell on the man like a net, so that he seemed momentarily to leap out of the darkness, or to catch fire. He only turned his head away from the glare and continued his strange wail. Shadows of the policemen danced across the garage, growing smaller and sharper as the men came forward. When they passed the corner of the house, they seemed very small indeed.

"You folks all right?" The officer who spoke was shorter than his companion, and also black and extremely broad-shouldered. His holster rode so low on his hip that it seemed it could not possibly stay in place. The other officer was white, paunchy, with a deeply creased face. He looked very tired.

"We're fine," Victor said. "He hasn't done anything but sit up there."

"He looked in our windows first," Janice corrected him. She stepped out of the house now and took hold of Victor's arm.

"All right, Jackie," the black officer called. "We'll get you down from there and you can come with us."

"How'd you get up there?" the other officer asked. "Hey? You hear me?"

The man answered with a wail.

"I left some ladders around back of the garage," Victor said. "He might've used those."

The black officer looked Victor's way and said, "Oh, Jackie likes to climb all right. He doesn't often need a ladder."

"You know him well?" Victor asked.

"We know him well," the white cop said wearily. "He's off his turf tonight, though. New neighborhood."

"Jackie, you going to make us come up there or what?" The black cop adjusted his gear, then folded his arms across his chest.

"You come up. Sure." The clarity of the man's voice stunned Victor. He realized he had been thinking of him as an animal of some kind, an ape or a bull, or a big dog. He hadn't expected *speech*.

"We don't want to come up," the white cop growled. "It'd be better if you just came down."

"Not better," Jackie said.

"Aren't you getting cold?" the black cop asked. "We'll turn the heater on for you, in the car."

"Not better," Jackie said.

"Come on, Jackie," the white cop pled. "Don't make us come up there tonight. We'll get mad if we have to climb up there for you."

Out of the darkness the man's voice drifted down again. "Die," it commanded.

The cops looked at each other, and then the black one turned to Victor. "You mind if we use your ladders?"

"Of course not," Victor said. "Just don't sue me if you fall."

"I hate this," the white cop complained loudly. "I'd just as soon shoot the sonabitch. Or let the dogcatcher handle it. This is ridiculous!"

"Jackie?" the black cop said. "Roy's getting madder by the minute. Maybe you'd just better come down."

"You're damn right I'm mad!" Roy said. "I got to risk my neck for a stupid jerk like you? I'm tired of it."

"Okay, Roy, simmer down," the black cop said, loud enough for everyone to hear.

"The hell I will," Roy said. "Do I look like a babysitter? You think we don't have more important things to do? Who the hell does this guy think he is? Wastin' our time!"

"Roy's really mad now," the black cop called up to the man. "Maybe you'd better just come down right now. I can't calm him down. You want me to help you?"

"Yes," the man said. The lump on the garage roof seemed to shrivel, and then rolled over, away from the lights.

"You think he'll really come down now?" Roy asked his partner.

"You get on that side, I'll stay on this," the black cop said. "He might slide down, then run for it."

"I don't feel like climbin'," Roy said, "and I don't feel like runnin', either."

They fanned out, the black cop stopping directly between the garage wall and the swimming pool, the white cop squeezing between the other garage wall and thick row of forsythia Victor had planted years ago to blot out the sight of his neighbor's yard, in particular a bare patch in the lawn created by the ceaseless ranging of an ugly black mongrel chained to a doghouse there. The dog barked all day long, "at everything that moves," as Janice had phrased it, but was quiet now, with a lunatic in plain view.

The man lay down on the peak of the roof and began to feel his way clumsily backward. Then he sat up and began to inch his way down, toward the black policeman, who encouraged his descent with friendly patter.

"That's right, Jackie. This way Roy won't be so hard on you. That's good, you're doing fine. Just a few more feet now."

When the man reached the edge of the roof, he looked down cautiously and then with frightening nimbleness—Janice gasped and her fingers dug into Victor's arm—hurled himself off, spun around in the air and landed squarely on his feet. The black cop grabbed him at once.

"Good work, Jackie boy! Now let's go home. Roy!" he called. "It's okay now."

But the man shrugged off the black policeman's grasp and walked away. Roy emerged from beyond the garage now, and it seemed to Victor he was actually holstering his gun. The man suddenly changed direction and marched toward the house. Janice gave a little squeal and slammed inside, but Victor was stricken by curiosity, rooted to the spot. The two policemen grabbed the man about four feet from Victor, one on each arm. The man tilted his head to one side and looked at Victor with terrible interest for a moment, and then asked, "Water? Please?"

"We got plenty of water at the station," Roy said.

"I don't mind getting him a glass of water," Victor said.

"We'll take care of that as soon as we're squared away," the black officer said, steering the man toward the driveway again, as though herding a cow.

The man looked over his shoulder at Victor as the officers hustled him along, and then disappeared around the corner of the house. Victor walked to the end of the driveway and watched the policemen install him in the back seat and then drive off.

Inside, he found Janice at the breakfast bar in the kitchen, trembling, and holding an awfully large tumbler of Scotch. "Darling, it's all right now." He tried to comfort her with a hug, but she pulled away.

"I don't believe you," she said. "You would have let him in the house."

"He didn't seem so terrible," Victor said.

"I just don't believe you." Janice was so frightened her lips were blue and her hands were shaking. The ice cubes in her drink gently tintinnabulated. "Don't you know what's going on out there? Don't you read anything but the business pages?"

"He was just a sad, miserable lump of a thing."

"But possibly quite dangerous. Did you see how he jumped down from the roof?"

"I had no intention of letting him in the house," Victor said. "I would have put the water on the little table and let him come and get it."

"He's obviously a lot stronger than he looks," Janice said. "And possibly not so dumb, either. And you're treating him like an ordinary houseguest."

"He wasn't armed. He was far away." Victor spoke matter-of-factly.

"Did you hear the sound he made?"

"Of course," Victor said. "He seemed so sad."

"Sad!" Janice laughed. "He sounded sick, and very . . . disturbed. Yes, disturbed."

"He's gone now," Victor said. "You can relax now, darling."

"He'll be back," Janice said.

"Don't be childish."

"You heard what the police said. He's done this before."

"Yes, but he's clearly harmless. They didn't exactly manacle him like some psychotic now, did they?"

"It could happen." Janice drank deeply.

"You're just being hysterical," Victor said.

"Goddamn it, Victor! If there had been no one out there, I might agree with you. But my God, there he was!"

"Finish your drink and we'll go to bed," Victor said.

"Not me. I'm not sleeping tonight."

"You'll just make things worse for yourself, staying up late, drinking too much."

"I'm not sleeping," Janice insisted. "Not tonight, not ever."

"And I'm not going to play along," Victor said. "I've got to be in town tomorrow, and I've got meetings, and I'm going to be there fresh and rested."

Sometime later Victor woke with a start as Janice slipped into bed beside him. The smell of the drinks annoyed him profoundly, and he turned away, drifted back into his dreams.

It was not, strictly speaking, true that Victor had to work in the morning. He could just as easily have conducted his business over the telephone, but he enjoyed being downtown and checking in with his broker and getting out of the house, away from Janice. He knew all this was a bad sign, and he had tried to think what the matter was and what he should do about it, but had also convinced himself it was just a phase, that it would pass and Janice and their relationship would return to normal in a little while. Besides, it was good for a man to get out into the world and see people, get the feel of things, talk to people who knew about this and that. He was looking forward to lunch at the new Antoine's with some of the traders at Chafee and Marks, and what conceivable good would it do to loiter around the house while Janice nursed her hangover and repented and went through all that tiresome business?

Janice herself, Victor reasoned, she was the one who would have to turn things around, take charge of whatever was bedeviling her. And if things got worse before they got better, he guessed he had plenty of patience. More than that, he felt he really didn't need her much now, for anything. He was loyal, but he was not dependent. The question of love didn't seem very significant any more, and even if it took a lover to renew Janice, Victor wouldn't mind, really wouldn't, he decided, as long as it didn't extend to divorce and disturb his assets.

It was not—was it?—that he didn't care. He did, he told himself, he did want Janice to improve herself, and the last thing she needed was a shock like that of last night. Damn it! She had been growing paranoid anyway and having some nut peering in the windows and clambering over the garage was most untimely. It fed into Janice's fears. She'd be a while getting the incident into perspective, Victor supposed, and then his mind turned again to his money and he was much happier.

He was going to sell off his steel and get into solar chips, and maybe ethanol, depending on what was floating. He also wanted to see what he could find out about a couple of little ceramic companies that might be going public soon, too. Some Japanese investors had already been nosing around, he had heard, and he could not stand the idea that they might be getting into this field first. He had plenty to keep him busy downtown, and by the time he returned home Janice might even be more relaxed. She would have had plenty of time to pull herself together and they might even enjoy a reasonably nice dinner. Janice knew how to do things right when she had a mind for it. After that, he could go off to his study as usual, and she could do what she liked—rent a movie or something, drive out to the mall—anything at all.

Victor's broker, Oliver George, was pleased to see him and had plenty to report. Oliver squinted, scratched his close-cropped beard spangled with gray, adjusted his glasses constantly. He was of the opinion that it might not, after all, be a good idea to dump the steel. The way Oliver saw it, the market was in for a real beating, soon, and he thought Victor should think about "survivability." He liked the long-range prospects of ceramics and ethanol, yes, but he didn't believe the little companies were going to weather the storm ahead, and there was really no way to predict which little guys would swim and which ones drown. Oliver also wanted nothing whatsoever to do with investing in computers or software companies, which he saw as a "crapshoot."

"Let's look at Japan," Oliver said.

"No," Victor said, "let's not. I want my money to stay right here, in this country."

"Okay," Oliver said. "Let's not. Let's not look at China, either."

"Definitely not," Victor said.

"All I was thinking of," Oliver said, "was getting your assets out from the epicenter of what's coming."

"You're really that scared?" Victor asked.

"Don't put your house on the market," Oliver said. "I mean it. Don't build any condos. I predict real estate is going to get splattered, too. I don't see many safe havens out there, Victor. I think the choices are really quite limited now."

"That hasn't been my impression," Victor said, and he and Oliver launched into a debate, interrupted by several telephone calls, that was to last all morning. In the end, Victor had prevailed. He dumped the steel. He bought ethanol and ceramics and put some cash in the bank, intending soon to purchase a couple of CDs.

At Antoine's he met Gary "Tiger" Moran, who had earned his nickname from ferocious handball tactics, and Bill Donati, who had done very well for his clients in newsprint and wire. Moran was tall and blond with smoky gray eyes and a perpetual cynical smile. Donati seemed always to be brooding, but was really quite unpredictable and could be outrageously funny and gossip wickedly. He frequently delivered comic pronouncements from beneath his dark eyebrows, and Victor had always felt that here was a man who didn't understand his success and didn't think he deserved it. Moran, on the other hand, seemed to believe himself gifted, a cut above, and deserving of every lucky thing that came his way.

Victor liked these men and trusted them about as far as he could throw Trump Tower. They were great entertainment, but you had to be on your toes around them. They took very great satisfaction in seeing you swallow a lie. "They would put butter on it and feed it to you on a golden spoon" was how Oliver had described their tactics. "They'd just as soon be the last investors on earth." They also, occasionally, dropped very interesting little tidbits of market news.

Today, however, they had nothing particularly stunning to reveal. They said they did not agree with Oliver's downbeat assessment of the market's immediate future and went on to something that interested them more: who the biggest grossing athletes were and what they were doing with their incomes. As far as they were concerned, anybody with any smarts could stay ahead of the market readjustments that new technologies and world progress would require.

"It's bad habits that kill everybody," Donati said. "Not bad luck."

"Stay loose," Moran said. "That's the key."

"These profundities have just cost you the price of the lunch." Donati handed Victor the bill.

"Bullshit," Victor said nobly. He passed the bill to Moran.

"Even Steven," Moran said, after cursory study, "it's about twenty-three bucks apiece."

Victor was a little disappointed by the luncheon, but decided to have another drink at the bar after the traders left. He opened the polarized glass doors to the bar, wishing he had put a few thousand into this product, for he was seeing it now in all the new automobiles and in yacht cabins, and somebody was cleaning up on it. He actually hated its use in car windows because you could never tell if someone saw you approaching or not, but he was angry with himself that he hadn't seen its profit potential.

Inside, his attention was immediately galvanized by two striking women who, with long, slender fingers, were tapping ashes into the tray before them and laughing with splendid abandon. They were sharing a bottle of champagne and gave every appearance of celebrating some success. Victor chose a seat close enough to eavesdrop on them but without seeming to intrude. If Moran and Donati had been with him, they would certainly have found a way to insinuate themselves into the women's conversation and celebration, but Victor was too shy for that and he even found the beauty and the polish of the two women a little intimidating. They were both blond and wore dresses that hugged their figures and showed off their shapely legs. Their eyes glowed, their complexions gleamed, and their smiles flashed rows of perfect white teeth. They were buxom and sleek. They could have been models, and sisters, but in fact their conversation was quite a technical one about principles of physics that Victor was only able to follow in the most general sort of way. Apparently, he decided, they were engineers.

It took him the time of one drink to understand that the women were involved in selling weapons to the American military. They had just returned from a convention in Washington, D.C., where they had apparently made a terrific deal or two and survived some tremendous partying. They were gorgeous, Victor thought, and they were giddy with success. He wondered what it would be like to attend a party with a pair of gorgeous predators like these, women who could describe to you the action of a missile or the latest developments in automatic weapons, in engineering terms, and who would think nothing of opening, as the tallest of the two was doing now, another and then another button at the bustline of their dresses.

Victor had to look away. Things were going on in this world

which he would never know about. Surely someone climbed in bed with beauties like these. He thought of Janice now, getting soft, deteriorating into some kind of awful, inhibiting fear that had begun to shut down both their lives, and he felt frightened himself now. Something about these women frightened him more, far more than even the lunatic he had encountered the night before.

The shorter of the two women spoke to Victor, with a little laugh. "Hey, guy." She held up a glass and her green eyes glittered merrily. "A little champagne?"

Victor bolted from the bar, followed by a squeal of dismay and outraged female laughter. The damned polarized glass doors were heavy and slow to let him through, and he resented them, the slight resistance they offered to his will to be gone from the presence of those sirens. Jesus, he thought, the cynicism of it, using tits and ass to get the attention of the generals. But then he mocked himself for his Puritanism, which he knew was insincere. He wasn't stupid. He knew what competition was; and he knew that in ten years the women celebrating in the bar would probably not have been kicked upstairs but would be doing something else, selling something else, or going soft, too. He didn't really begrudge them their champagne, begrudge them anything, and he knew it wasn't scruples propelling him back onto the street. He could rub shoulders with arms merchants. If his ethanol and ceramics companies landed military contracts, he would break out the champagne, too. He hadn't made the world and he wasn't responsible for its savagery.

But God they had frightened him!

Driving the freeway home, Victor could not understand himself and his own behavior. He was deeply irritated with himself, on the one hand, for passing up a chance to meet those women. On the other, he supposed—and the supposition itself was dispiriting—that he would only have been teased and dropped the minute someone younger, quicker of wit, handsomer, who knew the rules of the games, came along. Beauties like that would take scant interest in him. By escaping so quickly he was just being realistic. Why torture himself for nothing?

And yet: what was he going home to? He might at least have enjoyed the repartee in the bar and had those beautiful smiles and open buttons to think about as he fell asleep that night. Instead there was just the usual, and a bored, obviously unhappy and too often frightened wife awaiting him. And, of course, his portfolio which he now would have to update: new entries, new hopes there.

He pulled into the garage and hit the switch on the dashboard which lowered the doors automatically, slowly behind him. He remembered the fleeting impression of last night, how the interior of the car had seemed so peaceful inside the garage, and he lingered a moment to savor it now. He could see why people might choose such a spot to end it, the car engine murmuring them along to a dozing death. A last peaceful moment. Terrible idea, Victor shuddered, and then the wail of that lunatic filled his mind: nothing peaceful about that, was there?

Victor gathered his newspapers and briefcase and made sure the garage door was locked as he stepped outside. He glanced up at the garage peak, which normally would never have even entered his consciousness, and remembered the black policeman saying, *Oh, Jackie likes to climb.* What in God's name was that all about? Talk about things in this world you could never understand!

Or could you? Victor moved an empty glass on the table beside the pool to make room for his paraphernalia and walked to the rear of the garage. His painting ladders were there, rungs stained with the buckskin and redwood brown he had used to touch up some of the trim a while ago. The lunatic had leaned the lightest of these against the back wall of the garage and somehow mounted the gable from there. Victor thought it must have taken considerable strength, and some balance, to haul himself onto the roof from that angle.

He made sure the ladder was firmly planted, then climbed several steps, and then several steps more. He found that he could balance against the back wall, his feet on the penultimate rung, and actually see over the edge of the roof. The dark blue shingles rippled away like water. He cupped his hands over the gable and began to haul himself up, until his feet came free of the ladder and he had no choice now but to plunge forward and kick and haul himself, haul his own suddenly awful weight onto the rough, biting surface. He lay on his belly like a snake with his feet dangling over the edge, panted as the man must have done, but actually on the roof. The neighbor's dog heralded the feat with a paroxysm of snarls and yelps. The shingles were rough on Victor's cheek, but quite warm, and he actually enjoyed lying there. From his vantage now, the pool seemed to come right in under the eaves, into the garage itself.

He drew his legs up and steadied himself, and edged forward with the gable between his feet. The man might have rolled his way along, Victor thought. He seemed to like rolling. Victor tried a roll or two and the sky and then the shingles, sky and shingles, a cloud and shiny blue flakes crossed his consciousness. When he came to the spot where the man had sat and dangled his feet, he sat, too, and dangled his legs over the peak.

The view was really quite pleasant. He could see into the second story and attic windows of his own house, and although he was not so distant from the ground after all, the little odds and ends around his house seemed small, and to have been disarranged almost artfully. The neighbor's dog seemed small and huffy, and the neighborhood itself lay before him like a convoy of ships moving slowly across an almost placid sea. Victor felt released from any identity with all this, like an alien come down to attempt a closer understanding of all those points of light in the darkness of the earth, or the squares and triangles and the curving lines between light and light, circle and square. They were certainly a busy species, whoever they were out there, Victor imagined.

One difference between the lunatic and himself, however, was that the man had been naked, or nearly so. Absently, Victor unstrung his tie and peeled off his jacket and dropped them separately to the ground below. The jacket fell on the tie like a hawk on a snake, but did not fly off with its kill. Victor had started on the buttons of his shirt when Janice, holding a drink, stumbled through the back door. She shielded her eyes with her free hand, winced up at Victor a moment, and then cried out:

"What in God's name are you doing up there? Victor! Why are you doing this to me?"

"Oh, be quiet!" Victor said, coming slowly to his senses, but regretting also the dissipation of the mood, the seeming rectitude of the mood he had just experienced. "Can't you see I'm trying to fix something up here? What else could I possibly be up here for, but to make repairs?"

The Necessary Grace to Fall

GINA OCHSNER

From *The Necessary Grace to Fall* (2002)

All summer had been a medley of jumpers and fallers. The previous spring, simple dismemberment, and the winter before that, freakish hurricane-related deaths and injuries—deaths by debris, Leonard, Howard's immediate supervisor and cubicle-mate, called them.

"You're lucky. All I ever seem to get are the old folks," Leonard said, when Howard pointed out that his claims had been following these discrete and eerie patterns. "All natural. Nothing fishy—except that one old gal. One hundred and two years old, survived a fire in the nursing home only to die from a penicillin reaction in the hospital."

"What a shame," Howard said.

"Still. One hundred and two. That's beyond ripe. I'll bet she drank Boost or something."

Howard pushed his glasses up onto a tiny groove on the bridge of his nose. With all the power bars, energy drinks, and vitamins Leonard consumed, Howard was sure he would push a hundred at least. Before he started at Hope and Life Insurance, Howard had never met anyone as fanatical as Leonard about the maintenance of his own body, not even the gung-ho insurance sales staff on the second and third floors who formed weekend running clubs and circulated back issues of *Runner's World* on the break tables.

Despite his discovery that death was not as random as most people thought, a notion that for some reason gladdened Howard, he still found his job disappointing. When he'd transferred from medical data coding to investigations, Howard had entertained visions of dusting for fingerprints at crime scenes, determining whether or not his deceased policyholder was the victim of a poisoner or a strangler based on the friction patterns, those delicate whorls and swirls a simple piece of adhesive tape could pick up from doorknobs and medicine bottles. He thought at the very least he'd get to look at police reports, maybe even interview the bereaved. He had thought somehow he would be more necessary, able to see things others couldn't, for most problems came from being unable to see, not from not knowing or feeling. And so for these last nine months Howard had been processing claims, waiting for something to catch his eye: a murder disguised as suicide or a manslaughter passed off as a careless accident, large term policies taken out on people whose net worth didn't warrant insuring.

"You're an investigative *assistant*. So, it's not brain surgery. It's not like you have to do any real investigating," Leonard informed him on his first day. "It's pretty ordinary stuff really. Suicides—always the pink forms. We don't pay out unless the policy is at least two years old. We usually get a police report confirming it's a suicide and not, say, a homicide made to look like an accident. If it's one of those . . ." Leonard tapped his pen against a mini-file cabinet nearly hidden under his desk. "We wait for the coroner's report and for the police to clear any kin expected to inherit. Natural and accidental deaths—goldenrod—we pay out. Still, all you got to do is wait for the appropriate reports and file them with the policy. No big deal."

Howard's shoulders slumped and he could feel a space widening inside his rib cage. He had hoped for something more exciting. A little more murder. He wanted to study with practiced suspicion the beneficiaries. He wanted to know if they would glide, vapor-like, walking around as if undressed. He wanted to know how tragedy hung on the face and what he would say when he saw it.

The only excitement he'd found on the job was working with Ritteaur, the coroner's assistant. Occasionally, Howard couldn't read his handwriting and would have to call for clarification. Though he knew it was morbid, he couldn't help being curious about everything that went on in the lab and would pump Ritteaur for all the grisly details of the cases that came across Howard's desk. Sometimes when he was bored or, like today, wanted to dodge Carla, his wife, and her noontime phone calls, he phoned Ritteaur even when he could read his handwriting just fine.

"Ritteaur, it's Howard. I got a question on an older file, Pietrzak."

"Oh, yeah. I remember him. This one you would've *loved.*"

"So was he dismembered before or after death?"

"Both. But mostly after."

"Was the 'before' dismemberment accidental?"

"Sort of. It started out that way. Then the wife got ideas, seized an opportunity, if you know what I mean, and finished him off."

Howard felt his stomach tightening.

"They found most of his body cut into tiny pieces and stuck in a sump. The wife tried to flush him down the toilet, one flush at a time. There's a joke in there somewhere, but I can't find it just yet. Ka-toosh!" Ritteaur laughed, making a flushing noise. "You tell me the human creature isn't one sick animal," Ritteaur continued.

"Yeah. Pretty sick." Howard nodded his head in a mixture of disbelief and horror. He hung up the phone and studied the Pietrzak file. It never failed to amaze him how many husbands and wives, ordinary and sane people who'd sworn to love one another, killed each other. Before he started at the company, Howard had been optimistic about both hope and life, sure that life was good and so were most of the people in it. It never occurred to him that he might have to fear Carla, or she him, someday. And this made him sad, knowing that there were mysteries, little pockets of darkness people kept from each other. He wondered what it was that had set that woman off if it wasn't something small, very very small—that had bugged her for years.

At 12:05, Howard's phone rang and the white button indicating an in-house call began to blink.

"Lunch?" Carla also worked at Hope and Life, fourth floor, in the medical coding department. When they had first married, they always ate their lunches together in the break room. Now Howard made a point of being on the phone or out of the office during the lunch hour. Not out of malice. In fact, there was no particular reason why he wanted to avoid his wife. He just got tired of their regular lunches that over time began to feel forced, wearing on him like a habit that needed breaking. People need space, he reminded himself, though he knew she'd never let him get away with such a flimsy reasoning.

"Not today. I just got back from the coroner's lab and I haven't got much of an appetite left," Howard lied. "You know, all those smells."

"Right," Carla said, drawing out the word the way she did when she wasn't sure whether or not to believe him.

"Another bridge-jumper," Howard said, leaning forward to read the file label on the blue folder Leonard had deposited on his desk that morning. "Johnson, Svea." Howard tapped the edge of the unopened file with his ballpoint pen.

"She's dead, right?"

"Very."

"Good. Because if I thought, even for a minute, that you were screwing around, your stuff would be out on the lawn, Howard. You know that. Right?"

"Right," Howard said, wondering if Carla had really wanted to eat lunch with him at all.

Howard believed in human kindness, felt it was up to him to perform small acts of it whenever he could. But he wasn't kidding himself. He desperately hoped his good intentions would bring back to him some small act of kindness in return, he didn't care how small. Besides, life was too short not to try, he reminded himself. That's why before he was hired at Hope and Life, Howard had volunteered at a suicide hotline where he tried to talk people out of taking those fatal doses, out of pulling the trigger. *I know how you feel*, he had wanted to say. *I'm just like you.*

After a few weeks of doling out modulated and appropriate responses, Howard improvised, telling his callers about his grim high school summers spent chicken picking, about how he had worked at twilight, in that blue light of his grandparents' broken-slatted barn, picking the unsuspecting birds up by the feet where they sat in their own dung and dust. Sometimes, in the kicked-up dust, he thought he could smell their fear as he loaded them in cages on the back of the flatbed truck. That's when he'd hear them start talking, begging for mercy. "*Help*," they'd squawk, "*Please*," or worse, "*We'll come baaaaack*."

Though he hated that job, hated what he had to do, somehow sending those birds to their deaths validated his own life. This was hard to explain, even to himself. But he'd tell his callers anyway, desperate to make a connection. Smelling their fear, knowing their desire to live had worked for him, he'd tell them. Hearing a smaller animal plead, beg for the grace of just one more day, and these insignificant birds with brains the size of a pea. If a chicken could cling to life, then why couldn't he? This was what got him through each shift in the barn, each miserable night spent lying on his bunk with dung-lung, his voice split and cracking, frayed to a hoarse whisper.

There must be something to get you through, he'd urge. *Maybe buy a pet, a goldfish*. Invariably the callers hung up then and Howard would get that feeling, always accompanied by the taste of acid in the back of his throat, that he'd failed again. He had this same feeling about that Svea Johnson woman, for a cursory glance at her stats revealed she was his age, had lived in the same neighborhood he had grown up in. No doubt they'd gone to high school together, and yet he could not remember her.

Howard drummed his fingers on top of the blue file. It unnerved him how the fact of time and location forced a commonality between him and this woman he should have known but didn't. He leaned back in his chair and wondered, had she known him? Had she been one of those dumpy girls hiding behind a stack of books in the library, one of those disappearing girls with a disappearing face so nondescript it blended with anything? Or had she been beautiful, so beautiful Howard had decided she was unattainable and had thus relegated her to the deep pocket of his forgetfulness, for he knew his memory was like that: he could forget anything if he decided there would be no occasion to know it later.

Leonard pushed back in his chair and cracked his knuckles. With his conical buzz-top haircut, even his head looked muscular. As Leonard leaned over his keyboard, Howard noted how minute activities like typing brought into sharp focus the muscles in his forearms. Leonard pushed back in his chair again, this time to rifle through the lower drawers of his desk where he kept a large stash of energy bars. Then he unpeeled the metallic wrapper off a Tiger bar and took a bite.

"Want some?" Leonard offered the rest of the bar to Howard.

Howard shook his head and pointed to the unfinished cinnamon roll gummed to the corner of his desk.

"Treat your body like a temple, and it'll take care of you," Leonard said, his mouth full of energy bar.

Howard blinked and pushed his glasses back onto the deep groove at the bridge of his nose. He didn't know what to say when people discussed their own bodies. A body was what it was. Then he thought of Svea Johnson's body, falling head over heels perhaps. Or floating for a brief second before plummeting. He wished he could remember her, had some shred of recollection, for it was hard to conjure a faceless body, hard to imagine telling her what he wished he could have said: how unforgiving water really was, that of all the ways to jump off a bridge, none of them were good, this much he'd learned from Ritteaur.

Howard's phone rang. The white button blinked and he sighed before he picked up the receiver.

"Don't be late for dinner tonight, Howard." It was Carla again. "I'm cooking a Martha Stewart recipe." Howard knew that meant she'd spent too much money on hard-to-find ingredients, and would spend too much time trying to make the dish look like it did in the *Martha Stewart Living* magazine. "Presentation is everything," Carla had explained when he asked what difference it made if a salad had radichio or endive in it or not.

"Okay," Howard said, sliding the phone into the cradle. He pressed on his sternum. Before working in the coroner's office, Ritteaur had interned for a mortician. Ritteaur had told Howard how corpses, once pumped full of embalming fluid, tended to bloat overnight and it was necessary to push on their torsos and vent the gases through a plastic plug inserted in their abdomens. Howard thumped on his chest with the heel of his palm and wondered if he might not benefit from just such a hatch incision to let bad air out.

Sometimes Howard imagined himself utterly split, a ghost Howard, his consciousness hovering next to the corporeal Howard sitting there now, his fingers gripping the ribbed steering wheel of his blue Skylark. For it seemed clear to him that in all things there were two Howards at work: the Howard who wanted to arrive home in time for dinner so as to please his wife and the Howard who knew even as he promised that he would, he wouldn't. The Howard who knew he shouldn't leave work early, would have no good excuse should Leonard notice his absence, and the Howard who secretly hoped he'd be missed, knew that questions would be asked. How else could he explain it? For here he was, four o'clock, his foot heavy on the gas pedal, driving toward the Laurelhurst neighborhood where both Howards knew he would troll the old streets, the one Howard not sure what it was he thought he'd find over there at 745 Madison—hoping, in fact, it was a vacant lot of thistle and beer bottles, the other Howard knowing it wasn't so, knowing too that neither Howard would rest until he saw the house Svea Johnson had once lived in.

As he drove, the hills in the distance turned smoky under the late afternoon August heat. Howard rubbed his forehead. He should be at work. He should be inputting data, he said aloud even as he turned onto Weidler. He told himself he had no idea why he was doing this, though the other Howard knew this drive had more to do with making reparations, with jostling a faulty memory to reveal something of Svea Johnson. For Howard had either never known her or had forgotten her, forgotten her completely, and it bothered him that this could happen, that the same thing could and would happen to him someday.

You could read a lot about people from the houses they lived in, he reminded himself as he drove past the Laurelhurst park, past the huge iron posts, the remnants of an ancient gate marking the Laurelhurst neighborhood from the Rose district. And then he wondered, could sorrow leave its mark on the brickwork? Would he read the traces of grief in the troubled surface of stucco, in the warped panes' suggestions that theirs had been a family full of secrets and hidden hurts?

Howard nosed the whistling Skylark onto Madison. He circled the block, even numbers on the left, odds on the right. In his squeaking car, idling at five miles per hour, he was as obvious as a headache and he didn't like the oily feel of what he was doing, felt he was trespassing, though in truth he was idling along the very same streets over which he'd once ridden his bicycle hundreds of times as he delivered newspapers in the inky darkness of night. Still, it didn't feel right and he drove away, willing himself not to read the house numbers. He looped past the park three times, drove by the house he had spent his boyhood in, past all the houses along his old paper route. Then, delinquent both in fact and intention, Howard turned toward home, toward Carla and her dinner.

When he pulled into the driveway, he turned off the engine. From his car he could see Carla's shadow at the kitchen window, her dark form moving behind the scrim of the lowered window shade. Howard thought of the Johnsons again, tried to imagine their shapes moving from room to room, and he felt acres and acres of empty space growing inside of him, pushing everything else out of the way. His heart, his lungs—none of it mattered— and he could swear he felt them shrinking to the point where he could see himself reflecting pure sky, the vastness of that inner space.

"Where've you been?" Carla met Howard at the door, a spatula in hand. "You missed my Capillini pasta with red caviar. Endive salad and marinated artichoke hearts."

"I got held up." Howard pulled the door closed, felt the bolt slide home under his hand. "I'm sorry," he said, his mouth tasting like he'd swallowed a fistful of change.

"I called at your desk and left a message with Leonard. He said you left early." Carla set the spatula down on the stove and followed Howard to the bathroom where he pulled down his pants. Carla crossed her arms over her chest. "If there's something you need to tell me, you can just tell me. You know that. Right?"

"I'm okay," Howard said, flushing the toilet. "I just feel a little different, that's all. Like there's an itch in my arteries."

Carla went back to the kitchen where Howard heard a whole battery of kitchen noises: savage rips on the roll of tinfoil, garbled choking from the garbage disposal, all the sounds women make in a kitchen when they're angry. After a while Carla came back to the bathroom. Howard hadn't moved except to pull the lid of the toilet down and sit on it. She wanted a scene, he could tell, and here he was, full of guilt and too many character faults to count. For starters, Howard did not have the energy to give his wife what she wanted and rightfully deserved: a real fight, something, anything to prove to themselves they still felt the way people should.

"An itch in your arteries?" Carla rocked back on her heels and studied him. Then she turned on the tap, pulled out her toothbrush, and began scrubbing her teeth so vigorously Howard knew she couldn't really hear him.

"Like how you feel when you hang your head out a car window, how all that wind crowds your throat." *For a moment it scares you, and then it's pure joy*, he wanted to add.

Carla spat, turned off the tap, put the toothbrush away. "You're so late, I already sent Kevin to bed." Kevin was Carla's eight-year-old son from a failed marriage. For an eight-year-old, Howard thought Kevin seemed strangely devoid of life, ghosting the hallways, ducking past Howard when he'd stretch his hand out to rumple his hair. Kevin spent most of his time holed up in his room, fiddling around on his computer, and Howard sincerely hoped he'd do something risky one of these days, get into some trouble, sniff rubber cement at school, smoke a cigarette, anything. Just to be on the safe side, Howard had tried to tell him a little about the birds and the bees a few months back. Kevin had sat cross-legged, looking at him and blinking rapidly. The point is, he'd told Kevin, life and love are ultimately cruel but fair, breaking each and every one of us down to bits, "and disappointment, just get used to it."

"Can I go now?" Kevin had asked, still blinking, and Howard realized then these were things you did not say to an eight-year-old.

Carla pulled her ratty yellow nightgown over her head. "He needs you, Howard. More than you know. Boys need a strong male role-model."

Howard stood and stepped out of his pants. "They need fresh air, too."

Carla sighed, climbed into bed. "Kevin's got that karate test at the Y tomorrow night. 7:30. Don't be late, okay?"

"Okay."

She turned her back to Howard and switched off her bedside light. In a matter of minutes, he knew she'd start mumbling data codes. Her favorite: 99803: Venipuncture. He used to think it was cute, her bringing her work home with her. When they both worked in the coding department, they'd spout codes over dinner dates, during commercials, a sort of foreplay and mounting evidence that they shared the same sense of humor: 66701, Bipolar manic depression; 39099, Male pattern baldness. All one of them had to do was pick a person out of a crowd or in a restaurant, point and recite a code, and they'd both bust up laughing. 41000: Liposuction. Now he had to work hard not to smother Carla with the pillow when she began her nightly litanies, and remind himself that once he had thought her funny. But then Howard recalled his own quirks: his wearing the maroon-striped tie every Tuesday and Thursday, wearing the brown paisley every Monday, Wednesday, and Friday. Maybe they were all just forgetting how to live.

———

Howard spent most of the next morning avoiding the Svea John-son file. By 10:05, when the exodus for the coffee pots had died to a trickle, he duckwalked his squeaky-castored chair closer to Leonard, who had his fingers laced behind his neck. Leonard gri-maced and twisted first to the right and then to the left. Oblique crunches. Leonard did these every morning during their allotted ten-minute coffee break.

"People always overlook their obliques," Leonard explained.

Howard nodded. "I've got this strange feeling," he said, thump-ing his chest with his knuckles. "Like I'm gulping sky, can't get enough of it. Other times I feel I'm drowning on air. Can a person do that?"

"Fish." Leonard flapped his hands at the side of his neck, indi-cating imaginary gills. "They do it all the time."

Howard pressed on his sternum again, then untucked his shirt and lifted it to show Leonard his chest. "No, really. I think there's something wrong with me," he said.

Leonard leaned forward in his chair and narrowed his eyes. "No kidding. Your obliques have completely disappeared. If your ribs weren't there, your insides would be sliding all over the place. Too many beers, Buck-o."

"No, that's not it," Howard said, tucking his shirt back into his waistband. "I think it's more serious."

Leonard shrugged. "Nothing more serious than a bad case of underdeveloped obliques."

"Right," Howard said, adopting Carla's habit of drawing the word out as she exhaled.

For over an hour Howard sat at his desk trying to work up the courage to process the Johnson file. But the mere sight of it, of knowing that she was most likely a jumper because it was Au-gust, the month of jumping, depressed him. Howard looked at the blue file and felt that space expanding, pushing against his lungs. He laced his fingers behind his neck as he'd seen Leonard do every morning. Maybe his problem could be isolated, squeezed into form by a series of isometrics. Maybe this was why Leonard worked out so much. Howard grunted and leaned to the right, then to the left, repeating the movements until he could feel a tingle in his armpits, the first signal that his deodorant either would or would not fail him. After five minutes, he gave up. He pushed on his rib cage, lightly fingering the spaces between the bones, feeling as spacious inside as before, if not spacier.

Outside, the sky was a cloudless blue, so pure Howard had to look away. He picked up his phone and dialed the coroner's office.

"Ritteaur, it's Howard calling on the Johnson autopsy results." Howard had his fingers crossed. He was hoping against all odds that she had been a faller and not a jumper, feeling that either way, he was responsible for her.

"Come take a look for yourself. We'll get a beer after," Ritteaur said.

Howard grabbed his keys. He knew it was against company policy to drink on lunch hours, but it was a Friday and he was feeling that space again, was hoping Hope and Life would catch on fire, was hoping every office worker would steal staplers and envelopes, hoping every beneficiary got paid in full.

When Howard pulled open the metallic doors of the coroner's lab, he walked into the sharp smells of formaldehyde and antiseptic, thick in the air and carried as a stinging slap to the nose. On a table lay the body of a woman, a white sheet peeled back to her feet. The yellow laminate toe-tag read *Johnson, Svea*. Even though her skin was bluish and dark circles ringed her eyes, Howard could see that she had been a beautiful woman and he regretted he'd come.

Ritteaur pressed a forefinger into the woman's arm, leaving an indentation. "The body's a glorified sponge," he said, pulling out a skinny measuring wand that looked like a cocktail swizzle stick. He measured the depth of the pitting, then tossed the tiny ruler into a stainless steel sink. "At first I thought it was suicide. The bridge and all. At any rate, she got to the morgue quicker than most of our water-victims do and we had to wait a while to see if any bruising would appear. Anything suspicious—ligatures or marks around the neck or on the arms. Bruises don't always appear on the body right away, especially on submerged flesh. So we let her dry out in the cooler."

"And that's when you found bruises?"

"That's just it. None. Zippo. So I'm thinking suicide. Then I look at her fingernails and I see tiny bits of moss under the nails and two of the nails on her right hand broken off."

"She fell." Howard felt a surge in his chest.

"Or she intended to jump but at the last moment had second thoughts."

Howard closed his eyes, imagining what he would have said if Svea had called in on the hotline, feeling again that maybe he owed her something, should at least be able to locate her in a dim memory of a school assembly, the taking of a photo, but there was nothing.

"So what's the verdict?" Howard swallowed, tasting metal in his molars.

Ritteaur shrugged. "I still got to do the Y-incision, poke around in the stomach, run some blood tests."

"Do you believe in dignity for the dead?" Howard draped the sheet over Svea Johnson's body.

Ritteaur laughed. "Are you kidding? In this business? You think this is bad," Ritteaur poked the dead woman's big toe, "wait until the mortician gets ahold of her."

Ritteaur pulled the sheet back and looked at the woman's face. Her eyes were open, but chilled and empty, the way the eyes of fish look when set out on ice. "She's in pretty good shape, all things considered." Ritteaur forced the eyelids closed with his thumbs. "We had a decapitation in here a month ago. The family wanted an open-casket funeral, if you can believe that. But I'm telling you, those embalmers can work miracles. They trimmed the ragged edges, splinted and sutured the head to the neck, and painted liquid sealer over the stitching. Then they threw a turtleneck and some makeup on the guy, and I swear to God, if I hadn't seen him on my table just a day before, I wouldn't have even suspected."

"No." Howard put his palms on the examining table and leaned on it. "That's not what I meant." He adjusted the sheet to cover Svea Johnson's pitted forearm. "I mean on the paperwork, 'accidental death' sounds more dignified than 'botched suicide,' don't you think?"

"Hey. I'm not going to tell you how to do your job. I just wanted you to see for yourself what we got here. My opinion is it could go either way."

"But your report—"

Ritteaur pulled off his surgical gloves with a loud snap. "It's still incomplete. But judging by what we got so far, I vote for accident."

"Okay." Howard patted down his stomach, his hands fluttering. "Okay," he said again, backing out of the two-way door, away from the smells of the lab.

"How 'bout that beer?" Ritteaur untied his scrubs, pivoted, and tossed them into a steel clothes hamper at the far end of the lab.

Howard shook his head and waved his hands out in front of him. "Another time." He felt his throat seizing tight, like a drawstring being pulled, and he didn't know if the formaldehyde was getting to him or if he had brushed against a true sorrow for this Svea Johnson, a stranger.

———

Howard checked his watch. Though Leonard would be back from the gym any minute now and Carla would have called and left messages, Howard could feel that other Howard unpeeling like the silver and felt backing from an old mirror and his heart began to beat faster. He closed his eyes and pinched the bridge of his nose. Before he knew it, he'd eased the Skylark toward the Laurelhurst neighborhood, past the long and low elementary, school, one six-year complaint of noise and misery. Howard turned onto Madison Street and sat two doors down from the Johnson house, considering how he'd purposefully forgotten all those years, grade school and junior high. He'd willfully, willingly forgotten the awkwardness of his body, his body a menagerie of flawed parts as he had only been dimly aware then of what he knew now: how the body's mysteries lay not in the parts themselves, nor their shapes and functions, but in the naming of them, and in the particular nomenclature for how those parts could and would fail. And whether the naming came in the form of medical coding or as scribbles from a forensic pathologist, Howard was continually astonished by the subtleties, the lies such language imposed.

As Howard walked down the narrow corridor to his cubicle, he could hear his phone ringing and knew, again, it was Carla.

"Howard. Just a reminder: Kevin. Y. 7 p.m. Green belt karate test." Carla sounded like she was calling out a fast-food order.

"Sure. Okay," Howard said and slid the receiver in the phone's cradle. He hated these Friday night karate tests. It took forever to get through the hordes of White belts, all of them bad. Yellow and Orange belt tests were a little better; at least when the instructor counted, you could bet half of the students would execute the same move at the same time. With White belts, you could never be sure of anything. And Howard hated the parents, crowding the mats, the metallic flash and pop of bulbs, the edgy whining noise of film rewinding.

Howard leaned back in his chair and palmed his heart, bearing down on his chest with the heel of his hand. He hoped his internal organs would just disappear and he could give himself over to his internal gases and float, balloon-like, up and out of the office.

On Fridays, beautiful Fridays after everyone else had left early, the hours emptied and a calm filled the office, a liquid quietude welling along the corridors, around cubicles, lapping over the tops of Howard's shoes. Howard loved this quiet startled from the eventual lack of noise: the gradual winding down of the phone's nervous rings around five, the flurry to the elevator and the rubbery sound of its wobbled stop and the door bumping open. The copy machine, switched off, lid open as if cooling itself, made trickling noises like the ink was pooling somewhere. On Fridays after five, Howard felt he could think a little more clearly and he rolled in his chair, dreaming of policies that were never cancelled, claims never rejected, families redeemed by the careful and sympathetic coding a man with Howard's sensibilities could extend. In these moments of calm, the two Howards, his will and his action, neatly fused. This is what he was telling himself anyway, why he would even consider going back out to Madison Street. For this combined and profoundly optimistic Howard, the Howard who believed in doing the right thing, believed he could do right by everyone if only he tried a little harder, found himself once again, before he could fully comprehend the consequences, behind the steering wheel of his temperamental Skylark.

Howard sat in his car, drumming his fingers along the curvature of the wheel grip. He would knock on their door and with confidence, he would apologize for his intrusion. "But it would help if you could tell me a little about your daughter," he'd say, "anything that goes to character or state of mind." He would of course be professional, take notes, politely look at photos. And he'd be careful to give nothing away. They'd never know Ritteaur suspected suicide, never know of Howard's dilemma. He'd ask them, carefully, about high school. Perhaps he'd mention that he might have been their paperboy.

Outside the car, Howard could hear the crickets rubbing out the music of their long legs. The air was cooling and the sun dropped behind a thick grove of oaks at the end of the street. Howard started the engine, kept his foot off the pedal and allowed the car to idle past the Johnson house. Idling at this speed, moving in a straight and true line toward the darkness, he knew that the earth moved as well, turning in the opposite direction, moving entire continents and everything on them, including Howard and his whistling Skylark, turning so gently, so surely not even a dog stirred. Howard braked suddenly. He sensed more than saw motion behind him and glanced in his rearview mirror. He felt his stomach shriveling, for there in the mirror he watched Carla's blue Impala fishtail at the end of Madison and turn the corner.

At 7:30 Howard's desk phone rang. Howard straightened in his chair.

"I saw you." It was Carla calling from the Y.

Howard thought again of the woman of a thousand flushes. He moved his mouth, formed the beginnings of words on his lips. At last he settled, "I know."

"I don't know what's going on with you, Howard." Carla let her breath out in spurts. "But this has got to stop. People count on you."

"I know it." Howard pressed on his sternum, then followed the ridges of each of his ribs with his fingertips. He was feeling expansive again, like if he took a big enough breath of air, he might up and float.

"I forgive you," Carla said at last, but Howard could hear the mercury rising in her voice and knew that though he might in fact be forgiven, his transgression would be remembered on a long long list of grievances. "Whatever you were doing over there, I forgive you. But you had better stop. And you better be here for Kevin's test."

Howard swallowed. "I'll be there," he said.

Howard opened the driver's side door of his car and slid in behind the steering wheel.

He started for the Y, but as he approached the bridge, he slowed and parked in the soft sand shoulder. Overhead, August's moon, round as a month full of fallers and jumpers, glowed against the deepening sky. He walked to the bridge, ran his hand over the rough cement siding. His maroon-striped tie flapped in the wind, slapping his right shoulder. He didn't know where Svea Johnson had jumped or fallen. He knew now that there were five ways to fall off a bridge, according to Ritteaur, but as Ritteaur admitted, he was only an assistant, and there could be many more ways of falling than either of them had ever dreamed of. Howard knew that Svea Johnson had not been drinking, had not taken pills. She had probably stood first behind the spot where she would later sit. Maybe she had even held her arms up, like Howard was doing now, testing the air for flight. Maybe she was just having a bad day, a very bad day here in this extremely vexed land, and, like Howard, was looking for that one gesture, that break in the monotonous tide, the necessary grace to fall.

Howard planted his elbows on the cement and leaned over the railing as if to read the water. If a body is exiled, he thought, it's because it is contained by skin. Is that how she felt? Did she give herself over to the collapsing arms of the air, to all that space within and without, a falling between the ribs and then here between the arms, between fingertips and sky? Was hers an ordinary sadness that brought her to this bridge or a more resonant sorrow lodged behind the breastbone? Did she sit swinging her legs back and forth and then finally say, "Oh, the hell with it," and push herself over? Did she scream as she fell, or plug her nose?

Howard removed his shoes and in his stockinged feet balanced up on the thick cement handrail. Parsing through these borrowed thoughts, he could see now how easy it was. It wasn't so hard to imagine, no, not at all. A murmur of resignation washing over you, the body spinning in a full revolution between hope and despair. Howard felt light, giddy in this feeling of antigravity, and for the first time in months, Howard felt like laughing.

"Stop it," he muttered, climbing down from the ledge with caution, much more tentative about this minor action than any other in his whole life. He'd been right all along in feeling like he'd failed people, only they weren't jumpers and fallers, and it amazed him what he'd allowed himself, the lapses, what he hadn't learned yet. And for all of his empty spaces, this is what pulled him back. There was his Tuesday/Thursday God-awful maroon-striped tie, for starters. Kevin's Green-belt test and the knowledge that he should and could probably try a little harder with the boy, try to manufacture some genuine feeling. He could tell Kevin his chicken-picking story. And then, of course, there were all those things he hadn't lived to see: the appearance of new suns, distant limbs of the galaxy, the relief of intolerable urges, and other small kindnesses. This was something he could have told Svea Johnson. Howard slid his shoes on then, still feeling that lightness, but with it a sense of forward motion propelling him to his car.

Sophia Winslow's House

ANDY PLATTNER

From *Winter Money* (1997)

From the ages of twenty-one through twenty-seven, I worked on a horse farm in Midlands, Kentucky, called Burroway. I started off there as an ordinary hand, then became a yearling groom, then assistant to the yearling manager. I had four men working under me, and the owner of Burroway, Harry Linderman, would phone the barn every so often to check on things. He was a nice old guy and I was polite with my answers. I had a tenant house to live in, free of rent, and the last year I worked there I was paid to watch over the farm's young horses and teach new grooms how to handle them. I judged our stock for racing potential or how much they might bring at a sale. It was a good setup.

Then the horse business in Kentucky went bust. This is the mid-eighties I'm talking about. For years, there'd been over-investing, calculated profits, and this ridiculous go-getter mood. It took a while for all these greenhorn investors to understand racehorses weren't reliable for earning quarterly interest; most animals couldn't win back their inflated purchase price. These new investors were driven out of the game and, subsequently, sales prices plummeted. Horse breeders had borrowed money on projected earnings and the banks were nervous. They began calling in loans. Being attached to the horse business was now considered to be poisonous. The value of land dropped. I could go on. The result was that a lot of farms got wiped out.

Mr. Linderman didn't lose his place. It had been in his family for generations and that type of old money Armageddon can't loosen. But when the farm stopped showing a profit from its horses, he put them all up for sale. A couple of Texans came to look over our yearling crop. Somebody from Canada visited us. An English bloodstock agent representing the Arabs bought nine of our horses during a forty-five-minute tour of Burroway.

Mr. Linderman was generous enough about letting the help go. He gave each employee a month's salary and told me I could stay in my tenant house until I found something else. This was a fine offer, but I didn't want to just linger there waiting for some wonderful new job to come my way. Waiting can be a bad thing; you can get too used to doing it. The problem was, no other farms were hiring. Horsemen were being laid off everywhere and even regular jobs around Midlands were hard to find.

I decided to move to Lexington, about forty miles south. It was twice as large as Midlands. I thought there'd be better opportunities. I found a duplex on McGinney Street, the other half of which was rented by this fairly old lady. I began looking for a job. The economy was bad around Lexington, too. The whole town had been tied to the horse business in one way or another: nice restaurants for celebrating the profitable sale of a yearling; clothing stores that offered designer labels; new car dealerships—anything that meant a better lifestyle—and these places had begun suffering, too. Now, if there was an employment listing in the *Herald-Leader*, it had a dozen applicants by noon.

I got lucky and got on with a real estate company, Shively and Furman. They'd downsized, combining a maintenance job with a groundskeeper's. Neither man who'd held these positions previously was willing to have double workload at the same pay. Maybe they'd wised up and headed the hell out of Lexington. At any rate, I was hired the day I applied.

My job at Shively and Furman consisted of general fix-it work and looking after different apartment buildings, houses and vacant lots. If there was something I didn't know how to do, I'd call a plumber or an electrician. Lee Shively would scream about paying somebody extra, but I figured he'd rather have the bills than a house with an exploding toilet or ashes for walls. I was still a cost-saver for him—we both knew it.

I'd been at Shively and Furman about a month when they brought Joe aboard. Joe Albertello was his long name, but everybody at the office called him Spaghetti Joe or Joe Martini. When Shively first introduced Joe to me, he called Joe my "assistant." Joe had a dome of baldness for the crown of his head, thin black and silver sideburns, a salt-and-pepper mustache. He was six feet tall with a slightly stooping posture. Joe was wearing pressed slacks and a button-down shirt. Right away, I wanted to ask Shively if Joe knew what I did primarily was clean gutters and stick my face in cobwebs searching for breaker boxes.

"Joe can do anything," Shively said. "Just ask him." We were standing in his office. There were pictures on the wall of Shively with his arm around friends at a barbecue or some golf course. There was a photograph of Shively and his wife and weedy kids. Shively clapped Joe on the back. "Right?"

"Well," I said to Joe.

"Yeah," Joe said.

That first day, I didn't ask Joe to do anything that resembled grubby work. I dug up the ground around the septic tank at the Bakers Road property and Joe stood watching with his arms crossed. "This is it," I said. "This is what we do."

He shrugged. "I'm only gonna be here until I get something better going. You know?"

He showed up for work the next morning dressed in gray suit pants and a polo shirt. Our job was to take weedeaters out to Simms Circle and trim around the trees and the foundation of the building.

I took the weedeaters out of the bed of the truck and filled them with the gas/oil mix. Joe took one and started over for the building entrance. He stopped and pulled the cord to the motor a few times. It spit and began running. Joe stepped away from his work every few minutes to brush out the cut weeds that landed in the cuffs of his pants.

The stories that went around the office were like this: Joe was from Cincinnati and had gone belly-up in the catering business. Somebody said it was land development. Joe had been weaving his way in and out of bankruptcy court for the past few years. Loan officers held up silver crosses whenever he walked by. He was Shively's wife's brother or something and was working off a debt to Shively.

But Joe was all right by me. Any work he did was something I didn't have to, and he always had stories to tell. Once in a while we'd get a beer after work. We were sitting in the 427 Bar a particular time and I decided to ask him if he didn't own some old T-shirts or jeans or any clothes suited better for the type of work we did. He sat up straight on his barstool and touched his chest with the tips of his fingers. "I dress well because I expect good things to happen," he said. "I'm not down on my luck like these other bastards you see around. When my ship comes in I want everybody to know I never doubted it." He grinned. Everybody in life has their little speech and clearly this was Joe's. "Let's have another," he said to the bartender.

Joe and I didn't work together every day. When we were looking after the Shively and Furman houses on the east side of town, we'd split up. Lawns needed mowing, gutters had to be painted— one-man jobs that took a single afternoon. Joe and I would ride over to the east side in the mornings in my pickup and we'd divide assignments. I'd drop him off or he'd take over driving after letting me off. I always volunteered to do anything connected with the house at Vine and Conner and Joe let me. He knew I liked the woman renting there. Her name was Sophia Winslow. She was mid-thirties, with collar-length auburn hair and olive-colored eyes. She was home during the day whenever I worked there. The house wasn't much, a single-story brick deal with a concrete path to the front door and a carport at the end of the driveway.

The first time I saw Shively's car parked in that driveway, I didn't think much of it. He was there to check on the rent; maybe she'd been asking for improvements in the place. A couple of weeks later I saw his car there again. I was supposed to trim the hedges around the house anyway, so I guess I started near the windows. I was using these old manual, scissorlike shears with wooden handles, the kind that didn't make a racket. At the third window, I saw Shively and Sophia sitting on a tiny couch together, Shively with his stocking feet propped up on her coffee table. They were watching television and smiling at something.

It was funny, but I didn't see Shively over there again. I hardly knew what to make of it. Then one afternoon I was over at Sophia's house replacing shingles on the roof. I was climbing down the ladder, ready for lunch, and there was her face behind the rungs, staring out the window. "Come in and have a drink with me," she said through the glass.

We sat in the living room and had a beer apiece. I'd been trying to figure out how to work up to this point, then there it was all of a sudden. Sophia looked unhappy. "How do you like this work?" she said. She was in a tan blouse, jeans, no shoes.

"It's okay," I said. "Could be worse."

"I understand," she said. She stood up and headed down the hallway. After a minute passed, I heard, "Are you coming?"

When it was over, we just laid on our backs in silence. "Your boss is tossing me out at the end of the month," she said. "Did you know that?"

I was still. "No," I said. "I didn't know that."

It was quiet again. "He is so rotten," she said. She cleared her throat. "You better get back to work," she said.

I spent the rest of the day spidering my way atop her roof. I thought about the way Sophia looked lying there on the bed. Making love can fix your day, but when it doesn't, things look worse. I guess I hadn't helped much.

I returned to the house the following morning to finish the roof job. Sophia's car wasn't there and the door and windows were closed tight. She'd said the end of the month. I wanted to see her again. I got one of the secretaries to give me her phone number, but she never answered when I called. I drove by the Vine and Conner house in the evening a couple of times. Sophia's car was in the driveway. One time I walked up to the door and knocked. Lights were on inside and I could hear movement. Nobody came to the door, though.

Two nights after Sophia was evicted, Shively called me at my apartment. "When's the last time you were over at Vine Street?" he said.

"A couple of days," I said. I'd been over to mow the grass, which really didn't need it. The house had been shut up tight and Sophia's car was gone again.

"Garbage," Shively said.

"What?" I said.

"First thing tomorrow, get over there," he said. "You and Joe. Stop by the office and I'll give you the key."

The following morning I sat in the Shively and Furman office lot, waiting for Joe. The morning fog was dense and car headlights were haloed as they went up and down Carothers Road. Brakes would squeal intermittently. A horn would sound.

The only other car in the lot was Shively's Volvo. He'd been sitting at the receptionist's desk in the small lobby of his office when I went in. He held a key in front of his nose. Shively was about fifty, had a cone-shaped face and small ears. It was difficult to gauge what a woman might see in him, other than he was a landlord. "I want you to take care of this quickly and quietly." I shrugged. He flipped the key to me.

The key was in my jeans pocket as I sat in the truck now. That was the worst thing about a job like this: you couldn't tell your boss exactly what you thought of him. Forget it, fuck, I thought. You went around with something eating at you all day and that day would end up being about fifty hours long.

Joe pulled into the lot. He drove this ancient two-tone Seville. Light green top half, dark green bottom. It had a hundred and eighty thousand miles on it. A real piece of work.

Joe walked over to the truck carrying two steaming styrofoam cups. "Just took the lids off," he announced, as I pushed the passenger-side door open. He got in, handed me one, pulled the door closed. I turned over the engine. The tools in the bed of the truck rattled on the drive over to Vine. The fog was lifting. I traveled with one of everything: hammer, shovel, rake, ladder, two lengths of saws, a toolbox heavy with wrenches, screws, washers, etc. I had a small expense account for anything else. I tried to imagine what this job was going to entail.

"Old Shively playing fast and loose?" Joe said, when I told him we were going to the Vine Street house and that Sophia was gone.

"Yeah," I said. I hadn't told him about the afternoon the two of us had spent together. Not that Joe would've tried making a joke—I just felt more protective of what happened between her and me. I hadn't done much of a job there; she was gone now.

When Joe and I pulled up to the Vine Street house, the driveway was empty and swept. I'd just mown the lawn within an inch of its life. Joe and I got out of the truck and walked to the front door. The windows were shut, the curtains were drawn.

"I smell something," Joe said.

I stuck the key into the knob of the door and pushed it open partway. A terrific smell rushed out.

Joe laughed. "Jesus."

I shoved the door all the way open. The living room carpet was covered with trash, bags and bags of split-open deep green plastic. It was a foot high along the walls and in the corners. There didn't seem to be any air to breathe.

"A little unhappy with things, was she?" Joe said. He shook his head and there was a hint of admiration in his tone. "She must've gone out and brought this in from somewhere. Raided the dump." He set his hands on his hips. "I knew a guy once who tried filling a motel room with water. Turned on the spout in the tub, faucet in the sink. A maid noticed water dribbling out the front door. Kid stuff." We just stood there a minute and looked around the room.

Joe began stepping carefully over the piles. I followed. The kitchen was the same, worse actually, because the garbage was stuffed in the sink and crammed into the drawers. Everywhere, there were newspapers, rumpled frozen dinner trays, cereal boxes, beer cans, egg cartons, plastic soda bottles, magazines, rancid vegetables, filthy clothes, brand-new clothes, hardback novels, wine jugs, stray parts of household appliances, plastic toys, shower curtains, greasy pizza boxes.

"Another satisfied customer," Joe said.

I went down to the pay phone on the corner and called the office. "What exactly do you want us to do about it?" I said to Shively when he came to the phone.

"I don't want you parking a dumpster on the property," he said. "I don't want a lot of attention called to this. Can you just bag the stuff up, set it around back until the end of the day? Throw the bags in your truck and take them to the Simmons Road complex. There's a nice dumpster there."

I went back to the house and reported what Shively said. Joe sort of snorted at this. We drove to Sears and bought two 50-pack boxes of garbage bags. We returned to Vine Street. I got the shovel out of the truckbed. We pulled on our leather gloves.

I'd take a turn shoveling while Joe held an open bag, then we'd switch. There would be something interesting every few shovelfuls. We found a photograph album that began with pictures of a wedding; a perfectly good Texas Instruments calculator, which after a brief discussion we returned to the pile; a half-dozen shot glasses, each bearing the seal of a southern state; a three-iron with a badly bent shaft—there were other clubs like it; a little diary-like book with an X-rated lyric printed on the opening page. The rest were blank. Joe had looked over one of the shot glasses for a moment, then tossed it into the bag I was holding.

By the end of the day we had filled forty-one bags of garbage. We weren't anywhere near finished, either. It seemed like Joe and I had merely removed a layer of it. It was fairly disgusting work overall. We had to make three trips to the Simmons Road complex. The dumpster there really was a big mother, blocked out the sun. After all this was done, I dropped Joe back at the office lot and went home.

The person who rented the other half of the duplex where I lived was Margaret Ellison. She mostly stayed in her apartment. She was in her mid-sixties and through the thin walls of our building I sometimes heard her moving pots and pans atop the stove. She never had friends or family stopping by. She liked *The Jeffersons*. I'd been in her apartment twice, both times to fix something. Shively and Furman had offered me a one-bedroom in one of their buildings at a discount rate, but I knew what that meant: I'd be a twenty-four-hour handyman for the place. Every time something went wrong, people would be at my door. It sounded tiring. The problems Margaret had—loose hinges, faulty cable connection—were nothing. She held a five-dollar bill out to me each time I was finished. "Come on," I said. She pushed it closer. "You're young," she said. "Every little bit helps."

Joe and I met at the office and rode back over to Vine Street the following morning. We started the same process as the day before. A hundred different smells hit at the same time whenever I leaned over to thrust down at a pile with the shovel, but overall it combined for this mildew, rot odor. I couldn't tell if it was worse than yesterday.

We were working over in a corner of the bedroom and I was about to spear another pile when Joe said, "Hang on a minute." He leaned down and brushed a pocket-sized thesaurus aside. There seemed to be an ashtray or something there.

Joe lifted out a dinner plate. It was trimmed in gold. He reached for a torn-out arm of a flannel shirt and wiped a streak of coffee grounds from the plate. He held it out to me. It was a commemorative plate. In the middle of it was a picture of the Houston Astrodome, more like an architect's drawing actually. The dome of the stadium looked like the top half of a tremendous eggshell with beams stretching across its surface to keep it from floating away. In a half-circle above the drawing it read:

Coming Soon, The Astrodome
Eighth Wonder of the World

Under the drawing was a tiny red star with a "T" in a white ball at its center. "Texaco" was written under the star.

Joe looked at me. "This, I can sell," he said. "I know a guy in Louisville who handles things like this." Joe stood slowly. He brought the plate closer to his eyes.

"Somebody had it all these years," I said. "Why would they throw it out now?"

"They figured it was crap. Got tired of looking at it. Who knows?"

"How much is it worth?" I said.

Joe glanced up. "Fifty bucks, maybe a hundred. You never can really tell. It's worth a drive for me to find out." Something was clicking behind his eyes. "You drive me over to my car. I'll run the plate to Louisville. On the way back, I'll pick up some bourbon, wine, stuff to eat. You come over about nine. I'm throwing a party. The more we get for the plate, the more people I'll invite."

"Fine," I said. "Okay."

"This is great," he said. He slapped me lightly on the back. He let out a short laugh. "We find commemorative silverware, we'll have another party tomorrow."

"Grits and Fritz salt shakers," I said.

"Seattle World's Fair gravy bowl," he said.

I drove Joe back to the office. The plate rode on his lap. I returned alone to the Vine Street property. I discovered it was fairly impossible to use the shovel and hold a bag open decently, so I laid the shovel aside. Working with my hands was harder, but I didn't mind. If Joe hadn't been here, I probably would've just thrown the point of the shovel at the Astrodome plate—breaking it to pieces without really knowing what I'd done. I was working more carefully now.

It was midafternoon when I heard a car pulling into the driveway. Bits of rock popped under the tires. I was still working in the bedroom and heard the front door open. I didn't rise from my crouch. If it was a burglar or somebody, they'd just stepped into their worst nightmare. After a moment, there was someone in the doorway of the bedroom. It was Shively. He was in the Lee Shively uniform, pressed white shirt, tan pants, shined boots. "This isn't dream work, I know," he said. He glanced around. "Where's Joe?"

"Wasn't feeling good," I said. "All this stink was giving him a headache."

Shively nodded. He looked apologetic, different from the way he was before. Maybe this room and what was in it was working on him. "When I stopped by here a couple of nights ago, I couldn't believe it," he said. "She kept this house so nice." He leaned against the door frame.

I was resting my hands on my thighs. "Something must've provoked her," I said.

Shively let his eyes roll across the garbage.

"Did you know the woman who lived here well?" I said.

He glanced at me, the look on his face indicating I'd asked an inappropriate question. "I know all the people who rent from me," he said. "What they do for a living, how much they make, if they're having financial trouble. Kid needs braces, daddy's gone off to AA. The rent's late, I get all the stories." He watched me evenly. "Just checking on my property." He looked at one corner of the room. "This whole damn thing is going to need a scrubbing, a new coat of paint, new carpets. Just a write-off, the entire thing."

It was an odd thing, but I thought something about Shively then, that somewhere along the way he'd found a bad set of instructions and was used to following them. Here I was cleaning up what Sophia had done, but there was nothing about it that made me want to forget her.

What I said was, "It's not that bad."

Shively's face seemed stern and he stepped back from the door frame he'd been leaning against. "Tell Joe to take some Tylenol and get back to work. You ought to be through with this tomorrow. I've got sagging gutters over on Rollins." He turned and walked out. As he went, it sounded like he was trying not to step in something.

I stayed in my crouch for a minute after his car pulled out. I held my hands together.

When I'd gone into Sophia's bedroom that afternoon we'd spent together, she was naked except for a slim silver chain holding a St. Christopher medal around her neck. The curtains were drawn. I started taking off my clothes. Sophia sat on the edge of the bed and I walked over to her. "Kneel," she said. I did. My eyes were level with her breasts. She brought the back of her hand to my forehead. "You're sweating," she said. She leaned closer and blew softly on my forehead. She moved her lips past my face to one collarbone. She blew on that. She did the same to the other.

It had been an unexpected moment—extraordinary. And I thought now that she was someone who understood things. She might be a real survivor. I didn't think I was being pie-in-the-sky imagining things turning out all right for her somewhere.

I decided to knock off early. I set the bags I'd filled outside the bedroom door. I went outside and got in my pickup. I rode over to the 427 Bar. The regular bartender, Mitch, was there. "Where's your friend?" he said, after I ordered a shot and a Coors.

"Day off," I said. "Day off for everybody."

"Not me," he said, wiping out a glass that already looked clean. I shrugged. I had two more rounds and we watched a soap on the bar television. Then I drove back to my duplex. I laid on the couch and closed my eyes.

When I woke up, it was almost dark out. I went to the bathroom to brush my hair. I walked to the refrigerator and made a sandwich. I thought I heard some rummaging coming from Margaret Ellison's side, some light movement back and forth. I'd been getting used to the various sounds coming from there, but I felt more alert now. She was a fairly old lady and I guessed staying busy all the time was a real trick, the one that mattered most.

Then it was time to ride over to Joe's and see how he'd made out with our plate. Joe lived over on Wagner Terrace, in an apartment complex called Juniper Oaks. Juniper Oaks was actually two large, squarish, brick buildings, which contained twenty-two living units apiece. There was a large parking lot between the buildings and it was poorly lit as I pulled in. Silhouettes of a pair of empty picnic tables were next to one building.

Joe lived in 12A. The parking lot hadn't looked crowded at all, but as I stood in front of Joe's door I heard soft music and people talking inside. I guessed he'd found a buyer for the plate. I knocked on the door, and when it opened, Joe was standing there like a proud father. "I told you it was worth something," he said. He held the door open further.

Talking *Mama-Losh'n*

CAROLE L. GLICKFELD

From *Useful Gifts* (1989)

The siren sounded just as my mother and I jammed together in the window, leaning out over the fire escape, our elbows on the sill. Melva had the next window over to herself. Across the street, apartment windows got black as lights went off, one after the other. Within minutes the lampposts were out. It was completely dark, except for tiny flares of matches lighting cigarettes or the glowing embers of those already lit, from the people who hung out across the street from us.

Down the block a shrill whistle blew. "HEY! YOU! Turn that light out!" boomed my brother's voice. "This is your air raid warden speaking."

"Oh God!" Melva said.

It was my brother's first night as an air raid warden. Sidney's loud voice came through his megaphone like thunder in the dark. Since there was enough moonlight, I told my mother in sign language what we heard.

Ruthie and her deaf parents communicate in sign language, as is explained in the first story of the collection *Useful Gifts*. When they spell words out, a hyphen separates each letter. Words they denote with a single shortcut sign receive no special typographical treatment.

"Like b-o-s-s," my mother said, meaning that Sidney liked being a boss.

For a long time Melva and I didn't hear anything else, except the voices of our neighbors from the windows above and below us. We didn't even know where Sidney was, until we saw the beam of his flashlight shining into the front window of a car in the middle of the street.

"Pull over," Sidney's voice boomed. "I mean NOW!"

The car rolled slowly to the curb and turned its lights out. Sidney's flashlight went out, too, and then we lost track of him again.

It was hard for me to believe that my very own brother was out there in charge of Arden Street. Even if he hadn't told me about the Japs who could fly over our block and bomb us if they saw the lights, I would of been impressed. I knew he felt proud, because when the notification came he'd said, "They wouldn't have given any old *shmuck* such an important job." I didn't know what *shmuck* meant but later Melva said it was a really bad word.

After a while the all-clear siren sounded. Apartments across the way lit up again and the streetlights came back on. We put the screens in the windows and went into the kitchen to wait for Sidney.

"Listen to this!" my brother said when he came in. My mother held out her hands, like she wanted to take his helmet. Sidney waved her away.

"S-i-l-l-y," my mother said. She brought him iced coffee and sat down with us at the kitchen table. The whole time Sidney was telling us what'd happened, he kept his helmet on.

First he told us about Mrs. Sheehan, who lived just two steps down from the sidewalk, in the next building. She had run outside during the first siren. "I told the buttinsky to get her ass off the street . . ." my brother said.

"Sidney . . ." my sister interrupted.

He looked over at me. "Sorry," he said.

He took a long time telling what he'd said to Mrs. Sheehan and what she'd said, back and forth, and how she kept standing on the sidewalk, letting him know which lights were still on, in case he couldn't see for himself.

He imitated her Irish brogue: "Mr. Zimmer, sure and I'm jes tryin' to help ya." My brother was terrific with accents, even though he hadn't taken any languages in high school, like my sister was doing.

"Then what?" Melva asked.

"I told Mrs. Sheehan she could help the U.S. of A. by getting her goddam ass inside."

Melva kicked me under the table. I kicked her back. Then I told my mother about Mrs. Sheehan, except I cut it short.

"Irish, nosey," my mother said.

"What else? What else?" Melva asked Sidney, like she was real curious, even though when she was mad at him she used to say he was full of hot air.

Sidney told us about the man who lived over on Sickles and was walking his schnauzer on Arden. "I instructed him to get the hell back to his own block," Sidney said, "because I wasn't putting my neck on the line to have his dog crap in my territory."

I started giggling.

"This is goddam serious," he said. "There's a war going on. You don't have your dog take a crap during an air raid."

I bit the inside of my cheek, but when Melva kicked me again, the giggles burst out. Soon she and I were in hysterics.

"Jesus Christ! Girls can be so damn silly," my brother said, taking off his helmet and slamming it down on the table.

Being an air raid warden wasn't my brother's first choice. When he was seventeen he tried to join the Army, but they told him he had to get his GED, since he'd dropped out of high school. Up until then he was happy-go-lucky, going out with his friends all the time, dating Lori Steinfeld and giving her lots of presents with the money he made as a stock boy at Greenblatt's Grocery. But he became real serious, staying home nights to study, which made Lori mad. When he got his GED, though, she said she was pleased as punch. She was two years older than him and already in nursing school. She didn't want him to volunteer for the Army but to wait till he was drafted. He went down to the recruiters anyway, only it turned out he was 4-F, on account of his flat feet.

"I'm not gonna take no for an answer," Sidney told us.

My father thought he was crazy, spending all his money on the foot doctor and on special metal arches they made to put inside his shoes. Every night before he went to bed Sidney did his exercises, grabbing pencils between his toes and walking on tiptoe. But when he tried again to join up, he was still 4-F.

Then Mr. Greenblatt sold the grocery to retire and my brother lost his job. After that, Sidney, who was tall and skinny, got even skinnier. His nose stood out like a parrot's and I hardly ever saw his big dimples anymore. His friends, who used to call him Smiley, started calling him Slim. "Disappointed, s-o-u-r," my mother said about him, behind his back.

The whole winter he was looking for work. He left the house when I did in the morning to go to school, and sometimes he bought me chocolate-covered raspberry jellies or dots (the kind that are stuck to paper) at the corner candy store where he bought the *New York Times* for the want ads. He got my sister to type his applications because she was taking the commercial course at George Washington and was a terrific typist. But most of the places wanted someone with college.

My brother spent everything in his savings account before he asked my father if he could borrow some money. My father had a fit. I could see them in the living room from where I was, sitting on the floor in the foyer, reading my library book. My father was in the big chair, in his undershirt and slacks, and my brother was lighting up a cigarette, standing by the lamp table.

"Smoke too much!" my father said right off, about the Lucky

Strikes. While he signed he made barking sounds that deaf-mutes make when they're angry, kind of a cross between a person and a growly dog.

"When take t-e-s-t?" my father barked. He meant the Civil Service exam, so Sidney could get a job in the post office, where my father worked the night shift on the New Jersey table.

"Not interested," Sidney told him again. He'd told my mother the p.o. was okay for my father, since he was a deaf-mute and couldn't do any better, but for him it would be a dead end.

My father got up from the chair, smiling real sarcastically. "Fine, fine!" he said. "Who s-u-p-p-o-r-t you?" He poked my brother in the chest when he made the sign for "you."

"Please, n-e-e-d money," my brother said, "J-u-s-t loan." He stubbed out his cigarette in the ashtray, looking like he was about to cry.

"Money? Go take t-e-s-t, you," my father said. He poked him in the chest again.

"You go h-e-l-l," my brother said.

That's when my father hit Sidney in the face. I started screaming, though my mother couldn't hear me and my sister wasn't home. He kept hitting Sidney, but Sidney didn't move away. All he did was cover his head with his arms, the way he'd shown me to do when he taught me how to box because, he said, even little girls needed to defend themselves sometimes.

Finally my father stopped hitting. He stomped across the living room, almost stepping on me before he saw me. He kicked my book by mistake but all he said was "D-o-p-e" about my brother, then he went in the kitchen.

I didn't see how my father could mean that. Sidney was always reading the encyclopedia for fun and memorizing things from the almanac. The only reason he had dropped out of high school was to get a job, because my father didn't give him enough of an allowance.

My brother came over and picked me right up off the floor,

holding me in his arms. "Don't cry," he said. "The sonofabitch isn't worth it." He had to put me down, though, because he started crying himself.

Not long after the big fight with my father, Sidney came home and told us he'd gotten a job as stock clerk for Baum Fabrics, a linen store downtown on Fifth Avenue. He was real happy about it at first. Then, for some reason, he wasn't so happy anymore. Every night he came home from work tired and sweaty, took off his shoes, lit up a Lucky Strike, and waited for the cup of coffee my mother always made him. He would read the *Daily News* without saying anything, have his supper, and then tell us stories that made fun of Mr. Baum, who he called the *tsadik*. "That means a good guy," he explained, except whenever he said it he meant the opposite.

Every so often, he would have Melva and me in stitches, imitating how Mr. Baum waddled up and down the store holding a pencil behind his back to make his fat arms meet. Then Sidney would change into another sport shirt and different pants and go see Lori or some of the guys he hung around with. When my mother would tell him not to spend all his money, he'd say that he planned to enjoy himself before buckling down. He was thinking about going to night school at NYU to study retail management.

My mother invited Lori for supper on Sidney's birthday. My father was at work, but we had a cake with candles and my mother made my brother's favorite, potato pancakes. I thought Lori was real pretty, with shiny black hair, kind of wavy to her shoulders, a big pompadour in front. She had a tiny nose like Jane Powell, which my sister called a snub, and she wore a big red flower over her ear. Not a real one, but the kind that came with a bobby pin attached.

My mother said she was stuck-up, after she tried to teach Lori to spell her name in the sign language alphabet and Lori pretended she was too dumb to learn. "Think high c-l-a-s-s," my mother said, meaning that Lori thought she was too good to talk with her fingers. When they broke up on Memorial Day, my mother was glad.

Lori wanted to get engaged right after she graduated nursing school, while Sidney wanted to wait. Breaking up with her made him sick. He stayed home from work, saying he had stomach pains. When the phone rang, he jumped out of bed to get it, but it wasn't her. I felt really bad. Later I was playing with my dolls in the living room, which was where his bed was, folded out from the couch, and I heard him sniffling. When I turned around, he was wiping his eyes with the sleeve of his pajamas.

"You know what? You're a natural teacher," he told me, about how I was teaching the dolls to spell. He made me promise to go to college and become a teacher, but I kept my toes crossed when I promised, because I'd wanted to be a nurse, like Lori. "You can make a good living teaching," he said, "until you get married and have babies."

The week after, Sidney came home and said, "You'll never guess, I've been promoted!" He said Mr. Baum gave him a job as a salesman in the front of the store. He would have to start wearing a shirt and tie with a jacket to work. My father raised his room and board from ten dollars to fifteen.

From then on, when Sidney came home at night the first thing he did was tell us how much he had grossed in sales for Baum Fabrics. It was always in the hundreds of dollars. He was still tired and sweaty, though, and my mother put Johnson's baby powder in his shoes. She said it would stop his feet from smelling. I never smelled anything, probably because of my sinus trouble.

He still didn't smile much, except the day he got his instructions and equipment to be an air raid warden (a megaphone, a whistle, and a flashlight) from the Fort Washington Armory. He came back grinning from ear to ear, with the deepest dimples, and put his new helmet on my head, laughing when it cov-

ered my whole face. For a moment he got serious, warning Melva
never to touch it when he wasn't around. I asked him why he had
to wear a helmet walking up and down Arden Street. That made
him double over laughing. "She's such a card," he kept saying to
Melva, but he never answered my question.

The night the inspector was supposed to see him during the
air raid, Sidney was a bundle of nerves. When he came home
from work, he didn't read the *Daily News* or tell us how much
he'd grossed. Instead, he kept trying his helmet on in front of the
mirror, finally asking Melva which way was best. He made me
feel his cheeks to see if he needed a shave and even combed his
hair twice in front with the Brill Cream. Then he got out his instructions, reading them over and over while he paced around
the whole apartment.

I guess he got tired of pacing because he said to me, "Hey,
cutie pie. Let's go someplace and talk *mama-losh'n*," explaining
it was Yiddish for getting down to business. He liked using words
he had to explain.

"Where are we going?"

His face lit up. "Guess!"

"You mean it?" I said, getting the idea we were going to Schillingman's on Dyckman Street, two blocks over from Arden,
where they had the best ice cream.

When we got there he said I could have anything I wanted. I
got two scoops, cherry vanilla and pistachio, with sprinkles on
top, which was extra. My brother got a single chocolate. He put
four dimes on the wooden counter while we waited for Mr. Schillingman to scoop the sugar cones. It was pretty dark in there,
with the lights way up on the ceiling where the fans were spinning.

Mr. Schillingman gave him seven cents change and wished
him a good evening, except he said, "Goot," because of his accent.

Instead of saying thank you, my brother said, "*Danke schön.*"

Outside the store it was hot, in the 90's probably. Usually I sucked the vanilla off the cherries, then chewed them, but the ice cream was melting pretty fast, so I had to lick my cone like mad.

"See those bums?" my brother said, pointing with his cone to some high school kids leaning up against a parked car. "They'll never amount to anything."

In front of Nick's Fruits the sidewalk was jammed with baby carriages and strollers every which way. Lots of ladies were standing around the crates waving their arms, yelling for Nick. He looked up when we passed by and said, "Sid, how'ya doin'?"

"The best," my brother said. "You?"

But by then Nick was weighing something on one of the scales.

When I finished my cone, Sidney said, "Now, let's have a *tête-à-tête*."

"A what?"

"Something between you and I," he said, just before a kid on roller skates almost crashed into us. "*Nudnik*," he shouted, so that people outside the fish market stared. Sidney didn't seem to notice. He looked at me, putting his big hand on my shoulder. "What you should do when you grow up is go into sales."

I didn't know what to say. Ever since he told me I should be a teacher, I thought that's what I was going to be. I had even learned to pronounce words like Mrs. Landau did, especially "dance" and "idea," after she told our class most of the world didn't appreciate a Bronx accent. We lived in Manhattan, of course, but it was pretty close to the Bronx. And when people asked me what I was going to be when I grew up, I'd been telling them, "Teacher."

I kicked a bottle cap on the ground, waiting for Sidney to say something else. He said I was smart enough to be a salesgirl, since I'd skipped a grade, and what with his influence Mr. Baum would hire me right away when I graduated high school. "Your big brother's looking out for you," he said.

"I know," I said.

I liked being out after supper, even if it was hot and muggy. The sky was orange and peach, with dark gray clouds that came sometimes before a thunderstorm.

At the top of Dyckman my brother said he was sweating like a pig, so we went inside Nedick's, which was one of the few places in our neighborhood that was air-conditioned. Everything was so white in Nedick's it hurt your eyes: the tile walls and floor, even the kid behind the counter. He wore a white shirt and apron and a white pointy hat, like the kind you make by folding up paper, except it was cloth.

The kid looked at my brother as if he was crazy when Sidney asked how business was. He put the orange drink down without saying anything. That made forty-three cents so far that Sidney spent. He was always telling my sister he was broke, but Melva said it was on account of the Lucky Strikes. After he and Lori broke up, he started smoking two packs a day and was up to two and a half.

When we got outside, Sidney said, "Sales is 90 percent personality. That *nebbish* has zip. He'll always be a soda jerk."

We turned the corner onto Broadway. Outside the park, old people sat on the benches fanning themselves. I knew their buildings didn't have air conditioners like those downtown, where I wanted to live when I grew up.

Glory was on the stoop when we got back to our building, playing Double Dutch with the O'Brien kids. They were twirling and she was jumping, but I felt her eyes on Sidney. Sweat was running down his face and his shirt was all wet under the arms and down the middle of his back. He stopped on the first landing to turn around. "The U.S. of A. is a land of opportunity," he said to me, "and don't you ever forget it." He said it so loud I wanted to get out of there real fast.

"Promise me you'll go into sales," he said, still too loud.

I crossed my toes, then nodded, making sure not to look at

Glory. Finally, he said he'd race me and we ran up the stairs. Near the fourth floor he slowed down to let me catch up, then he beat me to the door.

Once we got in the apartment, he rushed around, wiping himself off and changing his shirt. He didn't let my mother powder his shoes. He got all his equipment and then he was gone.

We didn't have to watch long that night before we heard Sidney's voice booming out to someone up near the corner. "HEY! YOU! Lights out!" After that, it was real quiet until just before the all-clear. "Get off the street," we heard him say to someone, but we couldn't see anything.

When he came back, he was real excited. The inspector told him they might make him supervisor of the other air raid wardens in the Inwood District. "Lori will be sorry," Sidney said. "I'll show *her*."

The week before school started I went with my mother to Fort Tryon Park where she always met her deaf friends in the afternoons. I got real bored so I told her I was going home to play on the stoop, but instead I went up to the top of the park and got on a bus that goes all the way down Fifth Avenue. I only had one nickel on me. Still, I wasn't worried when I put it in the box because I decided to visit my brother at Baum Fabrics.

I knew the route pretty well, since I'd taken the bus lots of times. Up by the park there were brown brick buildings with kids playing outside. Along Riverside Drive there were white stone buildings and people walking big dogs. Then there was the section that wasn't so nice. Garbage cans were lined up along the curb, and sometimes spilled into the gutter.

At 110th Street it changed again, because that's where Central Park began. The trees were so beautiful I could never get tired of seeing them. On Fifth Avenue there were gorgeous places with awnings and doormen. I watched very carefully for 57th Street, where Sidney worked.

The store was little, with a big sign, BAUM FABRICS. I stood outside, looking at the white and beige lace tablecloths hanging on cords strung across the window like washlines. I liked the kind we had at home better: a green and yellow plaid oilcloth.

Finally, I made myself go in. The store was air-conditioned, which I didn't expect, since Sidney always told us how hot it was. I expected to see fat Mr. Baum, but the short man with the white mustache who asked if he could help me was skinny.

"Is Mr. Zimmer here?" I said, like a grown-up.

"Who?"

"Mr. Zimmer? Sidney Zimmer?"

"Oh, Sid. Sure," the man said. "He's in back. I'll have to get him."

But then a woman came in and asked about a tablecloth. They went outside and she pointed to one in the window. He ended up taking out a big pile of tablecloths from under the counter before she bought. When she left, the man went to get my brother, but he came back without him. "Sid is unloading a shipment. Since the truck can't wait, you'll have to," he said.

We stood around without saying anything. I'd never been in a store that was so quiet. The man wrote something down on a pad by the register, then hummed "Begin the Beguine," which is a song my brother sang when he was teaching me to fox-trot.

Just then my brother came out from behind the curtain. He was all sweaty and wearing strange clothes: a brown shirt and pants that matched, instead of the white shirt and gray suit he left the house in that morning. When he saw me, he said, "Jesus! What's wrong?"

I told him I took a bus ride and needed a nickel to get back. He stared at me for a moment like he didn't get it. Then he turned to the man. "Hear that, Mr. Schinkel? This is the genius sister I've been telling you about."

"Pleased to meet you," Mr. Schinkel said. "You got a real nice brother there." He turned to Sidney. "Well, I won the bet with

Baum. Lady comes in off the street and pushes my gross over the record." Mr. Schinkel smiled at me. "Sid's working his way up to sales. Someday he'll be behind the counter here. I wouldn't be surprised if he broke my record." He winked. "But it might take him fifteen, twenty years."

My brother walked me to the bus stop, but he couldn't wait with me. He made me promise never to take the bus again by myself.

On the bus I felt sick and my side was killing me. I hardly noticed the scenery. Then we were at Fort Tryon and I ran down the park and back to Arden Street.

I was in the kitchen when my brother came home from work. As usual, he had his cigarette and read the *Daily News*. My mother put baby powder in his shoes. After supper Sidney told us how much he had grossed that day. "Over a thousand," he said, like nothing had happened. We played some gin rummy until it was time for him to go on air raid duty.

Right after Labor Day my mother and I ran into Lori Steinfeld on Dyckman Street. She was looking in the window of Miles Shoes when she saw us walking by and came up to us. She was in a white nurse's uniform and you couldn't see her pompadour anymore because of the white cap.

"How's Sidney?" she said. "What's he been doin' with himself?"

She was surprised to hear that he was an air raid warden. "Tell your mother I'm working up at Presbyterian," she said, meaning the hospital at 168th Street.

"Good l-u-c-k," my mother told me to tell her back.

"You can tell your brother you ran into me," she said. "Lori Steinfeld."

"I know," I said. Then, before I could help myself, I said, "Sidney got a big promotion at Baum Fabrics. He's in sales now."

"Really!" she said, putting her hand on my mother's arm. "I always knew he had it in him."

As we walked away my mother said to me, "H-o-p-e not telephone," but I wasn't sure which was better, if he called her or didn't.

Until we got back to Arden Street I kept going back and forth over it, knowing in my heart he was going to anyhow. But then I figured Melva would tell him to wait and not call Lori right away, which is what she used to tell him after he and Lori argued. I didn't think Sidney would call her before the weekend. Definitely not before he was done with air raid duty that night, unless, of course, he thought Lori would want to come over our house and watch the air raid with us.

In the Picking Room

RANDY F. NELSON

From *The Imaginary Lives*
of Mechanical Men (2006)

1

Okay, here's my baseball fantasy.

I'm somewhere in that dry wasteland between first and second when I look up, and what do I see? On the far horizon I see
a silhouette that might be the third base coach on a trampoline,
already four feet in the air, knees almost touching his chin, and
cranking one arm like a wild man. Which tells me I can make it
even though baserunning is not my skill. Because in real life? I
am too slow, too heavy, just too damn big for anything. But on
this particular night, with the stadium lights like Hollywood, it's
going to be different. So I round second, pushing off from that
bag like it was the end of the earth. Chugging for third. And about
halfway there, I fling myself into the atmosphere, flying like a
bulldozer dropped out of a cargo plane because I'm a hell of a big
guy, and I get maybe one gulp of free air before I'm plowing into
that powdery earth so hard that it cuts a trench under the glove.
I mean throwing dirt like a meteorite striking the desert. And I
slide, man, I slide until that left toe touches canvas at precisely
zero miles an hour. Like a ballerina, Jack. And there he is. Blue
is looking down on me like Sweet Jesus, dripping sweat and fan-

ning air with both arms, telling the world I'm as safe as a baby in its crib, yes sir. While the crowd goes wild.

And I know that's not much. But I don't have much. And it's the best I've got on most days because we live in a crumbling world and if I blink just once I'm back in the picking room. Picking cloth. I'll be holding one hand like this, getting ready to whack the dust off my uniform, and then there he'll be, Pardue or maybe Murtaugh, swinging around the end of the aisle, saying, ". . . the hell are you doing now, you moron?" And then I guess the crowd goes pretty quiet.

Because in the real world they don't use binners and pickers anymore. The textile mills are failing, and the jobs are leaving for Pakistan, and there's nothing on the horizon but scaffolding and empty bins. And maybe somebody yelling out over the floor, "Hey y'all! Riggs is in Las Vegas. Doing his act."

That's what'll make them laugh.

2

On the day they fired Kutschenko I was a binner, slow as an ox but steady enough to know I would last as long as Murtaugh. If the layoffs didn't get me first. It was a simple job. You pushed a dolly of cloth into the picking room, found an aisle with vacant bins, and stacked the rolls—aisle 13, row 6, bin D—the boom echoing every time a roll landed. It was like heaving bodies into the sea. Lift and toss, lift and toss until the paper-shrouded rolls had disappeared into the deep. Then going back for the next load. Eight to ten times and hour. Because the aisles of the picking room were too narrow for a forklift.

So here is the point. One roll of hard-finished denim, papered and spooled, weighs seventy-five pounds. Ten rolls weigh a minute and a half. A hundred rolls weigh a lifetime. So that after six weeks your shoulders and arms were like steel. After a year you were Murtaugh. It's why we earned what we did. They gave us money, and we gave them hideous strength until we were somebody else. Nobody lasted. Everybody was on the road to somewhere else. A binner is a machine that looks like a man.

So it was like six months before I mentioned it. At lunch, you know, laying back on a stack of boxes, Willie T. and Pardue rolling up their hot dog wrappers and shooting free throws, Murtaugh smoking one after another, and Kutschenko saying, ". . . the hell you doing in that notebook all the time, huh? You look like an ape readin' a matchbook."

"I'm working on material," I said.

"He's working on material," Pardue said.

"What kinna material?"

"What kinna material you working on, kid?"

"Ideas."

"He's working on idea material."

"Will you shut the fuck up. What kinna ideas you working on? Like science ideas or like a novel or something?"

"I don't know, I'm just thinking about giving it a shot, you know, doing a little stand-up. Sometime."

"You mean like comedy?"

"Yeah, like comedy." Which is what got the big laugh.

"Hey, you got a great start already, kid. All people talk about is how your head is bigger than a mule's. Lissen, you gotta have college for that. I mean, you can be funny looking, but that ain't funny, you know what I'm saying? You want to *write* funny, then you got to have the college."

"I don't know. . . ."

"Like whatta you got right now, right there on the page?"

"It's just an idea. It's not really a routine."

"We'll tell you if it's a routine or not."

"Yeah, we'll tell you. Is it a routine, or what?"

"It's just a note," I said. "It's not a routine."

"He's got nothing," said Pardue. "He's working on a science book. I knew it. He's a scientist."

"You don't know," said Willie T. "It could be a routine or something. Let's hear it, boy. Play your note."

"Okay. Okay, here goes. Like, I was just thinking . . . did you ever notice how on television they advertise drugs that you don't even know what they're for?"

"Heartburn," suggested Pardue. "You got heartburn, and you got your cholesterol."

"Cut it out, give him a chance."

"No, I'm talking about when some announcer says like, 'Ask you doctor about Thorexynol,' and then, bam, your Thorexynol theme music will start up and your Thorexynol theme couple will go walking on the beach and there you are wondering what just got cured. They do that all the time now."

"That's not funny, kid."

"I *know* it's not funny, you dumbass. It's got to be part of a routine, which I already told you I don't have. What you do is work it into a doctor bit, see, like you go to the doctor's office with a broken arm or, you know, impotence or poison ivy or something and ask the doc for some of that Thorexynol because that's what the ad told you to do. Right? When it's really for constipation."

"If it's for constipation, then what you puttin' it on poison ivy for?"

"How about I kick your ass because you look like a dwarf?"

"I'm just saying. We think you need some new material."

"Hey, kid," said Pardue. "Did you ever notice that you suck? That's what you ought to notice. That funny stuff happens to you all the time and then you tell it and it turns to crapola? Did you ever notice *that*?"

Which is when Meek appeared. Holding the clipboard down below his waist, with the white envelope stuffed in his shirt pocket. Striped tie, short sleeves, beeper clipped to his belt. Everyone knew what it meant. I remembered at that moment nights around our kitchen table with my mother talking about World War II, how the guy from Western Union would bicycle right to your house with his satchel and take out the envelope as he was walking to your door. Everybody knew what that meant too. Except back then we were winning the war.

We knew before he even stepped out of the elevator. All of us looking up when the hoist light came on and the pulley started humming, because no one ever rode the elevator into the picking room. It was a one-way drop, like the caged descent into a coal mine, and you used it twice a day—once going in and once coming out. When the doors finally opened, we saw it was Meek. The personnel guy. He looked like a child, alone, on a very broad stage, and he waited until the steel doors and the safety gate locked before stepping across the crack. We thought he was a bastard, I suppose, because it never occurred to us that he was simply afraid. When he got to us, he spoke in a low, mournful voice that we all recognized as fake. "Burkhard," he said softly, "could I speak with you? Down in my office?"

"Fuck no," said Kutschenko. "Do it right here. If you're going to do it, you little maggot, you can at least be a man about it. Do it right now.

And that's the funny thing. The paper in the envelope really was pink.

3

The picking room was like a library where the pickers went their dark routes pulling scrolls of cloth form the bins and dropping them into boxes bound for other mills. We sent out boxes by the ton. It's the way they measured us, not by the miles we talked but by the tons we lifted, until the numbers 12/25/E became only the rough coordinates of a seventy-five-pound roll of denim buried under twenty others just like it, headed for China, where it would get its real identity. Then get shipped back to this country as something by Levi, Wrangler, Arizona, Tommy, Ralph, Calvin. Who the hell knew?

It's hard to imagine. A picking room is not like anything else. Not like a warehouse or an aircraft hangar or a cavern. It's just different. I used to tell people to try to imagine a castle or, anyway, something that's old and big like a cathedral, ruined and re-built over the years and then one day gutted so that all that re-mains is a hollow shell and not any kind of building that can be reasoned with. Just an outer wall circling back on itself like some kind of shape a kid would make with building blocks. Then fill the shape with shelves. Miles and miles of them. That's your picking room. So that some sections of the outer wall might look like a ruined temple, like any stiff wind could blow it away particle by particle. Then in other places you might find a master mason's work, delicate art woven in stone. Nothing surprised you after a while. There were bricked-up doors and windows all along the walls. Alcoves, arches, and columns. A forty-foot section of the floor where iron rails pierced the brick and then simply stopped beside a nonexistent loading dock. There were squat tunnels done in yellow ceramic tile like the subway, with the same black vacancy at the extremities.

It was a huge and haunted place, more like a morgue than a li-brary. You matched your ticket numbers to the little tags hang-ing on every roll of cloth; then you pulled your roll out of the bin, cradling it like a child for a moment before dropping it into its shipping box, always an avalanche of dust and grime falling in your face from the dark upper bins, the paper ripping on extru-sions, the cloth unraveling like torn curtains. Until after a while you could convince yourself that they really were bodies, crum-bling mummies stacked in open crypts like those war atrocities.

And then I try to imagine a man like Murtaugh inside that same place for twenty years.

He was the one guy who lasted, and he looked like the fifties never ended. Every day he wore a white cotton T-shirt, jeans, and biker boots—a uniform so unvarying that I accepted it as normal after a few weeks. The hair he kept in a disciplined flattop. His eyes were pale blue pools of no particular depth. And his immense size was, in a sense, the only shape that stayed in your mind. Pardue told me that he had once served time for killing a man with a logging chain. "Don't mess with him," he said. And I did not. Murtaugh kept a Zippo light in his hip pocket that he flipped open with a single snap of his fingers, and he held his cigarette cupped, like this, against some imaginary hurricane. On weekends we did not visit him in the green boardinghouse on Broad Street, and on nights when they needed some overtime we did not volunteer to stay behind with him. Even during the regular shift, Murtaugh would sort through the packing slips, selecting orders that would take him to the farthest aisles, down the long tunnels, and out beyond the ordered bins where the only lights were hanging bulbs. On some nights we did not see him at the elevator drop at all.

4

Every once in a while Pardue would go off on Meek, about how he needed to be killed or at least thrown through one of the walled-up windows. "They're doing layoffs again," he would say. "And I think that asshole enjoys it. He needs killing. Did you ever notice that the personnel guy is the last one laid off?"

"I don't think he enjoys it," I said. "I think he's just doing his job."

"I'll *tell* you what he enjoys. He enjoys porking that little gal in the commissary what you been going out with, name of Patty. I hear he's been spending a lot of time down there."

I didn't say anything.

"Don't nothing rile you up, kid? You need to stomp that son of a bitch into the ground."

"Patty's not that kind of girl."

"Forget Patty! You need to kill that bastard. I'll tell you what you need."

"What do I need?"

"You need somebody . . . from West Virginia. You need a dynamite man."

"I need a dynamite man?"

"You need somebody from West Virginia, son, the Explosives State, where they mix gunpowder in your grits and a cook-off don't have nothing to do with the Pillsbury Doughboy."

"I guess you might know somebody."

"I *am* from West Virginia, boy. We got dental hygienists up there who use Primacord instead of dental floss, and when you hear a high-speed drill it don't mean your wisdom teeth are coming out, Jack. It means the whole damn side of your mountain is about to lift and slide, that's what it means. Hell, back home we got twelve-year-old boys can blow the wax out of your ears and not even wake you up during the sermon. In fact, you don't even need me. You don't need no dynamite man. You need a twelve-year-old. From back home. In West By God Virginia."

"I don't know," I said. "Maybe I don't need anybody who's from a state that's just a chopped-off part of another state."

"Now you're catching on. Hey!" he yelled out over the room. "Riggs is developing a brain! He's coming up out of the swamp! Go ahead, kid, give me your best shot."

"Like y'all ought to change your name. I mean, West Virginia's not a state, it's a direction. It makes you look small."

"It ain't never hurt West Consin none, has it?"

"So what were you planning to dynamite?"

"Meek, I done told you. I'm going to dynamite his ass into the middle of next week."

"You're going to blow up Meek?"

"Naw. Hell naw! A hunnerd times better than that. This here's a variation on your classic cherry bomb on the toilet, except we'll probably need a couple of sticks of c4 on account of we want him riding a geyser right after he flushes."

Willie T. gave a piercing whistle and yelled, "Bring 'er on in for a minute, boys. This is going to get good."

When he had his audience, Pardue said, "We'll need to cut off the water for most of this section of the mill, you know, to build up the pressure pretty good, and then reinforce the pipe at the actual point of detonation. I want it to blow an eight-inch column of water through his butt. I want it to rocket that son of a bitch through the ceiling tiles so that his head will come through the next floor and somebody will step on him. I want it to look like he's riding Old Faithful to the moon. You understand what I'm saying? I hate that cracker! I want him to pull down his pants, take a seat, pull that damn handle, and think that he accidentally launched the space shuttle. That's what I want. And I'm telling you we can do it. It's a matter a teamwork."

"Have you ever done anything like this before?"

"Not me specifically. But I witnessed something similar back in high school. It was sad, really. Kind of tragic in a way. And it caused an international incident you boys may have heard of, which should teach you the value of careful and strategic thinking and also something about the fragility of human life. So I reckon I'm going to have to tell you about it."

"I thought you might need to."

"Okay, there's this one old boy name of Pruitt who hated the assistant principal the way I hate Meek and who came up with something of the same plan but without the careful thinking. What I'm telling you is they forgot to reinforce the sewer drain pipe at a vital point. It makes me sick to this day to think about it, and, well, you can probably already imagine what happened. Pruitt and his boys stopped up most of the toilets on the third and fourth floors and waited for the crucial moment right before the assembly where the genuine Boys Choir of Wales, I'm not making this up, was going to give its international Christmas concerto for the backward children of West Virginia, you know, on account of they thought that would be a likely time for the son of a bitch to visit the toilet. And sure enough he did. Everything was going to plan. The little Wales children was warming up backstage. Pruitt and his gang was hulking over several toilet bowls like vultures with a couple sticks of dynamite and a Bic, waiting for a miracle. And, by God, it happens. The assistant principal comes in with one of the singers, a little tiny pissant of a Wales kid name of Cardiff Glendenning it turns out, showing him where the bathroom is. Well, Pruitt and his gang are all in this one stall, feet up off the floor hulking on the rim of the commode so the place looks deserted. And they hear their guy. Then they hear the stall door next to 'em close and the little lock go snick, like that; and they figure it's a go for liftoff. So Pruitt gives the nod, and ffftt goes the fuse and flush goes the charge. Fifteen seconds later there's this dull, distant boom like thunder rolling down the mountain. And, oh, sweet Jesus!"

"What happened?"

"Nothing happened," I said. "He's making this up as he goes along."

"I'm going to tell you what happened as soon as I get a grip on my stomach because it gives me the dry heaves to this very day. It makes want to puke just thinking about it. There was a tragic miscalculation. And happened, boys, is that one hunnerd yards downstream the pipe blew. It couldn't take the blast, see, and it was like one of them submarine movies except it was blowing high pressure sewage through that cafeteria and it was like the u-571 taking the entire eighth grade to a watery grave."

"I thought you said the entire school was in the assembly listening to the boys choir of some damn place you probably made up."

"I'm telling you they was in the cafeteria, and they was *fouled*,

fouled something terrible. But that ain't the worst part. Because . . . oh my Lord, that poor little boy. You see, it was him in the toilet and not the assistant. It was horrible, just horrible."

"It blew him up?"

"No! A hunnerd times worse. In fact, the exact opposite. When the pipe blew four stories below and every drop of water in the entire system headed toward the center of the earth, what the hell you think happened? It created a suction like a hurricane blowing through your empty head. I can hear his screams to this day. And I can imagine the horror. Just think of it yourself, poor little Cardiff looking down between his legs and seeing what? A tiny ripple and then, all of a sudden, a whirlpool like the damn *Titanic* was going down. And the force of the suction? Good God Almighty, boys, Superman couldn't pull himself out of a force like that. It threw his legs together and formed a perfect seal so damn fast it was foregone before it was foredone; and that ill-fated child was bent in the shape of a V and singing soprano for sure, fighting for his life, and praying 'Sweet Jesus, if you love a sinner, get me out of this American toilet.' In fact, those might have been his last words."

"His last words?"

"That's right. What I'm trying to tell you, boys, is that young Cardiff was never seen again. And I believe to this very moment it was the tragedy that turned my life in the direction it eventually took, ruining me for medical school or one of the higher professions. That little boy's story is in many ways identical to my own. It's why I stand before you today a broken and humble man."

"That's a damn lie!"

"It's no lie, boys. I swear on my sweet grandmaw's grave."

"It's a gah-damn lie on account of you never been inside a high school in your life."

5

When the layoffs began again, they started in the weave room and worked their way through the departments. The weavers were replaced by automatic looms, inspectors by scanning machines. And the weave room went from being as noisy as a field of crows to being as silent as the grave. And the dye house lost its steam. Then I guess they sent the carding and spinning operations overseas where they weren't as particular about brown lung and wanted to share the opportunity with folks making twenty cents an hour. That's what Pardue said. He said, "Boys, you better read the handwritin' on the shithouse wall," meaning, I suppose, that we were as obsolete as John Henry's hammer. Still, I took pride in the fact that binners and pickers were the last to go, though when they came for Willie T., he simply said, "Fellas, I lost my job." Never suspecting that it may have been lost for him.

When they came for me, it was like I had done something wrong, which I guess I had in a way. I should have tried some college after all. For a time I worked security at a country-western place called Boots, where they let me try my hand at a few stand-up routines, but it never clicked. You got to make the crowds go wild if you want to do real comedy. You got to leave them gasping for air. Which I guess I never did. Within two years the mill was down to half production and only one shift. Businesses closing on Main Street while the pawn shops flourished. I got reports from my sister, who was a photographer at the local paper. She told me the mayor was applying for federal grants. Within two and a half years everyone was gone from the picking room except Murtaugh.

In my mind I could see him working alone, in his world where he had been shaped by the accumulated weight of years, dark and threatening as a thundercloud. Muscles corded under the white T-shirt like bridge cables. Hands and arms, God, like he could catch a Volkswagen if you could throw him one. Sometimes I think he had just been waiting for the rest of us to leave. Which is the way, I believe, that monsters are made. He stayed until the mill itself closed, about the same time I moved to the mountains and took up carpentry. My sister Emily sent me a picture of the picking room when it had been emptied of cloth, but it had no human perspective. It was just a photograph of a junkyard, like you could go searching the aisles forever and find nothing but the dry emptiness of canyons. And after that I tried to imagine Murtaugh walking the streets of our little town at night. Up and down, across and back, following the grid.

Jimmy John Pardue went into the movies and was arrested within a year for making the wrong kind. He bought a used video camera and a Volkswagen bus, which he drove through the mill village, offering money to girls who would accept a ride.

"Hey, sweetie, where you headed?"

And they would tell him downtown or to the movies or none of his business.

Then he would ask them, "You need a ride? Cause we can give you a ride and even give you a little money if you'll answer some questions, me and Patty here."

"What kind of questions?"

"Hop in, I'll give you forty dollars to tell us the first time you ever kissed somebody."

"What's she need a camera for?"

"That's Patty. And, Patty, I want you to meet the love of my life, the most gorgeous and most talented girl without a ride on this street whose name I want recorded right now on account of she's got the best-looking little legs I've ever seen and a smile that would stop a train. Are you Sarah? Because that's what somebody told me and you sort of look like a Sarah, you know, in a real fresh and perky kind of way. Why don't you hop in, and we'll give you a ride down to the shopping mall. I mean, if that's where you want to go. And you don't need to worry a bit. Ain't nobody going to make you take any money that you don't want to take, no sir, not one dime of this fifty dollars."

In the film they used for evidence, there is no sound, only unsteady images of the girl herself and the occasional hand or foot of the person holding the camera. Jimmy John is at the wheel, and you can see through the windows that they are driving through the country, trees and pastures spooling by in a blur. The girl is adjusting her skirt and pulling her hair behind her ears and touching the buttons of her blouse as she answers questions from the front seat. She is smiling, handling the interview well. Relaxed and talking to the camera. At one point she giggles and leans forward, planting a mock slap on the side of Jimmy John's head. He cringes in pretend fear. And they all laugh some more. You can see the camera jiggling.

A few minutes later the girl covers her face in mock embarrassment and then answers cautiously, looking out the window at tasseled rows of corn. There's a shrug and a few more words from the front seat. Some folded twenties that get handed to the girl who stuffs them into her backpack and sits meditatively until the scene goes blank. When the light and motion resume, she is on her knees in an impossible position, her rump in the air and one shoulder and the side of her face on the floor in the middle of the van. She's smiling and talking to the camera as she lifts her skirt and tugs at the elastic of her panties. Everyone seems to be laughing and having a good time.

6

I did not marry Patty the commissary girl or play professional baseball or become a big star, but my life is all right. Today I am a wood turner in a furniture shop in the mountains where guys say things like "Hey, Riggs, run outside and get us a tree" and I feel like I am at home. At night I lie down in a bed that I made with my own hands beside a woman named Elise who gave me the one thing that I love most in this world. And she is so tiny. Normal and perfect like her mama and as light as a snowflake in my hand. At least that is what it feels like to me.

Sometimes I tell her stories. I am still pretty good at that, and as I tell, I remember. Like how you got there by following the yellow line. One foot wide, repainted twice a year by men who never got off their knees because for them it was a never-ending line that wound through the carding room like a country road on a map. Then across the metal bridge and into the weave room where you dodged air cleaners drifting about you like jellyfish, tentacles hanging all the way to the floor and sucking up the cotton fibers so it's like the cleanest floor you've ever seen, weavers bustling around in hairnets and masks like surgeons. Then you took the yellow stairs down. Punched through two sets of swinging doors and went down some more until you smelled vinegar or maybe heard the dyer himself slamming at a bolt with one of his wrenches. And pretty soon there he would be, sweating on account of the steam and not even wasting a glance in your direction. Most of the time you only knew him as a pair of legs and a leather apron there in the blue fog, but it would be him all right. He never left the dye house. It was like the laundry room of a prison, the air a roiling thundercloud of blue steam. But sometimes you could see him in one of the aisles between vats, where he'd be roasting like a pig, arms absolutely blue to the elbows and where, if you came close enough, you would notice the one startling fact that stayed with you all the years. That his eyes were perfectly matched to his arms, the cobalt blue of new jeans.

Those are the things I remember because there was no direct route into the picking room. You had to follow the painted pathway. You had to take the yellow stairs down. And once engulfed in that fog, you simply held your breath until you reached the freight elevator, which, everybody said, was a one-way drop, like the canary cage dangling from some miner's hand as he takes the long ride down. And I do not know how I got out alive.

Now I look back over my life trying to see where it went right, and I find someone four years old climbing into my lap, there in the big chair, on nights when the wind rushes up through the valley. And I try to think of what to tell her when she asks where the monsters come from.

CONTRIBUTORS

ROBERT ABEL (1941–2017) was the author of *Full-tilt Boogie, The Progress of a Fire, Freedom Dues; or, A Gentleman's Progress in the New World*, and *Skin and Bones*. His collection of stories *Ghost Traps* received the 1990 Flannery O'Connor Award for Short Fiction. His stories have appeared in *Playgirl, Contact*, and *Denver Quarterly*.

WENDY BRENNER is the author of two books of short fiction, *Large Animals in Everyday Life*, her first collection and winner of the 1995 Flannery O'Connor Award for Short Fiction, and *Phone Calls from the Dead*. Her stories and essays have appeared in *Best American Essays, Best American Magazine Writing, New Stories from the South, Oxford American, The Sun, Allure, Travel & Leisure, Seventeen, Guernica*, and elsewhere. She is the recipient of a National Endowment for the Arts Fellowship, a contributing editor for the *Oxford American*, and an associate professor of creative writing at the University of North Carolina, Wilmington.

DAVID CROUSE is the author of *Copy Cats*, which received the 2004 Flannery O'Connor Award for Short Fiction, and *The Man Back There*, which received the Mary McCarthy Fiction Prize in 2008. *Trouble Will Save You*, a collection of novellas, will be published in early 2021. David is full professor of English at the University of Washington and also serves as the director of the MFA Program. David's stories have appeared in such publications as the *Massachusetts Review, Beloit Fiction Journal, Chelsea*, and *Quarterly West*.

ALFRED DEPEW has taught at the Universities of Vermont and New Hampshire, the Maine College of Art, the Salt Center for Documentary Studies, and Haystack Mountain School of Crafts. He is the author of *The Melancholy of Departure*, winner of the 1991 Flannery O'Connor Award for Short Fiction, *Wild and Woolly: A Journal Keeper's Handbook* (2004), and *A Wedding Song for Poorer People*, which was a 2014 INDIEFAB Book of the Year Finalist. His most recent novella, *Odalisque*, is set in the Quebec City of *Les Automatistes* and their *Refus global* after World War II. He lives in Vancouver, British Columbia.

CAROLE L. GLICKFELD grew up in New York City, the setting of *Useful Gifts*, which won the 1988 Flannery O'Connor Award for Short Fiction, and *Swimming toward the Ocean*, a novel that won the Washington State Book Award. She was the recipient of a Literary Fellowship from the National Endowment for the Arts and a Governor's Arts Award (Washington State), and she was a fellow of both the MacDowell Colony and the Bread Loaf Writers' Conference. Her stories and essays have appeared in numerous literary journals and anthologies. Now living in Seattle, where she has taught creative writing, she works on a consulting basis with aspiring writers on their manuscripts when she is not indulging her passion for travel.

MONICA MCFAWN is a writer, comedian, and artist living in Michigan. Her short story collection *Bright Shards of Someplace Else* won the Flannery O'Connor Award for Short Fiction. Her comedy writing has appeared in *The Offing* and *The Belladonna* and has been staged at Second City's Mary Scruggs Works by Women Festival. McFawn is a recipient of an NEA Fellowship in Literature and a Walter E. Dakin Fellowship from the Sewanee Writers' Conference. She is an associate professor at Northern Michigan University, where she teaches fiction and scriptwriting. When she isn't writing, drawing, or teaching, she trains horses and cats.

MELINDA MOUSTAKIS is the author of *Bear Down, Bear North: Alaska Stories*, winner of the 2010 Flannery O'Connor Award for Short Fiction and a "5 Under 35" selection by the National Book Foundation. Her work has appeared in *American Short Fiction*, *Alaska Quarterly Review*, *Granta*, and elsewhere. She is the recipient of the O. Henry Award, the Hodder Fellowship at Princeton University, the NEA Literature Fellowship in Fiction, the Kenyon Review Fellowship at Kenyon College, the Jenny McKean Moore Writer-in-Washington Fellowship at George Washington University, and the Rona Jaffe Cullman Fellowship at the New York Public Library.

RANDY F. NELSON is the author of *The Imaginary Lives of Mechanical Men*, which received the 2005 Flannery O'Connor Award for Short Fiction, *A Duplicate Daughter*, *The Overlook Martial Arts Reader*, and *The Almanac of American Letters*. His stories have appeared in such publications as the *Gettysburg Review*, the *North American Review*, and the *Kenyon Review*.

GINA OCHSNER is the author of *The Necessary Grace to Fall*, which received the 2001 Flannery O'Connor Award for Short Fiction. Her stories have appeared in such publications as the *Bellingham Review*, *Image*, the *New Yorker*, *Tin House*, *Iron Horse Review*, and the *Kenyon Review*, and they have received numerous awards, including the Ruth Hindman Foundation Prize, the Raymond Carver Prize, and the Chelsea Award for Short Fiction. She is the author of *The Hidden Letters of Velta B*, *The Russian Dreambook of Colour and Flight*, and *Pleased to Be Otherwise*, among other books.

ANDY PLATTNER is the author of *Winter Money*, which received the 1996 Flannery O'Connor Award for Short Fiction. He has published three other books of literary fiction: *A Marriage of Convenience*, *Offerings from a Rust Belt Jockey*, and *Dixie Luck: Stories, and the novella "Terminal."* His fiction has earned two gold medals from the Faulkner Society, the Dzanc Mid-Career Novel Prize, a Henfield Prize, the Ferrol Sams Fiction Award, the Castleton-Lyons Book Award, and a silver medal in literary fiction from the Independent Book Publishers' Awards.

FRANK SOOS, a native of Virginia, is the author of *Unified Field Theory*, which won the 1997 Flannery O'Connor Award for Short Fiction. He is also the author of *Unpleasantries: Considerations of Difficult Questions*, *Bamboo Fly Rod Suite*, *Early Yet*, and *Double Moon: Constructions and Conversations*, with Margo Klass. He is a professor emeritus of English at the University of Alaska in Fairbanks.

NANCY ZAFRIS is the author of *The People I Know*, recipient of the 1989 Flannery O'Connor Award for Short Fiction. She is also the author of two novels, *Lucky Strike* and *The Metal Shredders*. Her second collection of short stories, *The Home Jar*, was named one of the top ten books of 2013 by the *Minneapolis Star Tribune*. After serving as the fiction editor of the *Kenyon Review* for nine years, she became the editor of the Flannery O'Connor award series for several years. She has recently finished a new novel.